A Thousand Paper Birds

Tor Udall

ISIS
LARGE
PRINT

First published in Great Britain 2017
by
Bloomsbury Circus
an imprint of Bloomsbury Publishing

First Isis Edition
published 2018
by arrangement with
Bloomsbury Publishing

A catalogue record for this book is available
from the British Library.

ISBN 978–1–78541–472–5 (hb)
ISBN 978–1–78541–478–7 (pb)

Published by
F. A. Thorpe (Publishing)
Anstey, Leicestershire

Set by Words & Graphics Ltd.
Anstey, Leicestershire
Printed and bound in Great Britain by
T. J. International Ltd., Padstow, Cornwall

This book is printed on acid-free paper

Jonah sits on a bench in Kew Gardens, trying to reassemble the shattered pieces of his life following the sudden death of his wife, Audrey. Chloe, shaven-headed and abrasive, sits by the lake, finding solace in the origami she meticulously folds. But when she meets Jonah, her carefully constructed defences threaten to fall. Milly, a child quick to laugh, freely roams Kew. But where is her mother, and where does she go when the gardens are closed? Harry's purpose is to save Kew's plants from extinction. Quiet and enigmatic, he longs for something — or someone — who will root him firmly to the earth. Audrey links these lives together. As the mystery of her death unravels, the characters journey through the seasons to learn that stories, like paper, can be refolded and reformed.

Doesn't one always think of the past, in a garden with men and women lying under the trees? Aren't they one's past, all that remains of it, those men and women, those ghosts lying under the trees . . . one's happiness, one's reality?

Kew Gardens, Virginia Woolf

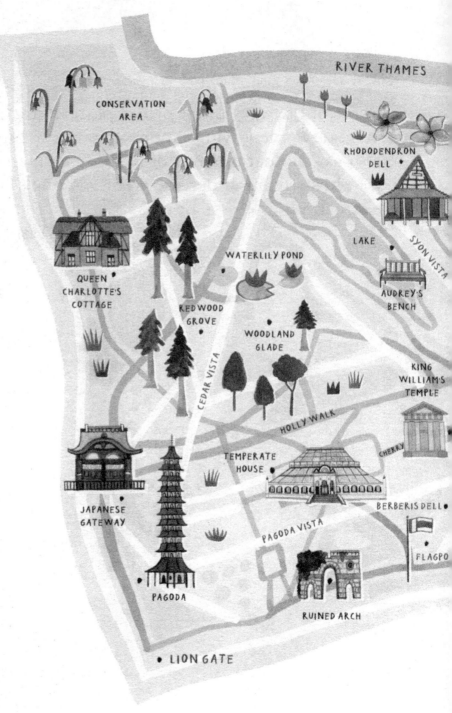

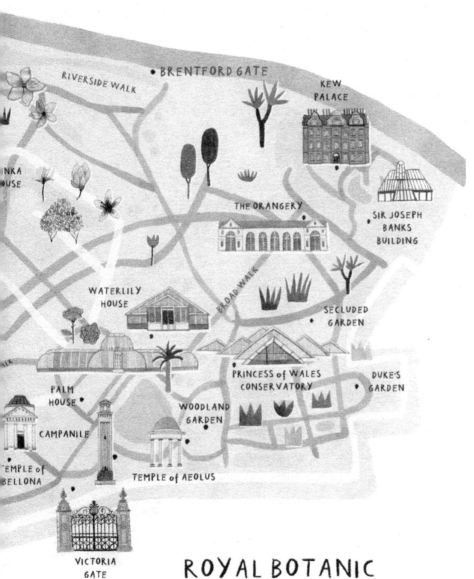

RIVERSIDE WALK

• BRENTFORD GATE

KEW PALACE

NKA USE

THE ORANGERY

SIR JOSEPH BANKS BUILDING

WATERLILY HOUSE

BROAD WALK

SECLUDED GARDEN

PALM HOUSE

PRINCESS of WALES CONSERVATORY

DUKE'S GARDEN

CAMPANILE

WOODLAND GARDEN

TEMPLE of BELLONA

TEMPLE of AEOLUS

VICTORIA GATE

ROYAL BOTANIC GARDENS, KEW
2004

Part I

The Opposite of Gravity

Written in pain, written in awe
By a puzzled man who questioned
What we were here for

"Oh! You Pretty Things", David Bowie

Audrey's Smile

Jonah stands at the threshold. His wife's scent hangs in the air, a perfume she has worn for years. He remains in the doorway, surveying the chalk-white walls, the varnished floorboards, the embroidered red throw. The shelves are crammed with books and the memories of reading them; times spent together yet alone, separated by different characters and continents. His gaze rests on a bunch of flowers that he bought three days ago, the yellow petals drooping.

Sun streams through the large sash windows, creating ghosts from avenues of dust. Particles shimmer. The room looks preserved, the tulips jarred in an antique glow. When Jonah steps inside he is unmoored in a place that should feel like home. Anything true is a memory.

Bile rises in his throat. He wades through the sunlight, searching for comfort. Here is a paperback splayed open across the arm of the sofa to bookmark her page. A cardigan on the back of a chair, a lipstick stranded by the kettle, a shopping list posted on the fridge; her handwriting hasty, impatient, her thinking perfect. Here is the laundry, his jeans with their stubborn, ink-stained pockets. These are the things she touched. Her fingers . . .

What she has left behind is delicate. It makes him feel oafish, his hands useless, mammoth. A photograph shows Audrey walking away, glancing back towards the camera, her red hair. Her hair that he remembers tangled against their pillow or salt-drenched from the Sicilian sea. She had burnt her nose that day.

This is the crease of time. The sag of an hour. Everything is so still it feels wrong to breathe. The silence stretches seamlessly through the flat while Jonah stands, gathering dust. He waits for Audrey to come in with a crooked smile and a mug of tea. The gap between her front teeth — beyond beauty.

The head of a tulip releases its grip. Jonah stands amid the petals, the dead light. But his wife never boils the kettle, or enters with that wonky, luminous smile.

Outside the window, Kew Road is dappled in spring and passing people. The sky is in its rightful place, as are the tops of the trees he can see behind the wall of the botanical gardens. Inside the flat, the fridge is still stocked with milk, the crockery still red. The furniture hasn't been moved, nor the streetlamps, or the bins on the pavement, but Jonah can no longer recognise this place. It is as if overnight the world has been rearranged.

A Book of Kisses

Harry Barclay catches sight of himself in the Paperchase window. Astonished. Wrecked. It's familiar, the face he has always worn, the blinking blue eyes — but he looks like a man who is lost, unable to find a way out. *Pull yourself together, Hal.* He plunges his hand into his pocket, where there's a roll of industrial tape, some litter (a lollipop wrapper, foil from a fag packet) and then, caught in the bottom, several seeds. Patting his other pocket, he finds his notebook.

It is soft-backed, the colour of cardboard. Inside is a bookmark of a black and white photo. Decades ago, Harry ripped it from a magazine, the well-thumbed page now folded into quarters. It marks the passage he is looking for: a list of train times from Paddington.

HB. 07.06.04.
District Line to Earl's Court
16.07
16.27
Every 10 minutes

Not knowing when Jonah will leave, he wants to get there early. It's only been twelve days, but Jonah is teaching. Undoubtedly he said something brave, like the kids need him, the exams are coming. A woman knocks into Harry. Unapologetic, she rushes across the forecourt, struggling to balance a takeaway coffee with her purse, her phone, her ticket. Harry feels someone watching: a boy in a pushchair a few feet away. What is the child looking at: a man in his early fifties, a well-cut suit that has seen better days? He hopes that his rusty-orange scarf marks him as artistic, but the kid is gazing at the darned elbow of Harry's jacket.

He stuffs the notebook into his breast pocket. Nodding goodbye to the infant's stillness, he enters the chaos: the shudder and snap of ticket gates, the rush-hour tide. The escalator takes him down into the filthy veins of the city, the lifeblood of London. He pulls off his hat, a gentleman's flat cap, and anxiously rubs the rim.

On the District Line platform, posters tell him what to buy and how to escape to "A Heaven Called Florida". While commuters fan themselves with newspapers, Harry searches for a man in his late thirties, carrying a beige satchel stained with red ink. It will probably be full of school reports, examples of Mozart minuets, a rondeau. He spots Jonah's head above the crowd — his hefty frame, the bag. As the train pulls into the station, Harry rushes along the platform. He elbows his way into the same carriage, his face pressed into another man's armpit.

Jonah Wilson is wearing a dowdy brown suit, and bowing his head as if trying to be the same height as the others. Through the array of limbs and luggage, Harry catches glimpses — the beard, jam on his shirt cuff. But nothing is the way Harry imagined. He weighs up the difference between this man and Audrey's description. He had expected someone smaller, not this reliable back, these broad shoulders. How can such an oak of a man be felled?

The tube stifles; the stench of communal sweat, smoke-stained clothes, the reek of takeaway cartons. Its tinged with a sweetness Harry can't put his finger on. Bubble gum, perhaps. Crammed against others, he notices the fractured intimacy between friends, a smile across someone's shoulder. He misses her — those unguarded moments. The way Audrey picked up a mug, or tucked her hair behind her ear. How she touched her lips with the back of her knuckles . . . her yawn building from a blink, to a gasp, as if her body's need for oxygen had ambushed her.

At Earl's Court, they change trains. As Jonah sits down, his sadness spills on to the upholstered seats; it leaks and drips. Harry remains at a distance, his tongue dry and useless. *The first time I met Audrey I saved her life.* As they continue their journey past Hammersmith, the crowd thins. Newspapers lie strewn on empty seats. When they finally cross Kew Bridge, there's a sense of space. Relief. Harry thumbs through his notebook.

. . . the alarming destruction of the world's flora. Rare palms are disappearing for ever. Our Madagascar

9

periwinkle is one of two left in the world. Five years ago we rescued the lady's slipper orchid from extinction. This is what we do, we stop things from dying.

No. No, I don't.

The entry was written three days ago. Harry has kept this journal for years, methodically charting the progress of plants, noting which trees are starting to weaken. On the next page is tiny scrawl.

They come to Kew in their millions — to appreciate the quality of time and their part in it. Some shoot the breeze with God, a bud or a falling leaf. This is a garden of grace . . .

The words blur, Harry's eyes cataracted by grief.

Kew Gardens station. Harry looks up and notices again the undeniable attraction of the man Audrey said yes to. As both men walk into the sunshine, the weight on Harry's back is heavier than all the rain in the world. How can a man made of mist shoulder it? Impossible.

Half-hidden among the cool green of the reeds, a heron stands on one leg, watching the sun glint on the water. Its wings are the colour of a bruise as it waits silently, like an old man wearing a coat of straggly feathers. There are four wooded islands on the lake, undisturbed by humans; stamping grounds for coots, moorhens and Canada geese. The air thrums with birdsong and damselflies darting between the campion and blanketweed.

10

Around the water, benches offer sun or shade, solitude or company, but each bears something in common: the name of someone who has died.

Under the sweet chestnut is Eliza Wainwright, "who so very much loved these gardens". Around a large English oak, a circle of benches faces outwards, naming the crew of Flight 103, who died in the Lockerbie bombing. On the westerly side of the lake, a concrete platform ventures ten feet out across the water. A solitary man sits on its wooden seat. His brown suit looks out of place with his matted hair, as if he is a tamed Samson from *The Book of Judges*. He has the same colossal bones, the beard, but without his wife, he has lost his energy, his talent.

An hour before closing time, this is the only place Jonah can bear to be, worlds away from the Paddington comprehensive. This morning, he believed he could do it — Sophie was struggling with her chord progressions, Ben needed a letter for his mum — but even taking the register made him want to weep: *Present. Present. Absent.*

As Jonah leans down for his satchel, the size of his back tests his suit's seams. After taking out a pile of essays, he tries to decipher a teenager's sloppy handwriting. He rubs his itchy eyes, tries again, but it's like he's suffering from sunstroke. He has no armour against the way the light is dripping through the trees, the day's warmth an insult. The simplest things injure: a damselfly landing on a reed, a drawing pin stuck to the sole of his shoe — Audrey had pointed it out a few weeks ago. Even drinking his bottle of water stings.

Without her, he has no pivot to give sense to the day's existence. What right, he asks, has the world to be beautiful today?

A mallard waddles out of the lake while a swan bullies two geese. The hole she has left stretches and crystallises, crushing his lungs until he can barely breathe. Without her, the air has thinned. The funeral is in two days. He still hasn't chosen the music. The floors in his home are covered in CDs: a "no" pile, a "maybe". A friend had suggested a track from Jonah's old LP.

"C'mon, there are twelve songs to choose from —"

"No."

"Twelve different Audreys —"

"For Christ's sake, how could I pick?"

Sitting by the lake, Jonah hums, yet again, the same four notes of an elegy, but can't compose the next phrase.

"I know nothing about Schubert," she had said on their first date.

"Says she, who can speak five languages."

"Six."

They were standing in this same garden, fireworks lighting up her wine-flushed face. The strains of "Ave Maria" still lingered in the air, and now the idea forms as if Jonah is hearing it. Inspired by a quote from Schubert, he knows what the inscription will be. But how do you order a bench for the deceased? Should he ask at the information desk or is it best to call — and will they, like the undertakers, bombard him with choices between mahogany and oak?

12

Jonah sneezes with hay fever. Head down, his eyes focus. A cigar butt litters the foot of the bench. As he nudges it with his heel, he recalls Audrey's lips around a cigarette. He said he despised her addiction, but perhaps he was just jealous that her lips weren't pressed against his. How many times did they kiss in the nine years they were together? A thousand times, a million? In his mind's eye he makes a list of all the kisses he has loved; the kiss hello that told him about her day, the sleepy satisfaction of their mouths after sex . . . a luscious lingering. There was the salt tasted on her cheeks after a fight, the I'm-late-but-I-want-to-stay kiss, or her lips on the back of his neck that suggested how many possibilities there were for the next. Then there was the kiss he hadn't known was their last.

Was it an accident? The witnesses said there was no reason for her to swerve the way she did. Jonah remembers the uncomfortable shrugs. "It's not your fault. Depression is an illness." Her friends talked of the waste, the fact that she was only thirty-six. But Jonah can't comprehend his wife choosing to leave. All the years he assumed were theirs, all that future taken for granted. He tries to imagine Audrey at eighty, how her mouth might then feel against his. Jonah gazes up at the sky. *But look at all the kisses you gave up.*

On the morning of the funeral, Harry scrubs the mud from his boots, hoping to scourge out the blame. Even at 5a.m. he knows the day will be humid. He finds some tape to bind a fraying lace. As he threads a carnation through his buttonhole, the irony of wearing a dianthus — the so-called "Flower of God" — does not escape him. He thinks about it for the entire train journey to Cornwall.

The church is close to the sea. Audrey spent her childhood summers here, and Harry imagines her running barefoot through the poppy meadow, a graze on her knee. But today there are only her family and friends, overheating in their Sunday best. The afternoon reeks of honeysuckle and sweat. Men, sutured up in suits, are restless. The headstones seem to be the only ones relaxed, leaning into the sunshine like drunkards.

The rhythm of waiting shifts, noise levels increasing and diminishing, as people talk about the weather then stop to stare across the meadow for Audrey's imminent arrival. Her mother, Tilly, circulates as if she's at a cocktail party. She talks loudly about Audrey's "illness" as if she could erase the word "suicide". She keeps playing with the pearls around her neck, and her constant, lipstick-smeared smile makes Harry think of a turkey. It's the creases around her throat, the way her smile pecks and grabs. She waves at her younger lover, but he's looking for a place to scrape off some dog muck, his foot hesitating against a gravestone.

The others continue their asymmetrical, repetitive dance. Scratch burning arm, look at watch, smile at someone in the crowd. Try to blink away the heat, the disbelief. "Audrey never did anything unexpected." Her father, Charles Hartman, walks up to the church, a debonair gent, once a fiend with the ladies. He now seems like a scuffed shoe in need of a polish.

The woman they are waiting for arrives. A second car pulls up and Jonah steps out, shielding his eyes from the sun. His hair is tied back.

The family walk behind the coffin. Once they have proceeded through the vestibule, Harry files in with the rest of the congregation. As he sits down in the pew, he realises that he's still waiting for Audrey to come down the aisle. He imagines her blinking as she leaves the bright day, her summer dress framed in the doorway. But she is already at the altar, inside that box, and no one else appears in the arch of light at the entrance.

The vicar takes his place in the pulpit and describes Audrey's academic brilliance, her excellent taste, her desire to be buried in Cornwall. When he sidesteps the suspicion of suicide and speaks of a car accident, two women begin crying. But it doesn't sound human. It's a strange kind of singing that echoes around the church until it sets off a domino of emotion. The organ begins, and the congregation cries in arpeggios, their resolutions not to weep breaking when they reach the high E. "He who would valiant be 'gainst all disaster". Harry's hymn sheet trembles, the words scattering and blurring into nothing. He gives up and studies Jonah's father. An old man, who has also lost his wife, reaches out and puts all his bony strength into his son's hand. As they both teeter, Harry catches himself thinking how wonderful this is, how wonderful to be grieved. What must this be like, Audrey? Can you see?

The wake is almost jolly; they have a picnic and a marquee. There's a low hubbub of polite conversation while hot red faces nibble on sandwiches, and bored children moan that there is no jelly. There are photographs of Audrey in a file, and people flick through, reminiscing.

"My goodness, doesn't she look young there?"

"I never knew she went to Israel."

"Do you remember when . . .?"

"I'm sure Jonah took that one."

"How's he coping?"

At least Jonah's dad knows there is nothing to say. He sits on a deckchair, nursing a beer, then a small child climbs on to his lap: "Grandpa, play horsey with me." On the other side of the marquee, Audrey's parents are enduring a polite conversation. Harry notices their other halves flirting with each other, then realises that Jonah is missing.

As he leaves the tent, the light is turning, the grass becoming wet. Harry walks through rows of gravestones, the names scrubbed away by sea-salt and wind. A silhouette hangs over Audrey's grave. It seems like Jonah is carrying the burden of the sky on his shoulders, then he glances up, and stares.

Harry's mouth opens. He's a stranger at the funeral, a gatecrasher, but Jonah raises his arm halfway and gives an unsure wave. Harry can sense his sleeplessness, his incomprehension. They both blink at the demi-light, the evening's veils shrouding them. Harry wants the ground to swallow him, or to duck behind a gravestone. Instead he attempts a smile as if he's supposed to be there. Perhaps he can be a distant uncle — someone who remembers a girl Jonah never knew. The air thickens, as if the gaze of two men is forming a bridge

... an invitation to travel between here and there. Perhaps Jonah feels it too. Aware of the danger, Harry doffs his hat. His action disturbs an intricate balance, and Jonah turns away, the atmosphere broken.

Back in the marquee, Harry tries to calm himself down by fiddling with a paper doily. He keeps looking back to the graveyard where Jonah's silhouette is still bent under the sky's weight. *How could I have let him see me?* But when the widower returns, Harry guesses that, from his perspective, the mourners' faces are blurring. Everyone is tired, but they try to smile; yet they aren't really smiling. It's more a slight ripping round the edges of their mouths. It reminds Harry of the invisible pain of a paper cut; that day they wear paper-cut smiles.

Practising Gods

Chloe Adams sits by the lake, sketching a heron. The bird seems to be the only thing calm this restlessly hot July morning. She should be enjoying these days of freedom, chuffed that she's earned a First from Goldsmiths, but she doesn't know how to pay the rent on a bedsit she has seen in Dalston. Her feet are sweating into her Doc Martens.

She shaved her head last September, her scalp completely naked. But recently she has let the dark down grow, her millimetre pelt as soft as a mole's. The heavy boots and shorn hair are designed to be her flicked middle finger, but her skinny shoulders are resolutely feminine. Her flimsy tea dress rides up her thighs as she reaches down for a packet of paper.

Each page is twenty centimetres square, the sheets embellished with ornate Japanese patterns. She picks out one with flowers outlined in gold, a background of peach and emerald, then she looks up again at the heron poised among the reeds. She works out its proportions so the folded bird can stand while bearing the heaviness of its wings.

She begins with a simple bird base, so basic she could do it in her sleep, but to anyone else it would seem she has conjured a shape in seconds: a magician's trick. Folding is a meditation, her mind pausing through the repetition of movement. Yoshizawa, the master of modern origami, insisted his students folded in the air. Without the support of a surface, the art requires patience and precision. Chloe calls it Japanese juggling.

She first learnt how to make a paper aeroplane at an after-school club run for kids of working parents. Her father was absent before her birth, and Chloe wondered if she was the result of an immaculate conception. At her C of E school, she escaped into the magic of a virgin birth, or the trick of turning paper into a boat or a fish. But at 6p.m. any illusion would be replaced by her mum's bitter smile, the disappointed slump of weight around her waist.

They lived under the flight path in Hounslow. Chloe spent her childhood trying to lift her mother's face, sing sound into her silence. But it was only when Mr Harris moved in that her mum brightened. This ruddy-faced man made Chloe feel like she was photo-bombing the perfect portrait. Chewing her plait ends, she became the pallid girl who made paper aeroplanes. She flew them around the house in an attempt to gain her mother's attention, then propped her elbows up on the table and scowled under her fringe. She folded a bird with unbalanced wings.

She left home at sixteen, exchanging creased paper for the crumpled sheets of an older boy's bed. She hoped that one day she would be able to accept this flat-chested ghost of a girl who wanted to disappear after sex into a puff of smoke, leaving a pile of dust in her wake. The parents of the morose teenage poet were kind enough to let her stay, then she moved on to Gary, the car mechanic, who suggested she apply for an art foundation year at the technical college. By the time she was nineteen, Chloe was creating large canvases in a classroom, the paint thick with rage.

It took five years to save enough money to embark on an art degree, and by that time she was officially a mature student. She continued to be sponsored by men who were happy to lend her their bathrooms, a mattress. She lived in a squat in Peckham, a flat in Archway, and for a few weeks became homeless. What kept her on the move were the men. As soon as they talked about forever, she would run away.

Chloe temped during her degree. While folding leaflets she creased the paper in half immaculately. She then remembered how to make a boat and a fish. Later that night she returned to a stoner called Dave, watching a B-movie on television. Shutting herself in the bathroom, she took a stolen ream of printer paper from her bag and cut several sheets into squares. She made one dove, then dozens, until tiny white birds were scattered across the linoleum among Dave's stray pubic hairs.

At college, Chloe began to research not only the art but the science. She discovered that paper folds are used to solve mathematical equations that can't be resolved with a straight edge and compass. But it was the study of patterns that intrigued her most. In origami, thousands of objects are created from the humble square — the challenge is folding anew each time. Discovering the right patterns in the correct order held a symmetry that Leonardo da Vinci explored. As Chloe studied the great masters, she fell in love with the precise geometry. Through Fibonacci and Fujimoto, she hoped to find proof that there was a pattern to existence, rather than a universe that bewildered. Soon she discovered that the Japanese word *kami* is not only translated as *paper* but *God*.

Chloe had loved the story of creation. As a kid, she was in awe of the vast imagination that made the sea, the fruits and stars — by Friday, a whale. If she *were* born in His likeness, what else could she desire but to create, like the Great Creator, playing with a paper-sculpted universe and breath? But on this summers day, the would-be god is making a mess. The heron topples over.

"For Christ's sake."

She dismantles the bird then tries again, the paper more pliable once broken into. But she soon becomes distracted by a minor fiasco on the other side of the water. Across the lake, a bearded man is directing two gardeners to move a bench on to a concrete platform. It juts out into the water, surrounded by reeds, and the guy is meticulous about the bench's angle. After the staff leave, he polishes the plaque with his elbow. He then sits down on the bench, smoothing out his trousers. His imposing body looks uncomfortable in tweed.

21

Hoping to capture his melancholy, Chloe reaches for a pencil but in doing so knocks over her takeaway coffee. It spills on to a pile of sketches. As she tries to salvage the paper, she is all elbows and drenched knees. A passing man stops to help.

"That's lovely." His office-smooth fingers hold a sketch of a little girl. "Is that your daughter?"

"No."

His clean-shaven face is so polished he must use moisturiser.

"My name's Mark. Gorgeous day, isn't it?"

"I guess."

Chloe is still trying to clear up the mess. She feels frayed by the heat, the bead of sweat dripping down the inside of her dress.

He scratches his neck. "Are you a member?"

"What?"

"I just wondered if you come regularly."

She isn't about to tell him how well she knows the lake's moods, its false serenity. She grabs the sketch, teasingly. "Can't you come up with something more original?"

Mark smiles at his navel; perhaps he thinks it's a bashful gesture, something charming. "OK, I'm sorry. But any chance I can persuade you to join me at the Orangery? I could replace your drink?"

"I've got work to do. Sorry."

He remains undefeated. His face is both satisfied and attentive — as if he's staring at a wicket that he wants to hit, the bails glowing in the afternoon sun.

"Ten minutes won't hurt."

She rakes her fingers across her scalp, trying to work out how to win her fight with the half-folded heron. "Now's not the right time."

"Well, nice to meet you."

"Yes."

As he walks away, she drinks the dregs of her coffee. Then, noting his pert backside, she calls after him, shouting out a series of digits.

Harry sits on a bench with his journal. On the open page are observations of the giant waterlily, the Victoria cruziana. The leaf now measures seven feet across; she is about to flower. Harry rotates the pencil stub between his fingers, then looks up at the Ruined Arch, one of the Gardens' follies. A central arch has a smaller archway on each side, creating three tunnels. Perhaps if he closes his eyes, Audrey will rush through.

"Sorry I'm late. I have a gift for you."

In her hands is a rusty-orange scarf, the softest muslin. But there is no sound of her elegant haste, no heels against concrete. Instead a large, fake crack runs through the mock-Roman ruin.

"Audrey?" he whispers. "Au?"

All morning he has looked for her — at the pagoda, the Palm House. He knows he can't turn back those crucial seconds, but desperate men cling on to magical thinking. A miracle would make more sense than this, this absence.

Harry takes out a packet of Montecristos and lights up a cigar. Through the veil of smoke, he peruses the ivy; it scrambles over brickwork that's pretending to crumble. A stone fragment leans against the wall: a Roman carved relief showing a bearded man and two women. One of them is winged, her body angled in such a way that Harry wonders if she's waiting or leaving. He returns to his notebook.

The Victoria is always hungry. Feed her with loam mixed with blood, fish and bone. Mould into feed balls. Leave to dry in the sun.

"Hal! Oi, cloth ears!"

The slap of plimsolls against concrete, a bowlegged rhythm. A child is running up the path, accidentally dropping flowers in her wake, a trail of fluttering petals. Her mousy hair is in pigtails, her beige cords rolled up beyond her knees. Even from this distance Harry can see the mud stains. As she slows down to a stride, there's no sway in her hips, no suggestion of a feminine shape. This eight-year-old hasn't yet realised the difficulties of beauty. Instead she has a boyish, angular bounce, as if, bat in hand, she is stepping up to play rounders.

When she reaches Harry, her face is flushed from running, and the pleasure of having something to give.

"Milly! I've told you not to pick the flowers. A thousand times, I —"

"Thought they'd cheer you up. Ain't they pretty?" She searches his gaze, then peers at his feet. "They were fallen. I promise."

Harry has always found rhododendrons garish, lacking the dignity of the rose, the mystery of an orchid.

24

But Milly is looking up at him with the hope only children can muster. For the last five weeks she has badgered him for details about Audrey's funeral, but he has only managed to describe the choice of hymns, the pretty napkins: "You could see the sea from the church window." Milly is still thrusting the rhododendrons towards his chest, as if these petals can make everything better. He can't bear it. To prevent her from seeing his eyes, he crouches down and rubs out the end of his cigar on the path, saving the rest for later. Still on one knee, he takes the flowers.

"Well, there's nothing for it, luv, we'll have to fetch some water."

As they walk away from the Ruined Arch, Milly's plimsolls scuff along the path.

"I've been looking for you everywhere. Where have you been?"

"Checking on the philadelphus."

She looks up eagerly. "The ones that smell of orange and jasmine?"

"Correct."

She does a little skip to celebrate her success. "What are we going to read?"

"How about *Swallows and Amazons*?"

A few hours later, Harry puts on his hat and strolls along the streets outside the Gardens. It is a sweet, warm evening. Through the litter and dust, he passes households and habits: a flickering television, a family dinner. As the indigo sky deepens, a man sings in another tongue — a Muslim prayer or incantation. In the distance, there's the sound of a train, a lorry, then the slash of shouting. A domestic row spills from an open window.

Five houses down, a boy is practising scales on a piano, a telephone rings, and a ginger cat walks along a brick wall then jumps down into the forecourt of Audrey's building. Her flat is part of an Edwardian mansion block that overlooks the Gardens. Swiping a fist across his tear-stung eyes, Harry stares at the foot of gravel between the perimeter fence and the building — the window to Audrey's bathroom.

He had thought he was a good man; doesn't everyone? How stupid we all are, he thinks, so occupied with holding our stance that we forget to question our impact, the devastation. "Look at the stories we tell ourselves," he mutters.

Behind the wooden slats of a blind, Jonah wrestles with bed sheets. The air is stuffy with his insomnia, his exasperated re-plumping of the pillow. Feet hanging over the edge, he discards the damn cushions, lies on his back, his belly, then stands up and leaves the bedroom. He lumbers from room to room, switching on lights, wearing only a T-shirt. His lower half is naked, as vulnerable as a child's.

A couple of hours later, it looks like the flat has been burgled. Audrey would complain that Jonah isn't separating her shoes from her handbags, the winter clothes from the summer, but finally, he is putting her things into black sacks: the nightie that has been lying on the radiator, the silk dresses and bras, the snakeskin shoes from her mother that she never wore. Ever since the funeral, friends have offered to help, bullying him with kindness, but he has to do this alone. Each item holds a memory — of a night out, a christening, a picnic. Even this jumper . . . it's still shaped like her, happily slouched on the sofa.

By three in the morning, Jonah's grief is a slow underwater dance. Each room feels liquid. In the lounge is a red throw, bartered for on holiday, embroidered with tiny, circular mirrors. When he blinks, Audrey is lying on this sofa, her limbs fragmented and repeated in the glass. In every chair, he sees her sitting naked. Over there, on that white armchair . . . but when he turns there's only a red-wine stain, spilt by her father at a dinner party in 1999. He'd brought his latest girlfriend with him; was her name Michelle? The piano stool is empty. The sheet music to Bowie's "Space Oddity" lies on an upright that is heaving under the weight of newspapers and unopened post. The Boyd London was a gift from Audrey on their fifth wedding anniversary; back then it was much more than a cluttered shelf. Next to that, the corridor leads to her study, where Post-its are still stuck to the desk, her shelves jammed with documents. Jonah has rifled through her personal files, searching for a suicide note or at least some sort of goodbye: a recommendation for a film he hasn't yet seen, a random snippet to keep their conversation alive. Paint samples are slashed on the wall in shades of pink and lilac. Instead of blocks of colour they tried out the testers by painting words. All of them are names: Bella, Amy, Violet.

In the bathroom, Jonah fumbles with a box of hairgrips, a little tree of hanging rings, her make-up. Then he notices her dressing gown hanging on the back of the door, a used tissue still in the pocket. As he adds it to the sack in the hall, each sound is louder than it should be: the tap dripping, his feet slapping against the floorboards, the zip on his wife's moleskin boots.

"Palimpsest."

Audrey had woken him to say it.

"What?"

"Fourteen across. 'A parchment from which writing has been erased to make room for another text.'" She fluffed up her pillow. "I know . . . I'm a genius"

"It's three in the morning . . ."

"I just woke up and there it was. Funny thing, the subconscious."

She leant across to the box of tissues, blew her nose. "Can you remind me that we need to pick up a card for your dad tomorrow. It's his birthday on Tuesday . . ."

As Jonah wades through the bin-liners, his calves throb. He has been diagnosed with restless legs syndrome. His muscles spark and short, but he has been refused more sleeping pills, leaving him a foreigner in his body. There have been too many times when he has compiled lesson plans until five in the morning, his knee knocking against the table like a kicking horse.

Jonah is beginning to understand that becoming a widower requires a physical disentanglement. A mesh, built up through years, is now being ripped apart, the many layers of her separating from his chest, his groin,

28

his fingers. When he finally goes to bed he imagines Audrey's weight hollowing the mattress. Here is the warmth of her spine curled against his stomach.

She rolls over and opens one eye. "Do you love me?"

"Yes."

She closes her eye. "A cup of tea would be nice."

On the bedside table is a photograph of his wife in an olive suede jacket. She knew how to tilt her head, just so, her gaze so incongruent with her tailored clothes that she invited you to move that little bit closer. More than anything Jonah would like to talk. He would like the phone to ring, for them to chat about nothing, just so he could hear his wife's quiet thoughts. He wishes he had taped her breathing so he could listen to it in the dark. Just the sound of her sleeping, her lungs moving in and out.

Jonah hauls himself up and turns on the radio. It is 6 a.m. He hopes to be distracted by news but ends up listening to gospel music. "Oh Happy Day". In the corner of his mind he hears the shower running, just on the other side of the wall. He picks at the memory as if it were a scab, knowing it won't do him any good. Audrey had hoped the cascading water would hide her tears, but still he could hear her. He could visualise her mouth cracked open, her forehead pressed against the tiled wall.

When the shower stopped running, Jonah tapped gingerly on the door, but she turned on the radio. It was gospel, played at full volume, pitting her tears against the garish hope of the music. All that friggin' talk about happy days. Audrey must have been smoking

— a pile of cigarette stubs gathering outside the window. The smell seeping through the cracks of the bathroom door was making Jonah queasy.

Each time was different. The first miscarriage was what they called "silent": the dead foetus found in a scan, an unbelievable, unblinking ten minutes. *You must be wrong, there must be a heartbeat.* Jonah flew home from Copenhagen where he was touring his second album. Crumpled from the plane, he returned to find her sitting on the floor in her study.

"I should ask them to try again — perhaps the scanning machine's broken."

He squatted down. "Oh, Jesus, Au, I'm so sorry."

"They've booked a D&C for Monday."

"But that's another week —"

"I kept asking if there was a heartbeat. But they wouldn't stop fiddling with the machine, waiting for a second opinion. They wouldn't answer me."

He kissed her damp eyelashes, her wet cheeks. As the sun brightened, she asked him to make love to her in the room they had planned for their child. She wanted him to fill the stillness inside her. He knew that the foetus was calcifying, but still he yearned to be part of that inexplicable connection between mother and child.

She let him in enough to understand, just a little. Audrey was so fragile he didn't try to come. As they clung on to the reassurance of each other's bodies, he ached to stay still within her, to learn again and again, love.

30

A few months later, they went on holiday in Sicily. Jonah remembers swimming in the sea, their sandy toes against the white bed sheets, the promise that soon they would start a family. He was astonished by the resilience of her body. Her scars began to blossom as they mined the furrows of their loss, and found themselves closer. Saying yes.

The second miscarriage happened in the bathroom. Jonah sank to his knees and fished the tiny foetus out of the toilet. He had held it in his palm, a sealed embryonic sac, about an inch long.

"It's good that you get to hold her," she said. "Imagine carrying her like this for nine weeks. This," she whispered to his unfurled fingers, "this is your dad."

Jonah was frightened he would crush the last bit of their child they had left. Should he speak to this remnant of a pregnancy or hold his silence? He felt terrible for wondering what was inside: a bundle of DNA and potential, an idea they had enjoyed of what could be, or a malformed, tiny-tailed monster.

It was over a year before Audrey became pregnant again. During this time, the money from Jonah's record label ran out. He stood in for a friend who was a music teacher at a sixth-form college.

"I don't think it's for you," Audrey worried. "Your talent —"

"But I need to earn. When the baby arrives —"

"I got my period this morning."

She was standing at the sink, elbows in soapsuds. He put down the tea towel, massaged her shoulders.

"Teaching will take the pressure off. I'll still write the third album, I promise."

In September 2002, he embarked on a PGCE and Audrey stopped smoking. The next March, she was pregnant. When they reached the three-month mark, the elation of the scan, she made plans to turn the study into a nursery, but a couple of weeks later she miscarried again. That was when the real grief began. He tried taking her to fancy restaurants, or buying her the latest hardbacks from her favourite authors. But all she could do was complain. Why hadn't he fixed the flush, or changed that light bulb . . . and what was that stack of coursework doing on the kitchen counter? Her friends reassured him that she was suffering from hormonal depression, but she refused to see a doctor.

It is different, Jonah thinks, the loss of a wife, compared to the loss of an unborn child. But, with all grief, there's the corrosiveness of absence, and something that makes people strangers. It happened to them. In the last three months, Audrey no longer cried in the shower but listened to lavish baroque: Bach or Vivaldi. Perhaps she was trying to fill the house with all the music he had stopped playing.

Jonah runs the scenes in his mind, as if he can recompose the past. But he can't alter the words that might have upset her. The news comes on and the shower stops running. He turns around to see Audrey opening the door of the bathroom. She is naked, wet. The mirage of his wife walks up to him and puts one soggy arm around his neck. She rubs

32

her face against his cheek then finally her lips touch his. What kiss is this? The one he is imagining in her absence. It tastes of smoke and tears. *Am I alone in this kiss?* he asks. She disappears.

A Place for Lost Things

Jonah walks down a corridor that reeks of chip grease and polish. Once inside the classroom, he shows his pupils how to diminish a perfect fifth into a minor chord, but his insomnia makes everything feel far away, like a photocopy of a copy of a copy. The hours are glazed. But sound punctures through: his foot pumping the piano pedal, his chalk chipping a clef symbol on to the blackboard.

There's only one week to go before the school breaks for summer. Jonah has done his best to fulfil his commitments, commuting to Paddington each day to teach Music GCSE to a bunch of teenagers. On the desk, his beige satchel, blotted with ink, looks like it belongs to a student. Last September he'd hoped it suggested he was still creative, a rebel. How ridiculous that he once cared what people thought. The bell bullies.

In the staffroom, the maths tutor, reading the newspaper, wets his finger to turn each page. It makes Jonah shut himself in a toilet cubicle for fifteen minutes. *Be functional*, he chants, *focus*. After lunch, he stands in for a sick PE teacher and oversees the

34

dilapidated outdoor pool, the whistles and shrieks slashing his eardrums. His voice bellows as he disciplines a couple of kids. Trapped in his throat is a rage. Unrecognisable.

"I am angry." He says it out loud to his therapist that evening. He is here on his GP's insistence.

"I thought she'd get over it, that we'd try again. How could I have been so stupid? I should have insisted on counselling."

Paul Ridley just contemplates him.

"Did I mention that I've already got Audrey's bench? Kate, one of her friends . . ." Jonah halts, tries again. "She's well connected."

He looks away from the pronounced eye sockets, the remarkably blond eyelashes.

The therapist leans forward. "I'm wondering if there's anyone else you're angry with?"

"You mean her?"

Silence.

Paul Ridley inhales nasally. "Whether it was suicide or an accident, I imagine you feel abandoned."

"She lost three children."

"So did you."

Jonah thinks of all the words he wishes he had said. He was not enough. He never was. A man of slender love, of thin ability. He thinks about his impotence, his failure to keep his wife alive. Happy.

Milly strolls around the Gardens. Every now and then she picks up litter, just like Harry showed her. She knows each path well, even some of the people: the mum in her fake-fur coat, pushing a pram — she always comes after school; then there's the old couple who perch in the Palm House. Packed lunch balanced on their knees, they hope the humidity will soothe their arthritis. One woman always sits on the same bench, doing *The Times* crossword. Further along, by King Williams Temple, there's another regular: a photographer with a tripod. Shirtsleeves rolled up, he focuses his lens on the twisted trunk of a Tuscan olive. As he shoots the picture, Milly bends down to pick up an empty water bottle, a fag end.

Along the Cherry Walk, the blossom is long gone, and Milly is struggling to hold all the tissues and lollipop sticks. Outside Temperate House, a woman sits on a bench, drawing in a sketchbook. Milly stops to study the shape of her shaved head, her crew-cut dyed as black as a raven. There's something familiar about her skinny limbs, her fragile posture.

She is perhaps in her twenties. Poking out of her canvas bag is a large book with the letters Modigliani. Suddenly the bag rings.

The woman picks up. "No, Mark. I can't make it tonight. I'm working."

Silence.

"No."

She angles her body as though she's shouldering the caller out of view. Putting down the phone, she looks at her sketch and breathes like she's praying. Milly moves closer, but the woman crumples the page into a ball. It makes Milly feel faint, as if she were as insubstantial as a paper doll.

The woman moves away from the glasshouse, throwing the drawing in the bin. Discarding her own collection of litter, Milly trails after her. The woman is wearing heavy boots and a dress that is too red for her pale skin. She walks with a wiry determination, the canvas bag slung over her shoulder. When she takes the short cut through the woods, it's obvious that she knows where the grass is boggy, or the best route to avoid a carpet of goose droppings. Milly thought only she and Harry knew the Gardens so well. She's been a dragon-fighting samurai under the ornamental cherries, or played pirates by the lake, and now, by this expanse of water, the woman crouches down. Rummaging through her bag, she fishes out a box. Inside are three white objects, each the size of her hand. When Milly hides behind the eastern hemlock she sees them clearly: birds made out of paper. Their necks are proud, their wing tips delicately arched.

The woman kneels at the edge of the water, the soles of her boots clogged with mushed dandelions. She lays the origami birds down on the surface as if placing flowers. They float for only an instant then sink. A familiar headache begins, a throbbing under Milly's right temple; she blinks. The woman is still on her muddy knees. There's no sight of the birds on the water, just the surface murky with weeds.

Milly fingers the wooden lump in her pocket. Her flower press usually comforts — the ridged carving, the metal screws — but the urge to run grabs hold. Plimsolls thumping against the ground, her knees shocked by reverberation, she races away from the lake, retracing her journey. Once back at the Cherry Walk, she rifles through the bin. Past the empty wrappers and sandwich crusts, she picks up today's newspaper. Delving in again, she finds what she's looking for, then opens out the tight ball of paper to discover the drawing of a child. Her hair is in pigtails, her smile cheeky, but there's something wrong with her eyes . . . as if they are too old, or heavy. Somehow, with only a pencil, the woman has conveyed the girl's question. It lingers, unanswered, between the page and the viewer.

"What's the matter, luv? What are you up to?"

"Collecting litter."

A smoky hand steadies her shoulder. "You look like you're about to keel over. Please tell me you haven't talked to a stranger?"

The only thing she can hold on to is Harry's gaze. As he crouches down, she strokes the grey bristles on his cheek. She likes the roughness of it, like a scratchy towel she has known for years.

His hug always roots her. Yesterday he taught her about the early-eighteenth-century sweet chestnut, otherwise known as *Castanea sativa*. As usual, he talked to her as if she wasn't a child. After learning how to spell it, she pressed her ear against the bark, hoping to hear the tree's ancient heartbeat.

"That's the sap scurrying from root to leaf. Can you hear it? Think of the thousands of conversations it has witnessed . . . how it has helped us breathe. For centuries . . ."

Harry pulls back from the hug and gives her shoulders a squeeze.

"I've finished for the day. How about we find out what's happened to the Swallows and Captain Flint?"

"Great. I'd like that."

From his breast pocket, he produces a large, yellow flower. "The *Allamanda cathartica*. I found it on the floor in the Palm House. Most people call it the golden trumpet . . ."

"It's perfect."

As she takes it, he doffs his cap. It's an honourable hat, made of tweed. He's wearing the scarf that Audrey gave him, the colour of brick. Milly straightens the fabric, kisses his cheek.

"Perhaps it's the trumpet of a fairy queen."

She loves how he laughs with his eyes — like sunshine on water.

"Go on," he urges. "What are you waiting for?"

Milly eases out the flower press from her pocket. The carved case is four inches square. She unscrews each worn, winged nut, then levers out the wood. The blotting paper is egg blue, dusty pink, pale apple green . . . all tatty at the edges, the pulp slightly puffy in places. A tiny bug is splattered on one of the sheets.

She takes a while to choose the mauve background. When she places the flower down, adjusting its angle, she can feel Hal studying the scar on her right temple. This is the place he kisses each night, the slightly puckered flesh like a baby rose, a lighter pink than the rest of her. He always believes she is asleep, but this is the one thing she stays awake for. Eyes scrunched closed, she clings on to this daily tenderness, like a sapling stretching towards sunlight.

Once the summer holidays begin, Jonah visits the Gardens daily. He always walks the same route, strolling past the Temple of Bellona towards the lake where he completes a lap around the water before settling down on Audrey's bench. Perhaps if he turns up at the same hour each day his wife will know when to sit beside him. He doesn't believe in this, but it doesn't stop him returning, as wretched as a dog seeking his master. The habit becomes a rut that he wears down, day after day.

Kew has its own patterns. There are more tourists this time of year. He prefers the people who ask if they can sit beside him, to those who barge in and make inane comments about the markings on the red-crested pochard. Right now, a young couple are walking towards him. Venturing on to the deck, they try to impress each other with their knowledge of waterfowl while an exhausted Jonah stares them out, bullishly defending the sixty square feet of concrete around his wife's memory.

The bench is as conspicuous as a fresh grave. Unscathed by weather or bird droppings, the redwood stands out from the other, greying seats around the lake. The plaque gleams.

Audrey Wilson
1968–2004
Her footprint on my heart and these gardens
forever

Unnerved by Jonah's unwinking gaze, the couple leave, their conversation stalling.

Jonah keeps his vigil. There is a particular hour when the birds take over, the hush of wings followed by the squawk and swoop of feeding time. A gosling in a running formation trips up and perhaps sprains its ankle; it limps on, trying to keep up with the rest of the gaggle. Jonah remembers what he hadn't relished enough.

"Jonah? I was right. It's a dove tree, because the white bracts look like wings. But sometimes it's known as a handkerchief tree, or a ghost tree. I asked one of the gardeners there."

On returning from her investigation, Audrey had tucked her arm inside his. Hands still in his pockets, he felt the weight of his wedding ring. Worn for only a year, it still held a novelty. He liked the sense of gravitas, of gravity, that it gave him.

"Its Latin name is *Davidia involucrata*."

Audrey paused to savour the ancient words, then told Jonah about the tree's heritage in the Sichuan Mountains. He was amused by the mass of detail she had accrued in her two-minute absence.

They had met in Kew Gardens in 1995. They were in their late twenties, enjoying a hot, hazy day outside Temperate House, a Victorian composition of white metalwork and glass. Its octagonal structures housed fuchsias, salvias and brugmansias; but on that fragrant afternoon, roadies were climbing scaffolding, their boots tearing up the beautifully mown turf. While they rigged the lamps for that nights concert, the Rolling

Stones' "Sympathy for the Devil" played through the speakers, and Audrey walked up to the sunbathing Jonah and asked him for a light. As the chorus sambaed in, he couldn't guess her name. Her smile was sunshine.

Jonah blinked through the shield of his fingers at the woman clutching a paperback of *Aimez-vous Brahms* in one hand and an unlit cigarette in the other. He took in her cream culottes, her pristine blouse, the red plait hanging between her breasts. Their first conversation lasted the time it took for Audrey to finish her cigarette. By then, Jonah had discovered that she was a translator. Despite literary yearnings, she mostly dealt with technical documents in Russian or Polish. As the music jangled jubilantly between them, a cocksure Jagger syncopating the air, there was rhythm between them. But it was her smile that disarmed. He wanted to unclothe her elegance, to explore that gap between her front teeth with his tongue.

In a rush of wanton curiosity Jonah offered to buy them tickets that he couldn't afford for that evenings performance. They met a few hours later, on the same lawn. Crowds had gathered with picnic blankets and hampers full of plastic champagne flutes. It was a balmy, scented night and everyone there knew they were lucky, graced with a warm evening during the British summer. There was the sense of not wanting to be anywhere but here.

Schubert was his favourite. They stood enraptured when "*Ellens dritter Gesang*" began, and the sky over the Gardens thickened with Ave Maria". In the

42

interval, they discussed the blessings and frustrations of a foreign language. Starting their second bottle of wine, Audrey offered to translate the German, but Jonah preferred to hear the emotional shape of the sound. To him, the lack of understanding allowed the step-by-step wonder of experience.

"I know you're a linguist, but there are just some feelings we can't get our mouths around."

She took a breath as if to explain, then laughed at herself. As they held each other's gaze, the garden hesitated, as if the word "love" was being pencilled in. It remained unspoken, a sketch of an emotion; too light, too amorphous. It was so foreign that they didn't share that word for a long time. Instead they held hands as the night exploded, the sky sparking with cascading light.

Once the smell of cordite had settled, they were ushered out into a Kew Road jammed with retreating spectators. They said goodbye by the bus stop, Jonah's boot shyly scuffing the pavement. Finally he kissed her, a question on his lips: non-intrusive, humble. Her answer was rapturous. Later that night Jonah lay alone in bed. All he could think about was the burn of the traffic, the glare of the streetlights and the quiet happiness of their mouths.

Their second date was at a pasta restaurant in Parkway. Over dimly lit meals, they felt an urgency to share their stories. Audrey retold a childhood full of exotic holidays and immaculate gardens. Her father taught his only child about ambition. Her mother, a glamorous socialite, enjoyed a mid-morning tipple.

"The only problem was, they were both screwing other people."

Audrey's memories were of secrets and strained silences, the chatter of strangers, the chink of glasses at a dinner party. When her parents eventually split, she immersed herself in her studies. She didn't lose her virginity until her last night at uni. What she remembered most was the damp on the ceiling, and the absurdity of the human body.

Jonah suspected it was her grand rebellion to date a scruffy musician. He tried to romanticise his middle-class upbringing by describing his early childhood in Devon. He painted a picture of a boy trailing a stick, scrambling over rock pools, spending Sundays crabbing. He told her about family evenings in the pub when someone would take out a harmonica or a fiddle, the room swelling with song. The smell of scrumpy and open fires, damp woollen jumpers, wet dogs.

When Jonah was thirteen, his family moved to Surbiton. Quick to lose his West Country accent, he still looked out of place, hemmed in, yet no one dared to bully him. A foot taller than his peers, he was the only one who looked old enough to buy beer. Despite his opportunist new friends, he still spent evenings alone, picking his guitar, trying to conjure up the cliffs or the taste of salt on his skin, his legs wobbly from chasing seagulls. As he attempted to capture the sound of a sunset, the music rushed towards him, then pulled back temptingly. When his sister was given piano lessons, it was he who showed the natural talent. He often skulked away from the dinner table to make racket and rhythm.

His musical skill won him a place at Bristol, where finally he escaped suburbia and mixed with the cool kids who listened to Patti Smith and Bowie. For his dissertation, he researched Celtic folk music — then compared it to the work of Cohen and Dylan. After graduation, he sent demos to A&R men, played covers at weddings and performed his own songs in beer-sticky venues. He mastered the seventies look that was popular then: brown leather jacket, flared jeans, all accessorised with unkempt hair and beard. But he didn't fit into the trip-hop scene in Bristol, and by 1995 it was the heyday of Britpop. He didn't have the compulsory swagger, just an acoustic guitar, sometimes accompanied by a cello. But eventually, at the age of twenty-eight, he was signed by a label.

On their third date, Audrey encouraged him to talk about his future, about whom, one day, he would become. In response, he shared one of his songs. It was about his mother who had died two years previously. It was full of grazed gratitude and yearning. As he sang to Audrey, he realised that the timing was exquisitely ripe to meet this woman. But her class and intelligence felt beyond him.

Afterwards, he was embarrassed. Keeping his gaze on the strings, he tried to impress her with talk of pentatonic scales and interrupted cadences. She teased him.

"Music? If you can't dance to it, make love to it, or cry to it, what's its reason?"

When he dared to look up, her eyes were glistening. He couldn't tell if they were tears; she glanced down and buttoned up her sleeve.

"You're absolutely right," he said.

"Always," she grinned.

When they made love, her immaculate façade began to crack, and underneath was a nakedness more bare than Jonah had known. She was inexperienced, but each touch was awkwardly sincere, each kiss loyal. That was the surprise, the pleasure, and he knew that she was the one to teach him. From her he could learn how to laugh gently, and to love fiercely.

In the summer of 1996 they met on the lawn in front of Queen Charlotte's Cottage, a rustic, picturesque building within the conservation area of Kew Gardens. Audrey was waiting under a birch tree when Jonah arrived, ten minutes late, carrying two large suitcases. He sat down, opened the first case and took out the Beatles' *White Album*.

"This is for you."

While Audrey grasped the vinyl, Jonah took out the next item: a toy lightsaber.

"And this is for you too."

Following that was a book of Yeats's poetry and several albums by David Bowie. There were photographs of Jonah's family on a windy beach, a pebble with a stone in it, then his mum's ruby-studded ring. Next came his first plectrum, a *Blue Peter* badge, and a Mozart concerto. Half an hour later, the presents were piled high on the picnic blanket: teetering towers of fishing rods, underlined passages in paperbacks, cassettes of his first compositions.

"What is all this?"

His smile was a shrug.

"Everything that means something to me."

They looked down at his lopsided proposal.

"It might take a lifetime to share all this. Is that OK?"

She tilted her head, as if to ask a question. Then it happened: the glory of her gap-toothed grin.

"I'd like that very much."

The sunlight, her tears, his fumbling for his mother's ring. He grasped her finger. "Promise me. Don't let go of my hand."

Click. A shutter opens and closes. Jonah looks up to see a thin woman taking photographs of the lake. When she puts down the camera, she searches the water, her shoulders as forlorn as her shaved head and flimsy dress. Jonah is unsure if she will find what she is looking for before the wind blows her away. A few feet along, a toddler and his mum are feeding bread to the ducks. Two women walk past, chatting about a problem at work.

"I told him to jump off a cliff!"

Later, Jonah realises that one of them has dropped her tasselled shawl. He wonders where the lost-property office is. Then he thinks that there should be a place in every town where people could put rescued or found things. Not just objects, but snippets of forgotten languages, or misused time — an hour that can never be lived again. It would be a place where lost faiths could be collected, as well as keys, gloves and love letters never sent. Here you could find extinct animals and old wives' tales vanished in history; a whole shelf of unfinished songs, discontinued books, deleted texts. It would be a safe for fleeting emotions — the first flush of love, or a particular scent on a sunny day that is never savoured again. Among the dog leads, phones and hats, there would be babies hoped for and lost. All this would be remembered: missed opportunities, mislaid friends, the smile of a wife. It would be a place for lost things.

The Gardener's Bible

Harry is always in the Gardens before the gates open. Stand in nature before anyone else has woken and most people find something to believe in. He holds no truck with traditional gods; if they exist, they're bastards. But still, right here, is the everyday miracle of petals opening, a sparrow turning towards the sun. He sees it all the time: the impulse to create at the core of the universe. It's in every sapling whose only ambition is to bear apples. He devoutly believes in the urge to flourish that is in every living thing. But more than that, if he is quiet, he notices the animals share certain rituals — like that squirrel over there, pausing at the rise of the sun. It's as if it is taking part in the whole, knowing something Harry doesn't. Whatever it is, it calls forth his humility, and he sees it in the people who come. They remember wonder.

These three hundred acres are buzzing with natural laws. But exactly a year ago, Harry broke them. He visits a little potting shed in the Redwood Grove and changes out of his charcoal-grey suit. In the mustiness of the shed, he takes off his waistcoat and hangs it up with his beloved scarf. On a hook is his old green jumper, the wool vanishing into ever-increasing holes. On this September day he imagines that if he pulls the right thread, all of him will unravel.

Once, this jumper looked smart, professional — as if Harry knew what he was doing, a man who understood his botanical craft. When he was younger, the female staff argued whether his blue eyes reminded them of Paul Newman or Lawrence of Arabia. They studied him tending to a new batch of seedlings: precise, attentive love seeping from his fingers. It seemed as though he were colouring in the tones of a tree, dabbing in the speckles of an orchid. The girls gossiped about the way he clocked-in at night for the giant waterlily to open. Some gathered in the temporary glasshouse under the pretence of learning. By nine fifteen they had waited two hours.

"Are you sure it's not ready?" a girl fretted. "It looks open."

"You can't rush her," said Harry. "You need to observe the final petals."

At 10.56p.m. the women held their breath as Harry waded into the inky-black pond. His cap placed at a jaunty angle, he looked like a matinée idol; but his hands held the delicacy of a calligrapher. Probing the anthers, Harry coated his paintbrush with pollen then went deeper inside the flower's hollow to complete the self-pollination. It was horticulture as an art form.

Raised annually from seed, the Victoria became Harry's obsession. There was no room for romance because he was already in love with these gardens. The volunteer girls yearned to unfold in his arms and

50

stretch towards the sunlight, but he never noticed the subtle pigments in a woman's lips, or the curve of her cheekbones. He was too focused on the swelling fertility of a stem, or the first sign of heart rot.

The girls soon discovered that Harry had been a soldier, but his love life remained a source of speculation. They didn't know about his childhood girlfriend, the scribbled notes in class, the cautious touching; or that when Harry went to boot camp, he had several one-night stands. But when Harry returned from fighting, he shunned the female species, too shocked by where his hands had been, and what they had done.

As time went on, he refused promotions, including Keeper of the Palm House. He didn't want to push paper or tell people what to do; he had a distrust of men in suits. But that didn't stop the foremen coming for advice — from the Tropical Pits, the Arboretum, the Herbaceous Department — and as the years went on, Harry moved between specialisms. He was civil enough with his colleagues, enjoying banter with the tree gang, but at the end of the day all he wanted was to go home and scrub the dirt from his fingers. Behind terrace walls, he read novels recommended by friends who had died in the desert. The sound of the turning page was a comfort. The paper was even familiar — that scent of pulped trees — and it was easier to trust these books over people; they didn't disappear.

On stormy nights, he lay awake, counting the hours. As soon as it was light he would go to the Gardens, to check on his friends: the chestnut-leaved oak, the

Chinese tulip tree, the Caucasian elm. Keeping things alive was his grand passion. Each morning he returned to the mess room to be part of an army that planted and pruned, and sometimes he did the most important thing in the world: he saved species from extinction.

In the passing years, the weather has dug lines into his face, flecked his hair silver, but Milly says the cragginess suits him. With her, he has found his apprentice. Together, they visit his favourite trees. He has pointed out the families — the great-great-grandchildren, the 200-year-old elders — and he has also told her about the great storm of '87.

"Seven hundred mature trees, luv. Never thought those great broadleaves would come down, but the wind plain pushed them over. We started the clean-up in the north end, working systematically through the Gardens, then in 1990 it happened again. It was a different kind of wind, a swirling wind, that got under the conifers, twisted them right out of the soil."

"Are you ready yet?"

Milly has popped her head around the door of the potting shed, her face masked by a cobweb. Harry wears a navy synthetic jumper displaying the Gardens' logo.

"Where are you working today?"

"Arboretum. Have you got your maths book?"

"Stop nagging."

After tucking his notebook into his belt, Harry and Milly walk hand-in-hand to the Victoria entrance.

It is mid-September, but the early morning still promises summer. There are many tourists this time of year, all the continents of the earth converging. As the gates open, Harry remembers what Audrey wore a year ago when she walked through this same entrance. There is a cacophony of languages as the visitors decipher directions, or try to explain to their companions what it feels like to be them in that particular moment. But once they are through these gates, the talk slows down, then stops. Everything is in the silence.

After his shift, Harry visits the library in Kew Green. He still whiles away his time off with reading. Before going to the poetry section, he sits down at a desk and takes out his journal. For the last few years he has dabbled with descriptive writing, surprised by what he can create with only lead and paper. He is slightly embarrassed by how much he enjoys weeding words, or pruning back an ellipsis; a poet trapped inside a gardener's body. Plant one word, watch it grow — but first, turn over the soil, start with the basics.

HB. 13.09.04. Richmond Library
Hardy cyclamen in bloom.
In Temperate House, the chillies are fruiting.

Harry gazes at his bookmark. The first time he saw this picture he was in the corner by the white pillar, leafing through an archive of *LIFE* magazines, dating back to the forties. When he came across the black-and-white photo, he stared at it for an hour. He tried to make a mental snapshot, but in the end he couldn't bear to leave it. The only member of staff was in the toilet and he quickly tore the page, a violent gash of sound. Even now, he wonders if he should tape it back in, perhaps leave an anonymous note of apology ... *I'm not normally a vandal* ... but what the camera captured in 1942 still transfixes him.

As he stares at the stolen image, he curses a God he keeps telling himself he doesn't believe in. The librarian passes, but Harry has no need to worry: the glossy page is now soft and dog-eared. Folded into quarters, there's only a glimpse of a woman's bare legs, a pair of black court shoes. That reader, two chairs down, might see the illuminated letters of the vertical word "HOTEL". But only Harry feels the lurch of the tall building. It stands on 530 Main Street, New York.

Harry tucks the photo into his pocket then returns to his journal. Milly is excited about the mass planting of bulbs that happens each autumn. He has drawn intricate maps of where they will be laying the *Crocus tommasinianus*, the *Fritillaria meleagris*. But he is struggling with the child's enthusiasm. Since Audrey's death, he can't look Milly in the eye. Trouble is, he's the only thing left she has to believe in. As his pencil touches the page, he thinks about Audrey's longing to be a mother. Was it this ache that brought the two of them together? He remembers that sleepy morning by the Ruined Arch.

Her kiss was the perfect trespass.

Bird Life

On rainy days the locals buckle down. Florists bring in flowers from the pavement, cafés pack up tables, and Jonah stands outside Kew Gardens station, his damp skin sticking to his collar. He misses the intimacy of being touched on the back of his neck, of talking so close to someone that he can feel breath on his face. He misses that complexity of sense.

His solitary footsteps chime out against the Surrey pavement. Once home, he orders a takeaway and remembers the nights when he cooked Italian. What do others do when they eat alone; use the TV as a companion? The freezer is full of Audrey's homemade stew, neatly packed in Tupperware, but he hasn't been able to swallow the onions she chopped, to let her nourish him. He can't even open the freezer door. He gazes at the pile of dirty plates, a thread of dental floss strewn across the sofa, then sits down in front of twenty-seven essays on the Romanticism of Brahms and Liszt. Like him, many of his students are struggling to focus. He looks up, wondering how to instil their passion, but becomes distracted by the colours on the shelves, books lined up like a rainbow.

There's a shaft of yellow on the third shelf and below that a wave of blue, becoming steadily darker until it reaches the black spine of *The Story of O*. Audrey found books easily, remembering the feeling of the cover, the font's curl. Garcia Márquez in the Penguin oranges, Murakami and Winterson in the white. A book about contemporary dance. They had seen the Nederlands Dans Theater at Sadler's Wells. In the interval, drinking wine on Rosebery Avenue, someone said, "His extension was magnificent." Catching each other's eye, Audrey and Jonah had started to giggle.

The clock taunts. Jonah pats out a rhythm against his thigh then moves to the piano. The maple wood is faded from sunlight, the varnish bare in places, the upright top covered in unopened post. He plays a middle C, then remembers when his fingers doodled for hours, the patterns revealing themselves: a lyric, an arpeggio. But now there is only a yellowing key, played over and over.

Time trickles through him: all those seemingly innocent decisions, like deciding to have a cellist play on his second album. *Between Your Smile* became a cult success, receiving rave reviews from *NME* and *Time Out;* but the indie kids made bootlegs. Touring was the only way to make decent money. Audrey hated him being away, surrounded by groupies. He explained that they were flimsy in comparison to her — that he would never behave like her father — but when Audrey fell pregnant a second time he decided to be there.

He refused a tour to break the album in the States. He pacified the label by saying he had the itch to write something new, but each time he sat with an instrument, his fingers were idle. He tried once again to write about Audrey, but her arms were constantly crossed over her belly. While she focused on her changing body, he lumbered around the flat, getting in the way, trying to help.

He's not sure exactly when his ambitions became flabby, but slowly he began to accept that he wasn't destined to become the next Jeff Buckley. During the PGCE, he put on weight, lost his style and self-belief; then, when he started work, he was shocked by the paperwork, the frustratingly poor budgets. Audrey blamed herself.

"Look at the sacrifices you made. For what? For non-existent children?"

"Let's be honest, I never had the showmanship."

"You were different. Perhaps if you'd toured America, or managed to write the next album —"

"Au, darling, it was *my* decision."

By three in the morning, Jonah is still sitting at the piano. He is peering at the patterns in the night, the soft fuzz of dots that swarm in the air; he first noticed them as a child. He squints closer, trying to manipulate the coloured flecks, then wonders if everyone sees this, or only those who have been awake for twenty-two hours. His legs involuntarily twitch, occasionally kicking the piano.

By four, he is watching porn. From the sanctity of her photo, Audrey witnesses her husband tugging and jerking his way to a blistered sleep. When he finally naps, his pants by his ankles, he looks like a Greek god that has been given salvation.

57

Masturbation becomes his way to relieve the monotony of solitude; but it only buys him short spells of sleep. The accumulation of five months of insomnia make the pavements topple as he walks down the street. The sky lists, buildings leer in puddles, and Jonah jumps as rubbish is tipped into a lorry: the clang of a metal bin. He struggles to complete lesson plans, his department so low on resources that he emails friends to see if they have an old instrument in the attic — an unplayed guitar, or violin.

Occasionally he is invited to dinner parties, where he becomes acutely aware of the uneven number of table settings. As he takes in the noisy camaraderie, it feels like he's looking down a wind tunnel. Friends, picking bones from their sea bass, ask how he is. After listening to his stilted reply, they agree that life can never be the same.

"But as time passes, it can still be good."

"Do you think, Kate?"

He stares at Audrey's friend. Pregnant for the third time, she looks exhausted. Repeatedly she has explained that she's not drinking. Each time she pours another glass for her companions, she is the epitome of passive aggressive.

"I was thinking about my colleague, Nicky," she says. "Just become single. I know you're not ready yet. But —"

"You're right, Kate. It's too early."

In November, the islands on the lake are vibrant with tupelo trees, a tapestry of reds and russets. As Jonah sits on the bench, his eyes flutter between sleeping and waking. He catches images of falling leaves, Audrey's hair brushing against his face — but she is always ephemeral, slipping between his fingers, impossible to touch.

A week before Christmas, Jonah douses his grief with whisky in a local pub. A third drink, a fourth drink later, the words on the coasters are blurring and a woman asks for a light. Audrey? His gaze focuses on a blonde with fuchsia lipstick. An hour later, he confesses he's widowed and she looks at him in a way he vaguely remembers. She is perusing him as if he is someone whose hair should be ruffled, a man who could suggest going home with just his eyes. Perhaps he really did seduce the crowd at The Borderline with only a love song, and now this woman is putting her hand on his shoulder and asking if he lives nearby.

Once they are in his flat, Jonah cannot comprehend the position she prefers, her excessively sweet perfume, but the trophy is this: afterwards he sleeps for a few hours, soothed by her arms and her wine-tainted breath.

He wakes to find a stranger in his bed. He moves to the wicker chair by the window then cumbersomely folds his knees to his chest.

"Good morning." The woman wraps Audrey's green-swirled duvet around her unfamiliar breasts. "Jim? Are you OK?"

"I'm sorry, I'm not . . . I . . ."

She gets out of bed. He blinks at the soft patch of hair between her legs.

"Your wife?"

"Yes."

"I guess I should be going. Perhaps I'll leave my number? If there's anything you need, or if you want some company . . ."

"Thanks"

The woman gets dressed. She pauses by the door. "Call me."

"Yes."

After suffering his first Christmas alone, Jonah agrees to go on a date. Who knew a noodle bar in Richmond would feel such a hostile place? He doesn't know the rules, the etiquette.

"Each week, Mam calls me," says Nicky, her chopsticks snapping the air. "She tells me about her friends' grandkids, then says, when are you going to get a boyfriend, Nic?"

Come on, Jonah, pretend everything is OK — but he is remembering the winter when he and Audrey toured London pubs searching for the perfect banoffee pie. She had charmed a headwaiter called Pierre, and although Jonah had no idea what they were saying, he loved their mock-flirtation, the luxury of watching his wife from a distance. Jonah remembers the day they first met, the book she was reading.

"*Aimez-vous Brahms?*"

Nicky sucks in a noodle. "Pardon?"

"I was saying Brahms, do you like him?"

"What books has he written?"

"Doesn't matter. What would you like for pudding?"

In early February, a drummer takes Jonah to a pub along the Thames. He has decided that Jonah doesn't need a relationship; he simply needs to get laid. They walk along the dark cobbles then enter the warmth, shaking off the rain. As they go up to the bar, there are other people looking for a canopy of skin to sleep under. A refuge is not only made of bricks and mortar. His mate points out a glorious yacht of a woman, then a pretty, ramshackle girl, but Jonah shakes his head and suggests playing snooker.

While he digs around for his wallet, his mate offers three girls a round.

"This is Jonah," he introduces. "He's a singer."

"Yeah, right, pull the other one."

"It's true."

"What kind of stuff do you sing?"

Three pints later, the girl with the kindest eyes notices his wedding ring. The conversation blurs.

"I hope I'm not boring you."

"No." She touches his arm.

"The thing is, my wife . . . she passed away."

"I'm sorry, what?"

"That reminds me —"

"Mind if I smoke?"

Jonah swigs his beer; she reaches for a cigarette.

"Well . . . freezing weather."

"Whether what?"

"Whether I could come back?"

"Can I have —?"

"Just a little piece of you?" She twirls her hair around one varnished nail. "Tell me something fascinating."

"She broke her neck."

"Do you believe in —?"

"Never." A cough. "Sorry, after you."

"You must be lonely."

"Yes."

Under the watchful eye of his wife's photos, he takes the woman back to his flat. Everyone needs company, some kind of consolation. This is the rough comfort of strangers, the sympathy of touch.

"All neurotic behaviour is a substitute for grief."

Jonah laughs with a grunt, as if he's been punched in the stomach.

Paul Ridley rubs his deep-socketed eyes. "You've had sex with four or five women — but you refuse to see any of them twice?"

"They help me sleep. But then I hit some part of my brain pattern where I realise it's not Audrey's arms and —"

"You wake up?"

"Yes."

Both men cross their legs, inadvertently mirroring the other.

"What else do you get from these encounters?"

Pity and passion. Relief. Jonah tries to think about the different women, but all he sees is the view from Audrey's bench: peacocks, swans, geese.

"I just want to get some sleep. It's only for three hours, but that's a bloody gift. It may seem callous, but . . ."

He breaks the reflection. He's been seeing this therapist for nine months, this balding man, who has no idea what it's like to lose a wife, or endure three miscarriages. But there's some comfort in their continued acquaintance, some sanctuary in this tiny, neutral room, beautified with paintings of landscapes and pastel cushions. It is the one place he can slosh around in his ugliness; revel, even.

"After nine years of monogamy I might as well enjoy my freedom. Each woman is different . . ." He rolls his shoulders, tries to be manly. "I'm having fun."

"Fun? That must be it."

A stalemate. The two men wait for the other to give in. Both blink.

The branches remain barren. In late February, Jonah is tempted to use sex to punctuate the dark hours, but he can no longer bear his whoring. He feels too guilty about not calling, the empty flattery, the waste of a woman's kisses. But alone, he faces the consequences. At three in the morning he paces the flat, berserk with exhaustion. His legs spasm and he falls, kicking the door of the bathroom. He beats on the door with his bare feet until he breaks the wood — then he spends the rest of the night on the floor, picking out the splinters.

When he finally gets up, he washes his sunken features, then stares at the bathroom mirror. Gone is the idealistic musician who proposed to Audrey. Instead, there is a hard-faced thirty-eight-year-old, behaving like a teenager. Not even forty and a widower, he thinks; almost forty and nothing to show for it. Womanising is his only way to sleep; the alternative is to down a bottle of pills and never wake. Opening the cabinet, he stares at the ominous jars on the shelf and considers the gap between thinking it and doing it. What would make someone take that leap?

A Guitar Riff

The air is tinged with spring. At closing time, people
return to Victoria Gate, meandering from different
directions. Many walk slowly, begrudgingly, not yet
ready to leave this blossomed world; but the constable
stands at the gates, ushering them out on to Kew Road.
The street is jammed with cars trying to squeeze
through the bottleneck of the bridge to the M4. The
visitors, dazed by pollution, reluctantly disperse.

As dusk falls, the quiet settles in the Gardens like
dew. Windows are ajar at Temperate House. Inside
there is a silent city, the plants assimilating the day's
sunshine. Breathing. Parakeets gather in the treetops as
Harry takes an evening stroll towards the Princess of
Wales Conservatory. Inside this glasshouse, cacti are
blooming, and flowers are perfuming the twilight with
scents more exotic than any woman.

A cockroach crunches under his foot and Harry
curses. Pests are a constant bugbear: a plague of thrips,
an infestation of whiteflies. He walks past the baobab
trees, checks on the carnivorous plants — sundews,
Venus flytraps — then he enters another zone and
opens a glass cabinet.

Inside is a deep-throated comet orchid. Harry wipes his clammy hands against his trousers then stretches out his fingers. It looks as if he's preparing to conduct a choir; instead he reaches into his pocket and pulls out a toothpick. Gently, he prods the male sex organs of the orchid, dislodging the pollinia from under the flap of the anther. His toothpick carries this treasure to the stigma of a second plant, where he splits the tiny white cap of his load, exposing two balls of pollen. He carefully pokes the toothpick into the stigma's delicate opening. If accepted, the stem will become turgid.

As Harry checks whether he has caused any damage, he wonders how many times he has waited for the stink that announces a particular flower is ready. Here, men do the work usually performed by hummingbirds, moths and night-flying beetles. Once these seeds mature, he will sow them, then present Milly with her very own baby orchid. It might not be as playful as a kitten but it will give her something to care for, to nourish.

What was that? Something moves outside the darkened window. A smudge of white, Audrey's face — Harry rushes towards her. But there's no one there. Perhaps a gull flew by, or it was falling blossom. Harry knows all about the art of patience. With the flowerpot still in his hands, he repeatedly knocks his forehead against the glass, a bruise slowly forming.

Over by the lake, Jonah slides out from his hiding place behind the tangled branches of a red osier dogwood.

He sits on Audrey's bench, his chin buried deep in his collar.

The night brings the breeze and the whispered language of secrets. Jonah beats his arms for warmth, listening to the creak of the trees, the snuffling of an unknown creature. As the moon rises, he jumps at rustling leaves, then tells himself it is nothing supernatural. It's just other people doing things they shouldn't: couples screwing, a few kids on a dare. At closing time it's easy to hide in these three hundred acres, in one of the follies or dells. But once the darkness falls, there are no streetlamps to guide, just the scurrying of rabbits and a man's wishful thoughts.

He tries to ignore the cold by remembering yesterday's session with Paul Ridley. For the umpteenth time they'd discussed Audrey's death.

"She loved me. You don't kill yourself if . . ."

There had been no reason for Audrey to crash their Ford Ka. The police had checked her phone to see if someone had distracted her from the wheel, but there was no record of a call. Two witnesses saw her coming out of High Park Road and indicating right on to the A205. One was a mother in a Nissan Micra who'd been driving towards Kew Bridge. She reported that Audrey didn't stop for the Give Way sign, that she'd accelerated rather than braked. The other was a child on a skateboard. He had seen her right indicator blink, but Audrey had driven straight into the T-junction: a white wall. Her head must have been turned to the left, the coroner said, for her to break her neck the way she did. Jonah remembers identifying the body, her lacerated face. He thinks of the car hitting the bricks, the white dust, the moment of impact.

"Shit!"

The planks of the bench suddenly dip under another's weight. The crash of two bodies, the warmth of a stranger's thigh against his. Then the shocking heat disappears.

"What the hell?" The woman's feet resound against concrete. "What the hell are you doing?" She has dropped a bag, the rustling of plastic.

"Nothing," he stutters.

She sounds young, in need of reassurance. He tries to calm them both. He stretches out his legs, easing out the stress they endured mere seconds ago.

"I'm Jonah."

She makes to go.

"I was just sitting here," he adds, "minding my own business, then . . ."

"You freaked the hell out of me! I didn't see you."

The rising moon must have navigated her way to the lake, his silhouette hidden by the dogwood.

He tries to imagine what she looks like from her voice, which is pitched high, ready to fight. But she isn't fighting, she's fleeing. He can only just make her out, leaving the decking, her feet unsettling the gravel, and all of a sudden he doesn't want to be alone.

"There's always a few people skulking around," he calls out. "They're bound to bump into each other."

Why can't he think of a joke? Something funny and friendly — with a punchline that convinces her he's not Jack the Ripper. Her footsteps stop. As he senses her turn, there's something thrilling about not being able to see each other, the air charged with fantasy, imagination. The adrenalin contorts. He can still feel his heart beating; he can almost feel hers.

"Actually, I work here." He can hear her moving towards him, rummaging in her bag. "I should report you."

Shit. His mind races about possible fines, or worse.

"Wow!" He never uses that word. But he's all innocence, as if they've just been introduced. Perhaps she'll forget that they're not in a sunny, public place, that he's not supposed to be here at all. "What kind of work do you do?"

"None of your business."

Suddenly he is blinded. Her torchlight scalds him. The tyranny of a tiny, electric bulb.

She seems to be relishing the advantage. The light moves around his body, measuring him up, as if she is the one holding the man's gaze and he the object. He blinks, trying to seek out the shape behind her weapon: a knee-length skirt, the silhouette of an androgynous, angular figure.

"You don't look like a gardener," he mutters.

She strengthens her grip on the torch, her stance feline, aggressive. Instinctively he raises his hands, as if she's holding a pistol; then he splutters with laughter.

"It's not funny," she says flatly.

"No."

The darkness prickles.

"I'm researching stuff."

"Stuff? I'm not sure you work here at all . . ."

A tiny battle of a pause.

"Look," he says, "admit it. If this is where you want to be, I can go."

"I'm not lying. I'm researching trees . . . shadows in the moonlight." She rams her hand into one of her shopping bags and pulls out a crumpled ball. As she shines the torch on it, she reveals a tiny paper bird.

"What the hell's that?"

"Origami. What's your excuse?"

Jonah laughs incredulously. "You're as mad as the moon."

"Well," she says, "what about you?"

The light is on him again. He can imagine what she sees: his unkempt beard, his sallow, hope-drained face. He looks more like a tramp than a teacher.

"I'm going home."

"You know a way out?"

"Of course." He stands up, then looks her over. "You're hardly dressed for the occasion."

"I didn't realise it would get so cold."

He begins to stroll away. "Are you coming?"

She hesitates before following. He plans to avoid the paths, Victoria Gate, and asks her to switch off her torch. He wonders what kind of girl would trust a stranger, but she seems to be enjoying her recklessness, as if this is a story to revel in later. Or perhaps she'll tell her friends the truth: *There was a sad guy on a bench. There was no way he'd hurt me. He was as weak as a punctured balloon.*

As they make their way through the Berberis Dell, he begins to enjoy their shared crime, his accomplice's

70

stealth. They can't see their next steps, but she continues walking, as if trusting the land beneath her. He can feel her listening to it too — the sap moving in the trees, the stilling of wings in the branches. There's a spaciousness to the wide sky, the way they are working together. Each is sensing where the other is, where they might need to duck, or negotiate some nettles — then they halt as a large bird takes to the air, perhaps a spooked owl. He smiles at her, perhaps she smiles back — neither of them can tell.

They reach the path running parallel to the main road. Jonah asks for some light as he ventures beyond it, into the undergrowth. The girl shines her torch against the brick wall, the beam catching a disused door. It has a statue of a unicorn above it. Jonah leads her further into the shrubs where the ground slopes upwards. He invites her to put her foot in his hand. As she hauls her weight up, he supports the back of her woollen knees, her bony ankles. Once she has thrown her leg over the wall, he follows her, until they are both standing on Kew Road.

Under the streetlamps, she is older than he imagined, perhaps in her late twenties. Her short black hair reminds him of a pixie, her fringe asymmetrical as if she has cut it herself.

She celebrates their escape with a wry smile. "Thanks. I'll see you around."

"Got far to go?"

"Dalston." Her stare stretches down the street. She scratches her leg, perhaps stung by those nettles, then begrudgingly asks, "Do you know a café I can wait in?"

"It's well beyond midnight." He blows into his hands. "None of them will be open."

She gazes down, suddenly fascinated by the dimple in her tights, the way they sag around her ankle. He grabs the opportunity to take in this urchin. She has a boyish figure. Uninviting.

"I guess I'll wait for the bus." Gathering her plastic bags, she looks for somewhere to perch.

"That'll be hours."

He can't leave her out here, prey to the cold or worse.

"I live a few minutes away. I could put the kettle on. No funny business."

"No."

"You're freezing. There's a comfy sofa. Heating. A bathroom."

That clearly interests her. She stares at his hands then lifts her head defiantly.

"Won't your wife be at home?"

"What? No." He glances down at his wedding ring. "No, no chance of that. I'm widowed."

"Oh."

Here it is again, the embarrassed silence. Warily she mirrors him, stuffing her hands in her pockets.

"My name's Chloe."

The streetlamp catches the glint of a dare in her eye. He tries to match it.

"Would you prefer tea or coffee?"

His flat is filthy. There is grime in the sink, shrivelled peas in the cracks between the floorboards, piles of books half-read, the debris of nights not sleeping. As Chloe disappears down the hall, he worries about what she will think of the broken door then hears the flush of the cranky cistern. A minute later, the girl reappears.

"You play?" She juts her chin towards the piano.

"A bit. Not really."

As she rubs her arms, she takes in the many photographs of Audrey: walking duffel-coated in the woods, chatting at a dinner party.

"How long ago did . . .?"

"Last May."

Jonah puts the kettle on while Chloe studies the shelves, her fingers trailing along the books' colour-coded spines. As he turns to stare at her, he remembers that he's out of Zopiclone. The lack of sleep is making him queasy. He watches his guest through a smeared lens. Her scrawny body looks like it holds a library of experiences, as if she has been touched by many things — or many people. But he tries not to think of her as his latest sleeping aid, a little human pill. She has taken off her shoes and wears a thrift-shop dress that doesn't quite fit. It is only when she moves into the lamplight that he realises her skin is as pale as a ghost's. It contrasts with her eyes, a cornflower blue . . . and what would it hurt? He has never run his fingers through shorn hair, or kissed a mouth that is almost too wide . . . a reckless mouth, as if anything could come out.

"I think I've seen you before."

"What?"

She is staring at him curiously. "It *is* you. I've seen you at the lake — at the spot where we met. You're there all the time." She pulls a face. "You usually wear a brown suit."

"What's wrong with it?"

"Nothing." Then she laughs.

He had thought that he was invisible out there, that his suit was retro . . . He clears his throat.

"So — you make origami?"

"I'm an artist. I've been working with paper for a while." She chews on a cuticle; among the bitten carnage of her hands is one long nail. "I'm hoping to be commissioned by Kew. Next year there's going to be several artists making installations."

"So that's how you earn your living?"

"Nope. Temping pays the bills. Usual office stuff . . . administration. But sometimes I give workshops — 'Art for Alzheimer's' — or pottery. What about you?"

"A music teacher. Most of them don't give a damn about Beethoven."

She sits down on the sofa. Seducing the others was as easy as practising scales; but it's harder since they left the Gardens. There's just the stark reality of the strip-light in the kitchen.

"Your flat's a mess."

"I'm a mess. Sorry. How many sugars?"

"Two."

He stirs the coffee, the clink of a spoon.

"I haven't been able to sleep," he tries. "I've got restless legs syndrome. There's very little to help. Sometimes touch. Massage . . ."

"You must be lonely."

"Yes."

74

Her glance is too intimate. Jonah is accustomed to being the one in control but the way her gaze is stroking his . . . He becomes aware of his Adam's apple, swallowing.

"You know," she teases, "you're not very good at this."

"What?"

"Seduction."

He realises he is smiling ironically. It doesn't sit comfortably on his face, as if his features have been intruded upon.

"Women seem to like this kind of thing," he admits. "Being needed."

"It doesn't look right on you."

He wants to ask how she's such an expert, this waif who holds herself in a way that states she is unlovable. It's in the slant of her shoulder, the inward turn of her feet. But there is something explicit about her awkwardness, as if her body is trying to contain some ruin or triumph. Her elbows rest against her crotch, her hands gesturing . . .

"So what does come naturally? Music?" She picks up his guitar. "Why don't you play something?"

The frets are embarrassingly dusty. He has slapped that soundboard a thousand times, the cedarwood battered from encores and bus journeys.

He scratches his shoulder blade, his T-shirt riding up, exposing his out-of-shape waistline. "It's not tuned."

The last time he touched it was before the funeral. She is still thrusting the guitar his way; his ticket, perhaps, to getting laid.

He reluctantly accepts the instrument. As he sits down on the sofa, Chloe has to make herself smaller to accommodate him. Tuning the guitar, he's surprised to find there's some comfort in the wooden body, the strings that may or may not comply with his whims. He feels its familiar weight on his lap, its curves adapting to the crook of his elbow, and hesitantly he begins to strum and pick. His fingers are rusty, but there is the vibration of sound against his belly, the chords appearing like the ghosts of old friends. They begin to form around one of his songs, but he doesn't sing the lyrics. They describe Audrey browsing the bookstalls at the South Bank — her day described in Chapter 1, Chapter 2, Chapter 3. For the chorus, he stole from Emily Dickinson: *Hope is the thing with feathers . . . It sings the tune without the words — and never stops at all. And never stops at all.* His fingers easily find the bridge. He becomes lost in the contrapuntal melodies, the ragtag rhythms, the slipshod beat.

Jonah stops, his eyes wet. Her gaze is set on him. Blue in every sense.

"You know how to touch that, at least."

She leans forward and wipes the tears from his cheek, then pauses, as if tasting the distance between her mouth and his. The initial kiss is raw and blue; a grazing of lips. Such a fragile gesture, Jonah wonders if he imagined it.

The second kiss is full of earth. The uncrossable space between strangers caving in, his tongue discovering the inside of her cheek. Here is the consolation of touch, the solace of skin. When he undresses her, he discovers the cool white of her stomach, her flat chest that seems naïve.

In the bedroom, Chloe straddles his hips. With her back facing him, he discovers the tattoo travelling from her coccyx. It stretches up her spine, and he traces her undulating back as if he could read the Braille of the black outlines. Spiralling up her vertebrae are three sheets of paper, a fourth with wings, a fifth with a beak, then two birds flying away.

She changes position, her heels digging deep into his kidneys. She dictates the rhythm, her muscles expressive, greedy. As natural as a baby sucking its thumb, it seems like she is compelled to fill up the whole of her sex, so she can feel complete. He thinks he might drown in her, this devouring surge, and when she comes there is an animal shriek, a primal piercing. It overwhelms him, his own body shuddering, releasing, and now, after the doubt and the thrill, there are just the two of them, breathing.

When Jonah wakes, Chloe has gone. For the last few months it has been the same. There are the usual signs that the woman has been looking at Audrey's photos; a frame on his shelf is wrongly angled. He rolls over to see the slip of paper on the pillow — a phone number with the words: CALL ME. It's like a guitar riff that repeats again and again, a looped comedy of manners, but today there is an anomaly in the pattern. It is 11 a.m. and Jonah has slept for nine hours.

Beautiful Collisions

When Jonah has been here, Harry has kept away. Now he runs his hand along Audrey's bench, debating the choice of wood once again. It weathers well, naturally resists insects and decay, but is relatively soft, risking dents and scratches. Not for the ecologically minded, redwoods grow slowly. The fact that it is made from his favourite tree disturbs him — it is horribly perfect.

It no longer holds its just-out-of-the-factory glory. Nine months of weather, and the weight of Jonah's bottom, has worn down the slats, and there's a splattering of bird droppings. But still it enjoys a special view, and Harry turns to take it in — the lake, the islands — then he nurses a nagging feeling that Jonah might appear from behind the dogwood. Wishing to divert such a crash, Harry walks around the lake to the other side of the water where he can still see the bench. Ageing gracefully, it looks almost the same as the others; but, for him, each individual seat is a request. They ask him to remember the thousand moments the dead have lived. How they too celebrated the gleam of sunlight on water, two planes leaving a kiss of vapour in the sky, or the minutes they stole to contemplate the shapes in the clouds. *The world is bulging with memories. I was here. I lived.*

Taking out his notebook, Harry flicks through a page on the endangered succulents from Madagascar, a memo about a leak found in the roof of the Princess of Wales, and a misnamed plant in Duke's Garden. But he can't stop fretting about what he'd overheard earlier: a foreman had been telling ghost stories about the Gardens. His colleagues admitted it was easy to get spooked at night, especially in a Victorian glasshouse. The panes rattle, a lizard unsettles a twig, a bullfrog jumps out of nowhere. But however hard he tries, Harry hasn't seen any phantoms.

He looks for them now, in the daylight. He imagines them gazing up at the trees — as if they've forgotten something, or mislaid a part of themselves in the woodland glade. Or maybe they're sitting on these benches right now. Unable to release their grip on life, they grasp on to beauty. In their laps are invisible things and dead stories. Hold on, they say, hold tight.

In the library, Harry's discovered an entire shelf dedicated to grief and the afterlife, most of it bollocks, but one passage suggested that people are trapped here if their deaths are sudden. So Harry watches Audrey's bench, waiting for a change in the air, a shadow, then he angrily scribbles: Stop it, Hal. You're just a gardener.

His seat commemorates the couple that founded Kew Theatre, and along the way is William Dyson, "An American who often walked these paths". Harry aches to see him, but there's only a woman with a pram. As they pass, the baby gives a toothless grin and Harry waves back. When he finally looks away from the lake, he realises it's not the kind of day to be morbid: Kew's visitors are flirting among the daffodils. Harry bookmarks his page with the usual photo — a woman's skirt, a brick wall, a net curtain — and putting on his hat, he wanders over to the Minka House, where two strangers are on a first date. He can tell by the way they shuffle around the conversation, trying to lessen the gap. What will it take for them to reveal themselves, to halt the pantomime?

Twenty minutes later, Harry is noting down more than the language of flowers. After years of observing plants, he has extended his repertoire to preserving people; *one day, these visitors, too, will be extinct.* Pressing down each passing moment, he writes about two gents in their seventies lightly touching fingertips as they admire the old black locust. Then there's the young couple lying on the grass. It's clear he wants to speak but she is reading the final chapter of a novel.

The
last
page
of
a
book
is
a
sacred
space

that
even
lovers
respect.

Harry stops so suddenly he breaks the lead. Jonah is strolling towards him. The woman beside him has boyish hair, sticking up in tufts. Her hand is tucked inside the waist of her jeans. It looks both comforting and sexual, but before he can investigate further, Milly arrives, holding a fistful of flowers.

"I thought I'd make a daisy chain."

When she follows Harry's gaze, her mouth drops open; but it's not the bearded man she's interested in. She is staring at the woman with a wistful expression.

"What is it, luv?"

The couple are moving closer . . . closer still. Harry pulls the child away.

"Can you tell me which cedar this is?"

Chloe sits on the grass, her cropped black hair framing her pale face. Beside them is a carpet of blue flowers called glory-of-the-snow, but they look more like a shimmering sea, the flowers the same colour as her eyes. Jonah turns away from them.

"So you know you're free to do whatever you want?"

"Of course. Otherwise I wouldn't be here." She scratches out some mud caught under her toenail. "It's OK for me to sleep with other people, just like you do."

"Good."

She sears him with that petal-blue gaze. "So is it true — the nights you're not with me you don't sleep at all? I'm your Temazepam?"

"Kind of."

She peers out from under her fringe. "So — you're using me?"

"Exactly. Is that OK?"

After Jonah dialled Chloe's number, he made it clear he wasn't ready for a relationship, but she seemed nonplussed. All she wanted was to come to his flat and have sex with him, and afterwards Jonah slept all night. This woman is made up of sleeping dust, his very own sandman.

For the last few weeks they have been keeping each other company, playing their own version of *Catcher in the Rye*. Falling through the air, they hope to be caught by that pitcher glove, at least for a while. Sometimes they eat together or watch a movie. At night when he can't sleep, he reads to her or she reads to him, small acts of kindness. Her lovemaking remains unabashed. Their encounter may only be a passing sympathy, but it's been impossible not to discover that Chloe has just turned thirty, and her favourite food is sushi.

Jonah is uncomfortable sitting on the ground — his back hurts, his legs unwieldy. In contrast, her body is compact and nubile, her elfin hair trendily messy. Leaning back on her hands, she is staring up at the sky — cerulean, seamless, stretching for miles.

"It must have fingerprints behind it."

Such an abstract statement. She's grinning mischievously, as if she's put an exotic fruit in front of him and daring him to split it open.

He dutifully asks, "What?"

"Creation. I just don't believe an accident can be this beautiful." Her London accent is a little tatty; a puckish mix of rough and whimsy. "I mean, look at these flowers. There's no way I'll be able to make anything as majestic, as simple."

She's already told him that she's received the Kew Gardens commission. She'll be one of several artists. Even though the exhibition is a year away, he can see her panic.

"You know this place well, for an East London girl."

"I've been coming for about eighteen months . . . sketching stuff, taking photos" She hesitates. "Come on. I could murder a cuppa."

At the Orangery, Princess Augusta's coat of arms graces the classical white façade. Jonah and Chloe sit behind the opulent arch windows, sharing a pot of tea. She fidgets, fiddling with her paper napkin, biting her nails down to the quick. It irritates him.

"So — when did you first study art?"

"A foundation year in Ealing. Back then I was building installations: dresses ruined with footprints, a series called *Elegies*. That one featured bird skeletons" She shrugs bashfully. "Birds seem to have become a theme. Freedom. Flight . . ."

"And origami?"

"Since I was a kid. But it was only as an adult that I took it seriously."

"What about that tattoo on your back?"

"It's a copy of a wood-block print by Katsushika Hokusai. It has a snappy title: *A Magician Turns Sheets of Paper into Birds*. It's only part of it, though. In the original there's a man in a kimono sitting cross-legged, throwing the sheets into the air."

"I like it."

"Thanks."

Jonah takes a swig of tea.

"I once thought of getting a tattoo. But Audrey worried. What it would look like when I was eighty?"

"At least your corpse would be unique!" With both hands, she bangs the table. "Did you know Houdini practised origami? It's a magical science: pure geometry and make-believe. It's all about the patterns, you see."

She clears a spill of sugar, then takes a folder of paper from her bag. She creases one square into a triangle.

"This is a valley fold. And again." A smaller triangle. "Lift the top half up then press down along the middle line. Repeat on the other side and hey presto, you've got a preliminary fold." Her hands have moved swiftly, creasing the paper back and forth, quartering the size of the square. "Now we make a petal fold."

Jonah is already lost, his eyes glazing over.

"This bit's tricky. Fold and unfold the lower edges and the top point too. Now lift up the front flap. Keep lifting until its edges meet in the middle then press it flat. Then on the other side . . ." Somehow she has turned a square into an elongated diamond. "So that's your bird base."

"OK . . ."

"Then inside-reverse-fold the bottom left-hand point to make the neck and do the same at the point's tip to make the beak. You do a similar thing for the tail. Here's the best bit."

She brings the paper up to her mouth as if she is about to kiss it then Jonah realises she is blowing gently into the base of the bird. The delicacy of her mouth against the thin paper, her eyes fixed on him . . . Jonah crosses his legs. Focus. As the body inflates, she pulls the wings apart, until in her palm is a perfect bird.

She waves it in front of him. "No wonder Houdini loved it."

"Wonderful." Jonah's voice is not entirely enthusiastic. "So, um, are you into magic?"

"When I was a kid."

She drops the bird into her almost-empty cup. The remnants of her tea stain the paper, browning the wing.

Jonah wonders what's stopped the conversation, but it's none of his business. He's not supposed to care that she's snatching her jumper from the floor and saying, "I've had enough of this place. Let's get out of here."

They walk across the width of the Gardens to the Japanese Gateway, where Chloe is considering displaying her artwork. They read about the Chokushi-Mon, then stroll along the stone paths of the tea garden until Jonah stops at a dripping water basin. This is where Audrey dropped a coin for their unborn child . . . but Chloe is taking a step forward and back, waiting. He follows her along the path to the Garden of Activity, where gravel is raked in circles around rocks to symbolise waterfalls, mountains and sea. They both stare at the little stone bridges that no one is allowed to cross. But Chloe ventures.

"If you need someone to talk to I'm here."

He can't help himself. "I've got friends for that."

She shrugs in disbelief. "Well, where the hell are they?"

Tired of my not answering their calls. Given up on me. "Most of them are parents now. They're pretty busy."

They walk down Cedar Vista in silence. It feels good to leave the structured stone, to be amid spaciousness. Chloe bounds along, beating her shoulder blades, as if trying to hug herself.

"Do you believe in reincarnation?"

Jonah doesn't answer.

"If I did come back, I'd like to be a pigeon." She gives a kooky grin. "I could hang out at St Paul's all day. Check out the tourist spots without queuing."

Jonah focuses on his feet, walking.

"And you?" she muses. "What about you?" Passing a bench, she taps on the wood. "Ha! You should come back as a drumbeat. Movement . . . rhythm . . . what do you reckon?"

"I think we just die," he says.

Jonah is trying. He admires her creativity, its young bravado, but her imagination exhausts him. There's something about her that's not fully formed, as if she's still finding herself, or playing dress-up. It reminds him of a couple of friends from uni; people hiding, yet so

86

desperate to be seen . . . He tries to come up with something authentic to say, then stops moving.

This is the subtle substance of memory, what remains etched in his mind's eye. A couple are standing on the other side of the waterlily pond and at first he can't make them out. But slowly he recognises her green suede jacket. The guy has a familiar shyness in his shoulders, as if he can't bear to recall his physique when he was younger. He's just finished his PGCE — her, the third miscarriage.

The August day is cloudy. Together the couple create the picture of silence. The man is contorting himself into any shape he thinks this woman can love. He folds and unfolds his arms, as if he could fold himself into someone dependable, someone his wife could lean upon.

She sucks on a cigarette, holding the smoke in too long. The man waits, watching the still surface of her as she turns towards the pond. Even her shoulders are wistful. Her spine is bereft, the curve of her neck sighing with longing.

"I thought you wouldn't start smoking again."

She refuses to look at him. "I can't help it."

Jonah can taste it as he speaks. A futility that reminds him of stale breath. "It's going to be OK."

It is a lie they both recognise as faith.

"Let's go on holiday, Au. Go back to Sicily. You will be a mother, I promise."

A teardrop falls from her chin and he wishes he had a camera so he could capture this . . . this woman looking like his wife again.

★　★　★

Sitting in the Rhododendron Dell, Harry asks the flowers, "What makes us choose one person over another?"

How are we to find the "right one" in this
Atom
Scattered
Universe?

He flicks off some tobacco ash that has dropped on the page then continues writing. The paper, like Audrey, listens without interruption. Harry glances up, almost expecting to see her tilted face, but there's just a yellow brimstone. As it lands on the rhododendron, Harry worries that his closest companion is a notebook.

Looking up at the sky, he tries to stare out the sun. Are there laws of gravity and grace to guide us? Or is everything random? Harry rubs his eyes, then massages his temples. What makes some of these accidents significant? One person might only be a comma in your story, while another might be a bewitching dot dot dot . . .

His crabbed handwriting looks like it belongs to a physician. The cramped letters remind him of teeth too close together. A few feet away, a man is scoping out a woman. All it took was a momentary glance from her, the vulnerable turn of her shoulder.

How can one gaze hold such extraordinary power?

As the brimstone flits past, Harry scratches his brow with the top of his pencil. Like insects lured by certain flowers, perhaps some people are attracted to characteristics missing in themselves; for others it's something similar, a narcissistic thrill. But everyone is looking for that quiver of excitement. Like a finger brushing the skin of a drum . . . perpetual anticipation.

Harry turns to a new page and writes: A BEAUTIFUL COLLISION. He thinks about meeting Audrey — the distant glance of that woman as some unknowable thought passed through her like a breeze.

It was that which moved me. Then I made my biggest mistake. I said hello.

This is the body Jonah saw. This is the person he noticed. Audrey eating melon, spilling pips on to her knees, the small moments of her smile, the silent words in her glance; all memorised by heart.

This is where the camera never was: the line of her forearm, the soft curve between her belly button and pelvis. He recalls them trying to talk, and kiss, in the same moment.

In the early days, they would pretend to sleep, his arm under her breast, tantalising close. The air would alter, quickening with sex, just the idea of it. There was the anticipation, the doubt, the pre-empting thought, where every breath mattered, every inch that his fingers moved exquisitely erotic. There was that first tentative gesture, the acceptance when that touch was returned. Here was the gathering in and the spilling out, the sound of their lips and lungs, the tasting of each other until they tasted their tastes merged. Au. Awe.

"Stop."

His hand presses down on Chloe's fingers. They've been walking steadily up his thigh, but this isn't fair. A clammy pause.

"I'm sorry. But I can't make love to you."

"Why?"

He says it so simply it hurts. "I am not in love."

"You don't need to be."

As Chloe straddles him, Jonah looks beyond her slight breasts to the ceiling. He feels pinned down, claustrophobic.

Her voice is quiet. "Perhaps I should leave."

"No. Not yet." He touches the place between her shoulder blades. "Stay. Please."

He feels her resistance, but pulls her closer, spooning his body around hers, as if this will make it up to her. Gradually the fight in her breath softens. He spends the rest of the night feeling her shape. He traces her turned back, then ventures towards her chin, her belly. She feels different from Audrey, younger . . . wrong.

Jonah longs for the soundless sanctuary of sleep. But for now this is enough, this silence where things are real — like this quiet between Chloe and him when there is no need to speak. He imagines them as two shipwreck survivors clinging together in a storm. As this thought bobs in his mind, he watches the night shifting outside. The promise of morning casts a dirty tinge across the ever-lightening sky. It will soon be sunrise.

90

Five o'clock is a time most people miss. A beginning so unblemished, so absurdly hopeful, that anything that happens after it is likely to be a disappointment. There is even a soundtrack of birds. It is so close to being peaceful and yet; Chloe shatters the silence.

"What's your favourite smell?"

He can't see her face, but knows that by making her wait, she has frowned. "I dunno. What's yours?"

"Skin maybe. Or the sea."

"How about tears?" He remembers Audrey crying, then her swimming in the Mediterranean, the smell of her sun-scrubbed skin. His childhood in Devon. "Perhaps it's the salt?" he questions.

Chloe rolls over and opens one sleepy eye. "Did you know that tears are different depending on their reason for existing? Tears of joy are chemically different from those of grief."

Jonah can feel the edge of sleep, warmly now, its absolute, beckoning relief. But suddenly he wants to resist — as if it would be unfaithful to give in.

Paul Ridley presses his fingertips together, then bounces his hands as if weighing the air that they hold. Perhaps all he is thinking about is what he's going to have for supper.

"It doesn't look like you're getting much sleep, Joe."

"I haven't seen Chloe this week." Jonah runs his finger along the back of his collar, chastising himself for not changing his clothes after work.

"Because . . ."

"There's a nine-year age gap. At the beginning, there was a choice that I made, we made, every time we saw each other, but now it feels like it's becoming a habit. A 'relationship'."

"But since meeting her, you've started playing music?"

"Nothing original." He tries to straighten his posture, but the attempt feels false in his muscles. "It's not even been a year."

He's been counting. It's precisely eleven months and one day since he received the policeman's call.

"So you're not available —"

"Of course not."

"And you're worried that this girl is falling for you?"

"Not exactly."

"Or that you could fall for her?"

Jonah recomposes his limbs. "We've been reading to each other. A chapter at night, taking turns. It was her idea . . . thought it would help me sleep. We're probably only seeing each other so we can reach the next instalment."

"Which book?"

"*The English Patient*. But I'm going to end it. Soon."

Paul Ridley smiles. "You're ambivalent."

Jonah thinks about Chloe's hair sticking up in the mornings. She often sketches people in the margins of the newspaper. Biro between her lips, she'll reach for the cereal. The pale curve of her armpit.

"I've known from the beginning it's not going to work, but I always end up saying nothing. For ease. For

92

a good night's sleep. For the sex. Which is great, by the way. I suppose I don't like conflict."

He watches the little clock on the desk. For a moment he hates it.

His therapist squints. "Is there anything else you'd like to talk about? We have another few minutes."

Jonah stares out of the open window. A scraggy cat is skulking around the dustbins, and a car pulls up by the traffic lights; the smell of exhaust fumes. Ridley is waiting. Jonah stares down at his shoes, then splays out his hands, his fingers reaching beyond the piano octave. He then notices a splodge of jam on his cuff. He tidies his tie, straightens his trousers, then looks Paul in the eye.

"I still miss her."

Time is up.

The heron balances on one yogic leg. Harry lights up a Montecristo, relishing the smack of smoke against his throat, then spits out shreds of tobacco. It is 6 a.m. and there's a fine mist on the water; but Harry is not feeling peaceful. It takes the length of his cigar to consider why. This is not the place Audrey loved. He can see how the reeds create a barrier between Jonah and the world — but this was not her spot.

Only two ducks are watching. Harry drops his cigar butt and stands up. He wants to pick up her bench and carry it in his arms like a gallant lover. But that's impossible, even for someone younger. He heaves the cumbersome object upwards until one end is propped on his shoulder. He drags it behind him like a crucifix.

The bench legs leave tracks in their wake, imprinting the ground with his treachery. Even the dew makes way. As his knees buckle, he hopes that Milly is sleeping. The heat of his skin prickles against the curt morning air. As he passes Temperate House, he sees his destination in the distance. His towering love letter: the pagoda.

He takes a breather, wipes the sweat from his face. Not much further. Hauling the weight back on to his shoulder, he drags his feet onwards as if he is making a pilgrimage to a star, but it is only the gilded finial that looks like a spire. It beckons, and his back aches, but if he puts her bench where they met, maybe she'll find him. Jonah has been waiting in the wrong place.

Part II

Falling

I can hardly withstand the joy
Beating, like wings, in my belly:
This fluttering, thumping bliss
that demands I learn again
how to be here
and to love.

Audrey Wilson, 30 March 2003

RIP

Among industrial backstreets is a warehouse studio filled with light, containing a simple stove, a sink, coils of wire, paint pots, blank canvases and naked bulbs. Several pictures of a child are taped to the walls: drawings of her crying, smiling, rubbing her nose. Others are collages made up of fabrics and wool. There are newspaper images photocopied on different-sized paper, embellished with stitched flowers and paint. Some are creased as if they have once been folded, but the girl is still staring at the camera, her gaze confidently straight.

Smells from the outside trespass in — cleaning chemicals, engine oil and gutted fish; they waft over a man lying on a mattress, his back heaving with snores. Chloe can't remember if he's Christoff? Claude? She had wanted to spend last night with Jonah, but he had a therapy session, essays to mark, so she dropped by a party and met a photographer's assistant. His eyes, half-hidden behind a flop of ginger hair, had been ludicrously flirtatious. Above his skinny body, sewing machines whirr, dishes clatter.

Chloe sits on the concrete floor, creasing a sheet of paper, ten centimetres square. She wears vest and knickers, her thin thighs white as her underwear. Folded creatures are scattered around her while she focuses on her experiments with greaseproof paper, parchment and foil. She finds comfort in a crease, her reassurance in a square.

At art school, she studied the practice of folding one thousand cranes. Traditionally the folder is granted a wish. Twenty-five strings holding forty birds, each a burning prayer. She read about these *senbazurus* as wedding gifts, or offered at birth to wish the newborn a thousand years of happiness. There were pictures of cranes hung outside temples, left exposed to the elements. Tattered in the wind, the birds would slowly dissolve, the wish released.

Chloe wanted to try it. In her graduation project she used newspaper: the weather on a bird's body, a crossword on its wing. Others were feathered with headlines of genocide, sex scandals, football results, assorted carnage. She chose each cutting for its politics or its typeface, working until her hands were stained with ink and her joints sore from folding. She persevered as if it were punishment. When she was tired of angles and edges, she made pictures of a little girl in paint and charcoal. Many dated October 2003. During those autumnal, sleepless nights, Chloe shaved off her hair and repeatedly re-drew the shape of the child's nose or shaded in her cheeks. In the early mornings she would fold again, hoping that, in this act, her thousand yearnings would turn into peace. She experimented with different-size birds, hanging them in a variety of ways, until she had completed a chandelier of flight and wars.

The project is now suspended from her ceiling, holding the horrors and jubilations of the world. Beneath it, the studio is filled with folded animals, and photographs of Kew: details of blossom and swollen fruit. For a while now she has yearned to create there; she has unpicked the practicalities, what materials will survive the humidity of the glasshouses or existing outdoors. She considers a technique called "wet folding", then remembers Jonah telling her about a place for lost things.

Chloe's knickers are still damp with sex. She wonders when the man in her bed is going to wake. Her longest relationship lasted two years; it was Simon Caldous who had first taken her to the botanical gardens. Back then, she had a black bob that suited her gamine face, and had mastered the illusion of intimacy. She discussed the intricacies of art with this fellow student, but never revealed enough for there to be anything to fall in love with. But still he did.

The man in her bed moves his leg. Chloe takes out a pencil and draws his haunches, but as the life study takes shape she shades in another man's frame. The androgynous back becomes broad, Viking. She tries to capture the power of the sea, a tide through his muscles, but it isn't true: there's something of the fallen hero in the fragility between his shoulder blades, Jonah's softening bulk. At first she thought he was too old, his suit lame; but now she's interested in his body's contradictions. Where does he hold tension — in his jaw, his hips? Starting another drawing, she sketches his beard, a little longer than stubble, then hesitates. Why is she doing this? His hand supporting his head, she draws his fingers, trying to find the poetry that she knows is in his knuckles. Then she smudges his gaze, blotting it out until there is no expression left, just a blindfold of graphite.

A week ago, she googled him, but all she could find was a dozen grainy photos shot from the audience. She also downloaded his album. After listening to it twice, she sat in the bath for an hour, the music still lapping against her. The next morning, his voice was still with her, a refrain haunting her on the tube, or while queuing for a sandwich. The Jonah she heard was different from the man she knows — so emotionally expressive, so tender.

She's not accustomed to sharing a bed without sex; it strangely unclothes her. But their casual liaison feels refreshingly mature. Jonah's honesty about his unavailability takes off the pressure. There is, at last, no superficial infatuation, no constant texting, no juvenile fantasies about the future. But normally she is the one who is attentive, then doesn't call for days. She tries to reconcile his extremes, but only sages can dance cheek to cheek with paradox; and Chloe knows she is no saint.

This is the middle time. Chloe can see herself suspended between who she was before she met him and who she will become. She can't wrap her mind around Jonah, however much she unfolds him. She likes his being surrounded with books, and that smell of school, cleaning fluid mixed with a hint of teenage BO. There's something worthy in the way he stoops to meet her height, his piano-playing fingers and that awful brown suit that should have been burned years ago. But mostly it's his pain she identifies with — the horror of being the survivor in a crumpled, thrown-away world.

The man in her bed sits up and wipes his face.

"Where's your lav? I'm busting."

Chloe points to the door, and Christoff or Claude staggers across the room, his buttocks clenching.

"I feel like death," he moans.

Last weekend, Chloe had asked Jonah about Audrey's funeral, but he'd only described the church in Cornwall. She had told him about visiting her granddad's gravestone. Standing in her school uniform, she thought the inscription said "rip".

"To a child obsessed with origami, that word meant giving in."

Chloe could remember how cold she was in her knee-length socks, the sound of paper ripping.

"Tearing it means you've stopped believing in the infinite possibilities of a square."

Friday night is the beginning of the May Day bank holiday weekend. Chloe wakes to find Jonah's bed empty. Earlier they had decided to watch a DVD rather than participate in conversation. The credits led to sex, led to sleep, but now a piano plays, Vivaldi morphing into Bach's *Prelude in C*.

Chloe peers out of the blinds; it is still night, perhaps three or four in the morning. Stumbling over a pile of

103

clothes, she pulls on one of Jonah's shirts and stands at the doorway. Hunched over the piano in his boxer shorts, he is now playing Bowie's "Rock 'n Roll Suicide". His legs look cramped, but his fingers are articulate, arched above the keys. She walks across the room then sits down behind him, wrapping her legs around his torso. She presses her mouth against his ear.

"I'd like to watch you play the cello naked."

"I don't play the cello," he says.

She wants to talk about the strings on his album. Instead she asks innocently, "Did you compose anything for Audrey?"

"I was stupid enough to try for her funeral."

It wasn't the answer she was expecting. Jonah turns around, but at the sight of her he hesitates, as if she's too young, or inexperienced — as if he's thinking, you wouldn't understand, you've never been married.

He swallows, says softly, "Not even Bach was good enough."

As she searches for a response, he turns back to the keys. Believing she could be any woman in this room, she holds him lightly, her body offering the shadow of a confessional.

"There wasn't a melody that matched her. I spent nights listening to different instruments . . ."

"What about the piano?"

"Not enough echo."

Chloe studies his profile as if he were an extinct species that she has stumbled upon in a museum. She hadn't known it existed — this intimacy between two people; she's never witnessed it.

104

"It's good that you keep talking about her."

Is it? For a moment, she is jealous.

"It was like I needed a different key," Jonah continues. "Not major or minor. Not B flat." A wry smile. "A song in Q might have worked, I think."

Chloe gazes down at the worn pedals, the scratches on the wood — a piano that is well loved, well used. Then she curves into the cavity between Jonah's shoulder blades and reaches out a blind arm to play a single note, then another, a black key. His voice vibrates against her chest, almost inside her, oscillating.

"Mozart once said that the music is not in the notes, but the pauses in between." He stops her hand playing. "Like rhythm — it's between the beats."

This is the lull between one note and the next. Jonah turns around on the stool and Chloe steps away. It is a movement and a rest.

Suddenly she yearns for fresh skies, even the banality of Claude. But Jonah leans forward.

"I took the cowardly way out in the end. I was so set on writing something perfect that I ended up with sweet FA. She got hymns, for Christ's sake."

Chloe wonders if she should explain why she was by the lake on the night that they met.

"I doubt I could have created anything either."

"I wish it was easier to visit her grave. We often talked about moving to that village — a life by the sea. I would have preferred Devon, but . . ."

"I've only been to the sea once."

"Really?"

She grins sheepishly.

"Your first dark secret! You never say anything about yourself, your family . . ."

"We only meet at Christmas. Some years I give that a miss. My stepfather's useless."

"And your real dad?"

"Lost to the cosmos."

She swirls her arms in the air, then doesn't know what to do with them. She tugs on her earlobe.

"Mum met him at a disco. She didn't know where he worked, or lived."

She waits for the normal fussing, but Jonah remains on the stool, his eyes holding her steady. She widens her stance, juts her chin.

"She kept saying it was the seventies — as if that excused her. She couldn't remember if he was called John. James. I remember it distinctly. She was mashing potato." A bitter laugh. "She was adamant it was a mistake. 'It or I?' I should have said."

Jonah checks she's finished by tilting his head. "I'm sorry."

"It's nothing. Really."

Jonah reaches for her hips. He pulls her towards him, his head close to her belly. Then he takes her tightly curled fist and brings her knuckles to his lips. *Don't do that. Don't unravel me.* Moments later, they are breathing the same breath, their mouths only millimetres away.

As they lie down on the floor, it isn't love, nor is it pretty. Her leg is bent under him, her heel on his chest, his heartbeat quickening under the ball of her foot.

106

They both look for something to believe in, somewhere among the stains on the carpet.

It is a night of holding, of gathering in. She discovers the roughness of him, from his trembling arms as he holds up his weight, to the cracked dryness of his heels. Here are his edges, his abrasive beard, the hang of his belly. They talk while making love and it sounds halfway between a psalm and a blue film. It is littered with insecurities, them getting to know each other's demons and angels, but there is also the balm: the acceptance that everyone is screwed up on this strange little planet.

Jonah sleeps. He is still inside her, her body cradling the softest part of him. Chloe blinks at the proximity of his face, then takes a mental snapshot, as if one day she will paint him. It will be a day's work getting to know his body.

She has not done this with the others. An edge of light escapes through the crack in the curtains and cuts across his skin. She can just see jigsaw pieces of his eyelids, his cheek. There is something erotic about looking at him without his knowledge.

In the dim light of the lounge, she notices the white armchair sitting in the corner like a phantom. Somewhere in the dark, Audrey's photos are looking down at them, a rumour of sex still lingering in Jonah's unconscious muscles. Chloe commands herself to get up, get dressed, but her gaze is pulled back to his stubborn thighs, the hair below his belly button.

She is taken by his stillness. What should she do with this man splayed beside her, this soul on loan to her for just an instant?

Lying down, synchronising her breath with his, she realises it is possible to feel this. She finds faith in the soft place at the nape of his neck. She finds faith in the place in her heart where everything hurts, in the friction between the painful and the sublime. Then she finds a word she can't speak. It is caught in her throat, unable to be lessened by the sound.

A Dress Falls

Putting a bench by the pagoda is Harry's love letter. Sir William Chambers may have built the structure for Princess Augusta in the 1760s, but for Harry it represents everything he loved about Audrey. In the last five days, Jonah hasn't come to the garden, so the theft remains unnoticed. Like a child nicking sweets, there's a glee mingled with the nausea of scoffing the lot, the guilt queasy and ecstatic. Harry might look like any other gent, sitting on a bench, his face tilted towards the sunlight, but underneath is an illicit thrill, as if Audrey and he are stealing a moment.

On this Bank Holiday Monday, his backdrop is a blazing blue sky and a towering folly, the most architecturally ambitious of Kew's structures. Many said this pagoda wouldn't stand up to the weather or the wars, but here it is, two hundred and forty-three years old. A Richmond bricklayer carried out the construction, and the ten storeys are a hundred and sixty-three feet high, tapering upwards, each floor diminishing in height and diameter. It is a masterpiece of chinoiserie, the spectacle of the Orient slap-bang in the middle of Surrey.

The ten roofs are blue, but underneath each is a faded poppy red, the paint on the slats peeling. At the top is a gilded finial that looks like a spire. This spring the doors are open and visitors are climbing two hundred and fifty-threesteps to worship the view. The pagoda has been given a fresh lick of paint, leaving white specks on the floorboards. But the tourists' sun-lotioned sweat is eroding the reek of emulsion. They come out wobbly and elated, as Harry did that day when Audrey and he ran up the stairs, giggling like children. The interior, then, was a derelict shambles.

Outside there are blue wooden benches set into the recesses of the pagoda, but today Harry is sitting further away so he can take in the scent of the Philadelphus "Enchantment" — the fragrance of orange flowers and jasmine. He'd asked Audrey to plant them, and, after some hesitation, she got down on her knees, her white shirt becoming soiled. There were flecks of dirt in her hair, but as she dug deep into the flowerbed, she began laughing.

The white petals have bloomed a month early. Harry fishes out his journal, but before writing about the flowers, he unfolds his bookmark. He smooths out the tired creases, the paper flimsy, then stares at the building standing on a corner of a street in Buffalo, New York. A neon sign reads "Genesee Hotel".

Harry knows every detail. There is a coffee shop on the ground floor with a large, curtain-draped window. Signs advertise milkshakes and ten-cent sandwiches, and a small billboard asks passers-by to "Give till it hurts Hitler". On the left, a motorcycle officer is rushing into the hotel, but what draws Harry's eye is in the middle of the frame. A woman is falling through the air, on her last journey from an eighth-storey window. The image is elegant and brutal. The girl is horizontal, her arms reaching out as if to embrace someone rather than the pavement she is about to crash into. Her dress is tossed up, showing her petticoat, her knickers, her lovely legs akimbo. Her dirty-blonde hair flails in the wind, but she has tidy black heels, shapely knees.

Harry discovered that her name was Mary Miller. She walked into the women's restroom, locked the door and crept out on to the ledge. What was she thinking as she plummeted, her face set in a smiling grimace, her chin raised to brace herself against the looming gutter? Perhaps she is still poised mid-fall, neither living nor dying, but imprisoned in the choice she made, at that one moment when she surrendered. Perhaps she is trapped inside a stammering disbelief, an eternal spasm. In the photo, time repeats like a stuck record, the scratch scratch of the same second. She has stayed pinned against the sky, her mouth open.

On the ground floor, a well-groomed man is sitting at a table looking out of the coffee-shop window, oblivious to the fact that in the next second a woman's body will tumble past his vision. Behind him there's an innocuous, tasselled lampshade.

Harry glances up from the photo. Milly is playing beside her favourite beech, the *Nothofagus antarctica*. The tree has grown sideways along the ground, making one particular branch her perfect dancing partner. Grasping it lightly, the child balances in a quirky

111

arabesque, happily off-kilter. But her grin vanishes. Harry follows her gaze then freezes; Jonah is standing five yards away, staring at Milly. Harry desperately shifts himself to hide the bench's inscription, but this is only the first of his worries; it would hurt Milly to know that Audrey was married. Trying not to draw attention to himself, Harry ransacks his mind for wisdom, but dread fills him from his boots up.

"Move away," he hisses. "Quick."

Milly gawps at him, then runs off.

Jonah has diverted from his usual route to the lake. Having forced himself to spend two sleepless nights away from Chloe, he is still thinking about her dancing in his T-shirt — he even sang, for Christ's sake. Now he has arrived an hour early for their meeting, hoping a walk will clear his head. Those aren't butterflies in his stomach, are they? Not exactly — it's queasiness, he tells himself, from lack of sleep.

His jowls feel thickly bilious, his legs both heavy and insubstantial. He tries to take in his surroundings — the pagoda, some benches, a little girl playing by a tree trunk. She seems familiar, dressed like a tomboy — must be no more than seven or eight. Jonah tries to remember where he has seen her beige cords, her stripy T-shirt, but in the recesses of his mind there's only a voice begging: sleep.

Like most children, she's still joining up the dots — a picture not yet fully drawn in. There doesn't seem to be anyone looking after her — there's just a guy on a bench, holding a cutting from a magazine. So Jonah follows when the child runs off. Halfway down Cedar Vista she slows to a bow-legged stride, pausing every now and then to pick up fallen twigs and litter. The garden judders like a cine-film, focusing on grainy details, bleached-out colour.

At the lake, there's a nook in a particular tree where a small bottom can fit. The girl perches here, thought-fishing, her feet dangling over the edge. Jonah watches her blow the seeds off a dandelion clock, then polish a small pebble against her leg. He wonders if she will remember this when she is older: the intrigue of a burrowing worm, an iridescent feather, the appearance of a man, a stranger.

Jonah recognises a desire for solitude when he sees it, but feels a teacherly duty, some quasi-Hippocratic oath. He walks towards her.

"Are you OK?"

As he looms over her, she covers her face.

He squats down to make himself a similar height. "I'm Jonah. Are you all right? Where are your parents?"

She scrutinises him through her fingers. "My dad's a gardener. We live here."

"You mean onsite?"

Her words are strangely defined, as if language is still new to her: something that requires proper attention from her lips and tongue. She takes her hands away and peers up at his shaggy hair as if about to make fun. Jonah's thighs are beginning to ache. He tentatively rests his bottom on the grass and stretches out his legs.

"What's your name?"

"Milly. But don't worry — people have to pay to get in here, so it's safe." She squints in the sunshine, her head cocked. "Do you live in a whale?"

"Pardon?"

"Were you scared? How big was his belly?"

"That's another Jonah."

"I'm glad," she says simply.

The light blisters the sky with beauty. When Milly jumps up, the sun crowns her head.

"Do you want to see something special?"

She reaches into her pocket and presents him with a wooden flower press. Her dirty fingers are studious. Carefully unscrewing the winged nuts, she shows him the blotting paper where some specimens are immaculately preserved, and others mangled. It smells of paper must: a dead tree holding dead petals.

While Jonah admires a page of forget-me-nots, she scratches an insect bite on her shin then flops down on the grass, arching her back so she is looking at him the wrong way up. "Copy me."

Jonah looks behind him. "Where's your dad?"

"Working. He's in the Palm House."

After running through the lists of dos and don'ts from his safeguarding course, Jonah decides to keep her company. Getting down on the ground is another matter. He cumbersomely lies down, flattening the lawn, until eventually he is looking at the world upside down.

"The grass is giggling," she says. "Can you see?"

Close up, the blades are quivering in the breeze. Jonah notices a ladybird, then the goose droppings on

114

his elbow. Milly starts to sing, and it hits him: would his daughter have inherited Audrey's gap-toothed grin?

Jonah's vision becomes slurry. He doesn't know how to grieve for their three children, or the child that may have come, but a new realisation shocks him like a wave crashing against his body, like being swallowed up into the dark belly of a fish. Audrey is never coming back.

The girl has sat up. "The Bird Man's here."

Jonah props himself up to see an old man with a red bucket standing by the lake. The man's whistle is hurting his ears. Wiping the goose shit from his sleeve, Jonah glances towards where he wants to be. "I've got to be going." He gestures towards the moorhens, the birds blurring. "Why don't you go and talk with your friend?"

"The Bird Man? He's busy."

"Right." Jonah aches to be alone, sitting quietly on Audrey's bench. "I'm going now, so . . ."

"It was nice to meet you."

"Yes. Bye, then."

He takes a few paces, then looks over his shoulder to see the little girl walking towards the Palm House. He continues his journey towards the other side of the lake while the coots and mandrakes scramble for grain. The heron holds its stillness while the other birds flap and fluster, the sky full of screams.

Milly is trying to make Harry laugh. She pulls a fish-face, then waggles her fingers through the railings of Victoria Gate.

"Ta, ta," she calls.

"Wait, luv, please. You mustn't talk to him. You've no idea how much damage you could cause. Believe me."

She walks across the pedestrian crossing, pretending she can't hear.

An ice-cream van stands on the corner. Harry halts when he sees the boy on the skateboard then feels the usual lurch in his stomach. Milly stops too, her shoulders caved into love-struck shyness. They both listen to the continuous rhythm of the wheels sliding along the pavement, the challenges the ten-year-old sets for himself. It's like clockwork every day, as if he is marking time, procrastinating from homework. Wearing a tracksuit hood, passers-by don't see James Hopkins's eyes, but Harry knows what is scratched on to his retinas: that moment of screeching tyres, the look on Audrey's face before her head hit the windscreen. Back and forth he skates, chasing demons, and Harry wishes this kid would turn to Milly and explain the impact of collisions. But, tired of being ignored, she ambles away.

In Kew village there's a bookshop, the health-food store, the butcher and the fishmonger. People are browsing postcards or eating al fresco. Harry catches up with Milly as an overground train from East London pulls into the station.

"Please, luv, you mustn't talk to strangers."

"He's not a stranger. He's called Jonah."

"Milly, he's . . ."

116

"Lonely. He needs a friend. Besides he has time to talk to me, not like that boy on the skateboard, or the Bird Keeper. Please, Da —"

"How many times have I told you? You shouldn't call me that."

A tide of tourists washes in and out, like a sea dappled with litter. A woman in a bright-blue dress pushes through the smog of people.

Milly tugs on his hand. "Look! We've seen her before."

"When?"

"With Jonah."

The sway of blue silk reveals the shape of the woman's limbs, as if the body beneath is offering an invitation. Harry looks away.

"But, perhaps I've met her before. And before that."

"Are you sure, luv?"

"I can't remember." Her expression brightens. "How about I ask Jonah?"

"Don't you dare!"

Harry's voice slaps the smarting air. Immediately regretting it, he pats her hand. He has an awful sense that consequences are unravelling, that there is some momentum that he can't comprehend, and God, that dress is beautiful. The electric blue contrasts with the girl's crow-black hair. Distracted by the silk, it takes him a while to realise that Jonah has probably sat down by the lake. Perhaps he has already noticed that the redwood is a slightly different shade, or the back of the bench lower. He might have turned around and seen the inscription.

1901–1960
Andrew Mattings
He walked these paths often

I am a foreigner here. This is what Chloe thinks as she stands by Kew's wrought-iron gates. Despite the familiarity of her surroundings, her feelings are untranslatable, as if she has been transported to the centre of Hong Kong and is now staring up at the flashing billboards, a world of unknowable symbols.

Here is her love letter. It is not made of words. It is a dress worn especially so he can watch it fall. Later he will unzip the back, let the straps drop from her shoulders, and the fabric will flutter down to her ankles. Worn on various occasions, it has always been a success. If fabric could speak it would tell its legends: *The Multiple Adventures of a Blue Dress.*

She thinks back to Saturday morning, when Jonah sang a Bowie tune under his breath. *Wake up, you sleepy head. Put on some clothes, shake up your bed.* Touched, she had joined in. She teased out his resistance, encouraging him to sing louder, until he began bashing the keys on the piano. She danced across his living room, singing, "No room for me, no fun for you," until he spun her around, caterwauling in time with her. They made such a racket the neighbour knocked on the wall.

They made love on the piano stool. Afterwards, she wondered if he knew something had shifted. Surely he must have been able to tell by now that she grew a centimetre or two whenever she was with him.

He ran a finger from her nose to her belly. There was sadness in it.

"You're better than you think," she said, "as a lover, a musician."

He raised his hands. "I don't know if I'm cut out for —"

"You could give private music lessons? Or run a project at a community centre . . ."

"You mean, like you — 'Art for underprivileged youths'?"

"Kids aren't really my thing." She stood up then looked over her shoulder. "Let's go out for breakfast. I'm starving."

"What just happened?"

"Nothing."

He looks at her questioningly, but it's not long before he gets fed up with waiting. "I'm seeing my dad this morning. Sorry."

She knew by his face, he was lying. Something she had done had turned off a switch. She imagined him spending the day flicking through TV channels, his legs jerking.

As she was leaving, she stopped by the door. How many kinds of love letters are there? She had never sent a sentimental text, or kissed a man's toes, or run a bubble bath for him after a long day's work.

"How about Monday?" She tried to keep the hope out of her voice. "We could celebrate Beltane . . . dance the maypole?"

"Great."

Jonah threw her a backward wave as he walked to the bathroom.

Chloe took the tube to Tower Hill, where she had brunch with Claude. Over brioche he talked about his admiration for a famous photographer, and took a call from a girl named Natalie. Chloe stared out of the window, telling herself that all she was feeling was a chemical imbalance, a flush of hormones. All she'd ever wanted was a man to give her space; she should be ecstatic.

Despite her attempts at nonchalance, Chloe spent all morning getting ready. She now stands at the entrance, feeling overdressed, nervous. She waits at the corner so long that she begins to worry that she looks like a prostitute. While she stands stock-still, she thinks about movement. She has always adored rocking horses and swings, the sweep of a paintbrush, making love: different kinds of momentum.

"You run away," her ex, Simon, had said. "You run away, so you can come back."

He is twenty minutes late. Chloe walks towards the visitors' centre where staff are selling cards, plants and bath oils under a bright, artificial light. The gates will close within the hour, but she doesn't want to start their date with recriminations. Instead she thinks about the space between them. Her art teacher told her not to focus on the objects within a still life, but what lies between the bottles, bowl and pear. Relationship is found in the distance. Jonah said as much when he spoke about rhythm. What is the right distance to maintain the thrill? she wonders. How close, how far apart? Chloe stares up at the campanile by the entrance. The Romanesque-style tower has a monastic air, as if the arched glassless windows should house a clanging bell. It's getting late. She scrolls down to Jonah's number on her phone.

"Hello? It's me."

"Hi."

She can hear him walking; he is probably rushing towards her right now.

"Are you almost here?"

"Where?"

"Victoria Gate," she says steadily "We agreed to meet. Remember?"

It sounds like he has taken the phone from his ear. Muffled footsteps.

"I'm sorry, Chlo. Something's come up."

"Where are you?"

A pause. "Look, why don't you wait in my flat? The key's under the green flowerpot. I'll be back."

"But . . ."

He has already hung up.

Chloe looks down at her carefully chosen handbag, the red shoes chafing her heels. What is she doing here? She can't bear to let the entrance staff know she has been stood up, so she walks in, flashing her membership card. The man in the booth stares at the backless scoop of her dress.

She holds herself steady as she walks to the Palm House and climbs the steps. When she eases open the heavy glass doors, the heat hits her like a rainforest. Vast and fluid, the space drips with vines and bananas. She breathes in the damp, woody scent, the sheer aliveness, and when she looks up at the enormous fans of the Attalea palm, she remembers all the times she has come here looking for rescue. White steps spiral up into the foliage, towards the ceiling of glass. This will help her for a while at least, this bath of light, leaves and warmth.

Once he hangs up, Jonah continues searching with the sweaty panic of an abandoned child running through a supermarket. Just forty minutes ago, the lake had looked the same, the red osier dogwood was still behind him, but Jonah sensed at once that he was in the wrong place. When he finally looked over his shoulder, he saw Andrew Mattings's dates. He walked across to the nearby seats and found one plaque for a forecourt gardener. Another simply stated it was "Mums Bench".

He looks around, dazed. It's as if he's forgotten where he's parked his car. Walking chaotically from bench to bench, he drifts away from the lake and loses his bearings. He chastises himself for not visiting the Gardens for nearly a week.

He has lost Audrey all over again. He should have been here, stewarding his wife's memories — not singing and shagging. Another bench.

Do rest a while as she often did
to gain thoughts and pleasure.

122

Where is she? It's almost closing time, and the Kew constable will be herding people out into the rush-hour traffic. Perhaps it's this one.

In memory of my wife
Bertha Trauss
and the happy hours we spent here

Who the hell places these benches? Perhaps they're shifted to make room for the mowers. Jonah stumbles upon two benches choreographed to form a gentle encounter in a glade. Others have the best view of Syon Vista, seats perfectly placed for the sun's movement through the day. Here is a circle of benches facing inwards, a gathering of Second World War veterans, but Audrey is nowhere near. Jonah wants to drop to his knees and shout her name. As the day stretches into evening, he continues walking, searching for one bench that looks exactly the same as the other thousand that are here.

Chloe has been waiting in Jonah's flat for two hours, watching the sky turn. Uncomfortable in an ever-tightening dress, she debates whether to leave, or make supper for Jonah's return. As she texts Claude to see if he's free, she can't shake off the feeling that Audrey's photographs are staring. She deletes her words and studies the many moments of a marriage. She notes the endearing gapped grin, the tailored clothes, then enters the study, hoping to discover a wife's bad habits.

There are names on the walls: Bella, Amy, Violet. Chloe picks up a book, then puts it down, then takes another, rummaging through the shelves. She knows it is wrong, but she wants to understand this ghost of a rival. Flicking through translations and folders of invoices, she finds a hardback book in a box-file, bound in hardy yellow fabric. As she opens it, memorabilia tumbles out: a feather, a ticket stub and a cigar band with the famous branding of Havana. On the first page are handwritten words.

> I can hide inside you. And in your warm places I will write you love letters and tragedies . . . and you can post them out to the world.

Don't turn over, don't read any more. But Chloe can't take her gaze away from the italic. It is a confident, expressive hand, the indigo ink stylishly slanted. Jonah told her that he'd searched through Audrey's personal belongings, but this was in a file of copy about a Russian cosmetics company. Chloe struggles with the idea of sharing her discovery: this ex-lover who's barged into their lives, triumphant and surly.

The heat rises in Chloe's body. She glances at the door then gingerly peels back a corner. Careful not to make a fold, she glimpses the next sentence.

> H understands. It's only with him that I don't feel a failure.

124

Hesitantly, she flicks through the pages and finds a scan of a baby. She can make out the feet, the dome of the head. This is trespassing. But still she turns over to find thick, black pen.

WHO IS HARRY BARCLAY?

Thumbing through the book, she finds the question again and again. Chloe sees the decision in front of her as two visual choices. The first is the door to this study. She can return the diary to its hiding place, go and cook spaghetti. While the pasta boils she can decide how to tell Jonah, yet cover up the fact she's been snooping. The second is a treacherous door. Chloe tugs on one of her cuticles, then turns to the final entry.

26 May 2004
Today I'm going to find Harry.

A Sheet of Paper
(can become many things)

12 March 2003

Why haven't I told him? I almost said something this morning before he went to school, but . . . I want to write about the Gardens.

The crocuses are out. There was an old Buddhist monk standing at the ice-cream van, buying two Mr Whippies. He was bent over, counting out change. He looked ancient.

Beyond the entrance, a younger monk was sitting cross-legged among the crocuses. With his saffron robes and shaved head, he looked like a statue — but he was VIBRANT. He must have been waiting for his teacher, but it looked like he was meditating, peace saturating his face. He was surrounded by flowers.

As I walked past, our eyes met. He gave me the most beautiful smile — the world seemed to bend with the joy of it. I wondered if he knew my secret . . . if he had divined the gentleness in my womb. Hush, I thought. Don't tell.

I sat down under a tree and did the maths. I am six weeks pregnant. I know there's nothing to feel but somehow I sense it — like wings quivering in my womb. There is a fluttering, thumping bliss in my belly. I don't know how to describe it, this ELATION.

I pray that what they say is right. Third time lucky.

It is ten in the evening. Jonah hasn't returned; perhaps he is getting drunk, or sleeping with someone else. Chloe is still sitting in her blue dress, under Audrey's shelves. She stretches out her legs, notices some stubble on her calf, then crosses them again.

14 April

I dreamt about you. It was the day of your birth and you were exhausted by the struggle of becoming — the shock of life, your first day of breathing. You were so small.

My parents visited — and J's dad too. Everyone walked out a different person — melted, shaped, reinvented by the miracle of you.

There was lilac on the walls. But J says I shouldn't paint the study yet. What does he know?

Chloe walks to the kitchen, pours a whisky and swallows it neat. There are still Post-it notes written by Audrey on the fridge. As she picks up the diary, a fragment of cardboard drops to the floor, torn from a cigar packet. On the back is scribbled in ink:

Meet me at the pagoda. Midday Tues. Yours, Hal.

During the night, Harry is restless. He nudges furniture this way and that, but stubbornly leaves Audrey's bench by the pagoda. Acutely aware that she hasn't returned, he drags other seats to the exact spot where visitors can bask in the setting sun, or notice the symmetry of an avenue of holm oaks. He places one bench under the rhododendrons so people are encouraged to smell the "King George", a hybrid created with specimens from the Himalayas. Visitors might even become still enough to hear a nuthatch or a woodpecker. Harry would love to talk to these strangers, but doubts they will listen.

After moving a bench to the Woodland Glade, he sits down, taking in the quiet majesty of the trees, their constant compassion. This mysterious place breathes for the city. As the damp from the rotting slats seeps into his trousers, Harry remembers a bench he found earlier, decorated with blossom. It marked the anniversary of a mother s death. At Christmas, relatives will often place wreaths or mistletoe, and it's palpable, the love of those remaining . . . and the hungry distance between absence and presence. Probably no one will remember this moss-covered bench, but the wood still tells its story. It's reminding Harry that trees can be reincarnated into a seat or a coffin. A sheet of paper, a piano, a weapon . . .

A branch breaks. Then another. The footfalls are too heavy for a fox or a badger. A man stumbles through the dark. As the intruder navigates his way past unexpected trees, Harry sits as still as a plant.

Jonah lumbers into one of the clearings. He runs his fingers along a bench's inscription, then another. Harry looks up at the sky and awaits God's judgement. What else could love have done? he asks. What? Tell me.

Jonah moves on, but for hours he searches. It is dawn when he stands by the waterlily pond, where soon the lilies will unfurl. In this tender light, a white birdhouse shimmers. The swamp cypress has catkins and cones, both male and female flowers — and between this tree and a man is a memory. As Harry hides behind the New Zealand flax, he doesn't know that Jonah once stood here with Audrey; but he senses that the habits of humans are no different from those of birds. All creatures migrate home, and this is a place where Jonah once found relief, not knowing that in less than a year Audrey would be gone.

Hunching under the new sun, the robbed husband wears his solitude like a coat. How wonderful it would be if Audrey was looking down on them, but she has abandoned them both. How can a woman leave two men so gifted and disabled? Harry desperately wants to explain that none of it was Jonah's fault; but he just stands there, seeping pity, until the sky relents and joins in, soaking them both.

Outside the window, the Tuesday morning is sleepy with rain. Chloe sits naked on the toilet, the yellow book in her hand. There are only two hours before Jonah needs to leave for school. A crumpled blue dress lies on the bathroom floor like a puddle.

Chloe feels wretched. Having skipped dinner, she keeps thinking she'll get up and make some toast, but the only thing that will cure her nausea is sleep. She's promised that after tonight she won't look at the diary again, but she can't find a good place to stop. She's trawled through Audrey's complaints about work, pages of purple prose on the ecstasies of Kew Gardens. It is clearly written by a woman who enjoys language. Notes about favourite books, Saturday jaunts — a miscarriage.

> I woke up and didn't remember. I stroked my belly, then realised that this is just the space where you once were.

The next page holds a scattering of biscuit crumbs.

> Think of all the times I would have kissed your head, or your feet. WHAT HEAVEN IS WORTH GIVING UP THESE THINGS?

Under a doodle of an inky maze, the handwriting becomes scratchy.

> Watching some mutant, slug-like insect. Why does it get to live?

14 May
Today I passed a pregnant woman on the street — the radiance of her rounded belly. Then I stopped outside The Shoe Station (masochist). I looked at the tiny sandals, then went home, undressed and stared in the mirror. Why doesn't anything grow in here?

Chloe peers out of the window. Between the house and the fence, a gravelled path stores the buildings bins.

130

Propping herself up against the wall, she continues reading, her bare toes scrunched against the lino.

19 May

The grainy image of that ten-week scan ... the many minutes of the professionals staring at the screen. A doctor came in and said, "Has anyone told her?" The sound I made — as if something inside had ripped. I couldn't tear my eyes away from the monitor. My womb had become a reluctant grave.

Friends moan about the sacrifices they make for their kids, then look at me with pity. I offer them another cup of tea — while wondering what would happen if I told them that I want to dig up the foetus. I want to devour all the membranes, the tiny vertebrae, the once-flickering brain, until she becomes part of me again. Is that why some beasts eat their children?

All these things I don't speak out loud. I'm still a Grade A student, but it doesn't matter how many languages I speak. It only gave me a sense I could control things ...

It feels like the ghost of a wife is sitting on the toilet. Two naked women in different times circle the same bathroom.

4 June

I was twenty-seven when J rescued me from my library tower. He smelt of wood fires and salt — kindling all the desires I had stifled. Back then I didn't know how to be intimate, not even with myself.

131

London became a windswept shore — and I, the net. He reeled me in; then he showed me how to spread my wings, my legs.

There are pages of collage: a cinema ticket, a postcard from an art gallery and an advert for a herbal supplement that claims to fix hormonal imbalances. Then a passport photo of Jonah, younger, untamed, his body taking up the entire booth. He had to hunch himself into the frame.

13 June

I first saw you perform in a smoky cellar. Hands like a sailor, but boy, could you play. You stood as if you only wanted the mic to hear, and everyone leant in to be part of that secret. I was mesmerised — by the emotion snagging in your throat, the awkward poetry of your body. Then the music shifted, and your voice, generous and unaffected, invited us all to join in. Guitar pounding, the audience bounced, girls shrieking your name.

But you were never at ease with the self-promotion. You were happiest sitting in the sunshine on a brick wall, highlighting Chatwin's *Songlines* or a novel by George Orwell. You heard words differently — scribbling music in the margins. Like a scruffy magpie, you collected things that glittered.

As time went on, I worried about your fans — their tight jeans, their impossibly straight hair — but then you gave me a demo cassette, *Between Your Smile*.

You had turned me into music.

Where is he, anyway? Perhaps Chloe should record him as a missing person, but it's most likely that he went to the pub and is now pushing a woman up against the wallpaper, kissing her neck. Or maybe that happened hours ago. Chloe's throat feels claggy. She really should get some water.

17 June

Early on, we talked about children — my ambition to do things differently from Mum. I couldn't stand being in that car with her bloody perfume. When my dad yelled at me for throwing up over the leather, I promised myself that when I had kids, I wouldn't care about appearances, or grades, but making things out of egg boxes.

12 July

PGCE done, you've had four or five interviews. Once, you only wore suits to funerals. With your extra weight, you're no longer able to get away with the slouch of younger musicians; you try to remain the rebel — with your seventies lapels, your retro hair — but somehow I have tamed you.

You were the only one who understood my jokes, and where to touch me — but now all you do is chastise me for smoking. But darling, it knuckles everything down — the grief, the boredom — even you, the way you look so disappointed all the time.

Last night, at Kate's, you told the story about that stray dog you found on Bantham Beach. I've heard it so many times — the anecdotes you bring out to amuse or impress — and we're both so talented at pretending everything's peachy. We still see friends, or share the crossword — after all, we have no gravestones to visit. I find myself mourning: the potential not just of our kids, but of the mum I know I could be. And what about you? You sacrificed your career to become a father. But without children or music, you are shapeless.

I can't remember exactly when you stopped playing. You had assignments to write, a wife to cheer up . . .

It's your muse I blame. She's no longer beautiful. Sassy. I've no idea why you keep framing her up on the walls. She doesn't live here any more.

4 August

Sex has become perfunctory. A means to an end. Sperm, eggs and timing and us trying so bloody hard to be who we once were — but we're like ghosts of the people we married. For most of the month our bed is frigid. A yard of mattress between your legs and mine — I could tell you the exact temperature of its coldness. My body is beached, voluminous, unattractive.

7 August

What kind of woman is unable to bear children? Even my mother was able. And still you try so hard to be romantic. The other day you surprised me with scrambled eggs and smoked salmon for breakfast, but when you stroked my hip I couldn't bear it.

Skipping forward, Chloe reads about Jonah starting at the Paddington comp then finds a place where the paper is crumpled. Some of the words have leaked into inky puddles, as if Audrey's hair has dripped.

12 September

In the bath, sunlight spills through the window. This could be the perfect journey. I could hold my breath underwater. Wait for my lungs to stop.

I'm sculling towards my children. They are in the corner of my eye, waiting — but then I sit up, spluttering. My lungs have a willpower stronger than my own. They insist on breathing . . .

Lying inside the empty bath, Chloe imagines Audrey cradled by the cold enamel. Is this what suicide feels like? Don't. Flicking back through the pages, Chloe retraces the entries she has missed.

THE POND, August

Just you, me and the view — the grey sky, the lilies — but between you and I there was an uncoverable distance. You coughed into your sleeve and it irritated me. I don't know the exact day it happened, when we lost our shine, but now we're like a faded version of ourselves, a tape recording weakened by time.

I tried to imagine what we would look like ten years from now, but I could only picture the damage of two people. I knew you were doing everything you could. You folded your arms, squinted at the pond. You tried to hide it, but your eyes were damp.

This is my husband, I kept telling myself. This is the man I love. But you kept fidgeting, making inane comments about the lilies, and I wanted you to be still. When your mind paused, I could almost remember your beauty.

135

You said it was going to be OK, but that was a lie, just childish faith. You talked about holidays, and I wondered what supports a love that endures — then I thought about the unfamiliar borders where love stops and something else begins.

I started crying because I realised I was sorting out the business of leaving a man. Perhaps you could meet someone else, become a dad.

Chloe pushes the diary away. She doesn't want Jonah to read this, but then wonders if it is herself she is protecting. She looks around the tiny bathroom and feels dirty.

It is eight in the morning and Jonah is either lying in another woman's bed or on the tube, travelling to school in yesterday's clothes. As Chloe gets out of the bath, her vision skips, the white patterns on the floor swirling. It's impossible to rub away her headache. She distractedly tears off a piece of toilet paper and begins to fold the tissue. Origami has shown her that nothing is set in stone. A bird can be refolded into a boat, a fish, a kimono, or any other extravagant vision. At other times it aches to return to its original folds. The paper begins to fray. It tires, rebels.

Stories, too, can be unfolded into different shapes. It depends on who is doing the telling. The truth is versatile; Chloe can pleat it and pleat it again. She transforms the tissue into a bird then a box — how much does paper bend?

A Day in September

Audrey's bench has been missing for three weeks and no one in Kew has been able to help. Jonah has tried to focus — organising a meeting with a troubled pupil, rehearsing the Year 10 concert — but he can't shake off the feeling that he is being punished. His dad disagreed, suggesting that this was a sign for him to move on; but to Jonah the missing bench is a mystery to be solved. There's nothing more haunting than a question mark.

Two days ago, on the first anniversary of Audrey's death, Jonah sat cross-legged on the lake's benchless deck. His aching back became a self-flagellation, but other than that, he felt surprisingly numb. He had scheduled in the devastation. It was easier than those times of ambush. Once, he had seen a woman walking down George Street, wearing a poppy-print skirt — one of Audrey's donated to Oxfam.

Chloe is sitting in his stained white armchair, sketching in a notebook. She looks like a scrawny stray cat that has wandered into his living room. The late-May evening lights up her pale elbows, her baggy T-shirt. She is wearing Union Jack boxer shorts and

137

snakeskin boots from the second-hand market; she has revelled in tottering around in them all afternoon. She has left a trail: a spill of coffee, a magazine by the toilet, pencils and pastels strewn across the floor. Audrey would have shuddered at the mess, raised an eyebrow at Chloe's leg slung over the arm of the chair. But her long, naked limb makes Jonah think of the strength in her thigh muscles, her joyous nocturnal yells. He craves it. He chastises himself.

The fish is ready. Over supper, Jonah remembers a night chatting with Audrey. Massaging the evening with whisky, they rewound their day, the candlelight warming their upturned faces. Over the wax-crusted table, the conversation waned. There was the cough of dawn, the crunch of morning. Her cigarette smoke lingered in the air.

"Joe? Did you hear what I said?"

"What?"

Chloe's eyes are hurt. "I was talking about the Kew Gardens commission."

"Sorry."

She is too close for him to see, his focus far away on a memory. Perhaps if she steps back a few feet?

"Perhaps you shouldn't have stopped seeing your therapist." She tugs on a tuft of hair. "Since the bench has gone missing, you've been getting worse."

"Worse?"

"Distant. Not sleeping."

Jonah shovels peas down his throat then puts down his fork. "Did you move it?"

"What? No!"

138

"It can't have vanished into thin air."

She looks at him steadily. "You'll find it."

As she tidies away the clattering dishes, Jonah has an itch to quarrel. He remembers that, with Audrey, sometimes fighting was more intimate than sex; it can be the best way to know a person. They would squabble over undone chores, opposing views about a mutual friend, her over-criticising her parents, but now he would give anything to have one more chance to argue. His fight wanes. Don't even consider it; Chloe needs a better man than him, a man who is, at least, present.

A bench was supposed to make his marriage indelible. But so much is being rubbed away, erased, and now he has to make a decision; he never expected this relationship to become serious. They both reach across to clear up the same bread-crumbs; but he withdraws and tidies Chloe's sketchbook. Inside is a drawing of Audrey copied from a photo above the fireplace. The cross-hatched lines feel blasé, intrusive.

"What the hell's this?" he splutters.

Chloe's lips part as if rehearsing an answer. Instead of shaking it out of her, he strides over to the piano. He insults her by practising scales; a private meditation. He focuses on keeping an even pace. As she hovers nearby, he persists: B flat minor pentatonic. Then she's behind him, trying to reel him home with a kiss. Her lips land somewhere between his ear and cheek.

His voice has a careful sheen. "I'm sorry, Chlo. But if you're looking for somewhere to put down roots, this isn't it."

"Lucky I'm not a flower . . ."

"Great."

A nod to check they understand each other. He smiles a smile that's trying too hard to please, then turns back to the piano. As he plays arpeggios, he congratulates himself for being honest, then wonders if there's another truth, so frail that speaking it would be prodigious.

"I'm having a bath."

He stares down at the scuffed pedals. "I'm sorry, Chlo. I wish I could be who you want."

She shifts position, hip cocked like a gun. Her snakeskin boots seem pitiful.

"Who's that, then?"

Her face is resolute, blunt. Jonah reaches out, hoping to escape the mess of words, but all she returns is a frigid child-like hug.

While the bath is running, Chloe slips down the hall to the study and levers Audrey's diary from the box-file on the shelf. Stashing it under a dressing gown, she makes her way back to the bathroom, where she sits on the floor, clutching the towelling bundle. Three weeks ago she'd returned the diary and spent the rest of the day temping in an office in Old Street. As she photocopied and stapled, she debated whether to let Jonah discover the book in his own time, if ever. But when she called to check he hadn't been run over, he informed her that the bench had gone missing. It was as if Audrey was asking to remain hidden.

Chloe thinks of Jonah's patronising, apologetic smile and considers whether she is gathering ammunition. At

140

any moment, she could walk out, throw this book across the floor.

Your wife was not who you think. Can't you see who is standing here instead?

A liar.

Perhaps she should storm out, go back to Claude. She's always been able to fold herself into someone new, to fly away . . . but she remains motionless. She chews on the inside of her mouth, feeling the satisfying mark made by her teeth, the sweet pain she can manage. The room is steaming up, the mirror clouding over. She becomes mesmerised by the ghosts lingering in the mist, the whitewashed walls, the mock-1950s radio the only bright-red excess. This is what Audrey listened to as she touched these towels and taps. She studied her reflection, as Chloe does now, stretching the skin across her cheeks, pinching her neck.

Last week, Chloe went to the market and bought Audrey's favourite book: *Bonjour Tristesse*. Despite Chloe's hankering to dislike her rival, she knows Audrey better having read the novel she loved. She can recognise the other woman's obsessions and doubts. As she read about an existential daughter, a promiscuous father, she wondered what it would have been like if they had met; perhaps they could have been friends. Then the penultimate chapter described a woman killing herself in a car crash.

Chloe sits on the toilet and opens the diary. She tells herself that she needs to understand what she's giving Jonah, but she feels like a child who says she hasn't eaten any cake while it sits like a rock in her stomach.

13 September 2003

At the pedestrian crossing, I thought the lights had turned green. I stepped out, sure the car would brake — but everything seemed involuntary.

The wind hauled me back, but it wasn't the wind. It was a stranger. I'm not sure if he held my wrist or elbow. As the car whizzed past he let go.

"Today is not your day to die," he joked.

I looked away, embarrassed. Pedestrian lights. Flashing. Once I'd crossed the road with the others, he had gone.

I don't know how to describe him. A stranger stood before me, and yet — it was the most intimate moment I can think of. It wasn't his appearance that was the beauty. His eyes knew me. Imagine that.

Harry thought it was a funny day — something in the weather. Kew Gardens was filling up with visitors, squinting in the mid-September sunshine. The afternoon glimmered with possibility.

When Audrey walked out on to the busy street, his arm reached out instinctively. He didn't expect to have an impact; the words came out of his mouth without thinking. He didn't stick around to see if she had heard him.

He saw her again an hour later, sitting on a blue bench set into the pagoda. He watched her quietly eating a sandwich as she stared into space. He wasn't sure what had happened. He was glad that this woman could still feel the warmth of the day, but the whole incident unsettled him.

13 September 2003

How stupid to believe this month would be any different. This morning, there it was, the red stain. I sit on my usual bench, the paint still peeling, the planes still flying low overhead.

I cradle a silence between my legs, pregnant with numbness.

Twin boys run around the tower, clutching wands made of twigs. They remind me of my early childhood, when the summer was filled with my parents' sunny snoozes, when the world felt small and safe.

If I am quiet enough, perhaps this ache will pass me by . . . if I just remain unnoticed.

What is this want and what would fulfil it? A cigarette? Some faith?

That man at the crossing?

Funny how these furls of smoke create a barrier around me. A little girl is playing near a twisted beech. Stripy T-shirt, pigtails, trousers rolled up to her knees. What would happen if I took her in my arms, rubbed my face against her cheek?

Audrey wasn't the reason Harry was there. Walking past Temperate House, a little girl had waved at him. She didn't seem to have an adult accompanying her, so Harry decided to keep an eye out. After a while, the child stopped by the horizontal trunk of a beech, her smile irresistibly cheeky. Then Harry recognised the woman sitting with her back against the pagoda. Despite the heat of the day, she was wearing autumnal colours . . . a red jumper with a rusty-orange scarf . . . her hair like turning leaves. She looked up from her notebook to the nearby cedar of Lebanon and there it was: the distant glance of a woman as some unknowable thought passed through her like a breeze.

She then looked at Harry. And Harry, the foolish dreamer, made his first mistake. He said hello, or good afternoon. He can't remember which.

14 September 2003

When I said hello the sound surprised me, catching in my throat. His suit and tweed cap made him look artistic. I thanked him for earlier, but my voice boomeranged back into itself, spooled with too much breath and not enough volume. So I gestured: please — sit.

The man glanced up at the sky then cleared his throat. Said no, then yes. Something about it can't hurt — just for a while. He hitched up his trouser legs to sit down. Sturdy boots, muddy hems. On his navy jumper was the Kew logo.

He was perhaps in his early fifties. The sparkle in his eyes, his grey stubble, reminded me of that guy in *Butch Cassidy and the Sundance Kid*. But on closer inspection, his jacket had lost several buttons. He looked like a painting in need of restoration — that at some point in his life he had been beautiful.

"My name's Harry Barclay. But, please — call me Hal."

"Audrey Wilson. How do you do."

There was her outstretched hand, waiting. Taking it, Harry became aware of the warmth radiating from her skin, the slight moisture between her knuckles. When he realised he was squeezing, he let go.

Looking up at the sky for reassurance, he said, "Good God, look at the moon." The celestial sliver

144

stood out against the broad blue. As Audrey smiled, Harry's intimidation melted. It was as if it had been sucked away into the friendly gap between her teeth. He noticed her freckles.

"Pretty," she said. "What a wonderful place to work."

"It is. But am I stopping *you* working?" Harry gestured towards the yellow notebook, then noticed a pile of papers by her feet. On them were words he couldn't understand: perhaps Russian or Polish?

"I was looking for a distraction. It's fine."

He shouldn't have been talking to her — there was work to do; he looked around. But there was no one to raise an eyebrow. Did he want to pull a joke, or stare at her, stunned? He decided to exercise his tongue.

"Did you know that there are over fourteen thousand trees in Kew? I particularly love the Old Lions — the maidenhair tree or *Ginkgo biloba*, the *Sophora japonica*, the *Robinia pseudoacacia* otherwise known as the false acacia . . ." Her eyes were unreadable. "Am I boring you?"

"No, not at all."

She asked if he had always been interested in gardens.

"Ignorant for years. It wasn't until I was in the army that I learnt about veggies."

He had planted them in a Welsh village, during training. But then his regiment was sent to the desert where nothing grew. There was just the stench of human flesh laid out in the sun. Harry remembered batting away a fly that had landed on the tip of his rifle. Focus. Shoot.

"One of the lads was a Kewite. He had this notebook full of botanical drawings. He'd heard of a conservationist collecting specimens, even under fire. But where we were posted there was damn all. Out there, he told me about these gardens — a paradise called Kew."

"So he was the one who inspired you?"

"I guess after all that fighting, I wanted to be with the earth."

He had a curious voice that made you wonder if he had spoken. Its power wasn't in its pitch or volume, but how the words bedded themselves into my belly. He peered into me, his gaze pulling out all the weeds, the roots, the flowers . . .

He took out a Montecristo then joked about the medicinal nature of plants. With a silver guillotine, he sliced off the end of his cigar. The smoke smelt sweet, and I was glad to have an excuse to light my own cigarette. The pause stretched, but Harry didn't seem to mind. He enjoyed the taste of his cigar with deliberate calm. Then he began a story. It was about the craft of folding leaves in the right order.

Harry was trying to remember how to cross the unfathomable distance between himself and another human being. He told her how tobacco leaves are blended to create the perfect *Habanos* or Havana.

"The *volado* leaf is used for its combustibility, the *seco* for aroma and the third, *ligero*, is the most full-flavoured. The slow burning of the leaf gives the cigar its strength."

He knew he shouldn't get involved with visitors but he didn't want this to end. Perhaps he was capable of

146

more than he thought; he had, after all, saved this woman. But as he told her about the *capa*, the last, supple leaf that forms the wrapper, he felt like an idiot.

I found myself looking at the crook of his thumb. He used his hands to articulate his words, and I wondered what those palms, good at growing things, would feel like on the curve of my stomach.

We were squashed together on the narrow bench. Hemmed in by the alcove, our proximity was uncomfortably thrilling. Behind him, graffiti was scratched into the eighteenth-century brick — love hearts, initials. The boys I'd been watching earlier were running around the pagoda again. One was panting to keep up. Then Harry said I didn't talk much. I have a hideous feeling that I might have shrugged coquettishly.

"I prefer to listen," she said. "Other people's stories are much more interesting."

Neither of them knew what to say after that. Harry started fidgeting.

"Are you OK to be doing this?" she asked gently.

"What? Oh yes, I've done my shift for the day."

Their words flew into the distance. The silence was punctuated by the repeated click of Harry's lighter each time his cigar went out.

"I could tell you about the pagoda in the war," he suggested. "Would you like that?"

He explained that the German bombs had destroyed many local properties, but the tower had stayed intact.

"It was the British bomb designers that wrecked it. They cut holes in each of the pagoda floors, then dropped dummy shells down."

"To test how they fell?"

"Yes. Bombs away!"

She laughed, a bit sadly. "I can't help thinking of school-boys dropping paper aeroplanes."

"Do you want to try it?"

"I'll race you."

Harry wanted to please her. She was that kind of woman. The risk rushed to his cheeks as he led her to the pagoda. There, he took out a large key from his pocket, the kind that would be appropriate to open a secret garden. After turning the lock, he pushed his weight against the surprisingly thin door. Checking no one was watching, they darted into the tower and stared up at the dilapidated stairs, the rotting wood, the magical shambles.

Audrey climbed the first few steps, peering upwards. The spiralling staircase made Harry feel small, but suddenly she started to run, as if some capricious spirit had claimed her. Up and up she went, her tailored skirt hoisted, and Harry chased after her, dizzy with the backs of her knees, the underside of her heels. As the octagonal walls closed in, he was dazed and dazzled.

They ran nine flights in all. Harry was nimbler than he thought but his heart beat against his chest like a wooden mallet. Once they reached the top, they were as surprised as the other.

Surrounded by windows, they stared into each others eyes like animals. No language, but still trying, insisting, to find the reflection of themselves . . . then the stillness broke into laughter. It was liberating, unadulterated — more intimate than anything Harry could have imagined.

Audrey brushed the hair from her face, letting the sunlight bathe her neck, her head thrown back with pleasure. Looking at her flushed features, Harry imagined her sitting up in bed, just a sheet wrapped around her. He was shocked by that. But then she glanced skittishly at the view as if daring to throw herself from the window. She stood at the top of the tower, arms outstretched, and Harry's stomach lurched as if he was the one plummeting from the tenth storey.

To fall or fly? What recklessness! To him, I was someone different. No history of miscarriages, just my bright eyes . . . and his. I could be anyone. I could run up stairs, make a racket. I was wide open for something not ordinary. I teetered on the edge of it — wobbly, woozy, intoxicated.

When I turned back, Harry was grasping a stitch. Rubbing his ribs, he looked out of the window. I followed his gaze to the little girl I had seen earlier. She was leaving the beech tree. I asked him, what now? But he just scratched his chest as if he had heartburn. Then he suggested we make our way down.

The civilised distance of strangers. I smoothed down my skirt, unsure what had happened. As I followed him, I clutched on to the railings. Rotting banisters. Rogue nails. I had left my swagger upstairs.

The Gardens felt spacious. We strolled along Pagoda Vista, the little girl a hundred feet in the distance. When she entered Temperate House, we continued walking.

In the Berberis Dell, Harry stopped and declared, "The mighty flagpole!"

A mast towered above them.

"It's a Douglas fir from British Columbia. In 1959 they transported it — all two hundred and twenty-five feet — to Kew." Worried that he sounded like a tourist brochure, he wiped his brow.

Audrey gave a courteous smile. "Perhaps I should get back?"

They returned to the path that led to the pagoda, but at Temperate House, he wasn't ready to release her. He bowed to a nearby bench.

"Good afternoon, Mademoiselle. You're looking mighty fine today." Christ, what was he doing? He nodded towards the inscription. "She sang '*J'Attendrai*' after D-Day. Can you see what it says? 'A wonderful mezzo soprano'."

Audrey bobbed her head in a curtsy. As she straightened her neck, they heard crying.

They both glanced towards the glasshouse, and saw the same young girl. One hand was held against her face; the other clutched a sunflower. Next to her, a woman with a black bob squatted down. She was rummaging through a rucksack.

Harry's gaze met mine. He began talking about what had happened earlier — that I had seemed disappointed when he

150

stopped me from walking on to the road. I stammered through what I hoped was an acceptable answer: there are days when I'd like to escape my life — or to change it, but . . . Harry searched every inch of my face, then leant back as if his suit was heavy. He told me I had a lot to live for.

When Harry looked at her freckled face, there was something vaporous about Audrey. They had spent the last hour chasing shadows. The little girl had left the sunflower, and was now walking away with the dark-haired woman. It looked like they were carrying something delicate, as if they had gathered up two wounded birds from the lawn.

Harry was torn. He looked down and caught sight of the gold on Audrey's hand.

"How long have you been married?"

"Eight years."

"He's a good man?"

"A music teacher."

She studied the horizon, lost in thought. Then she remembered herself.

"He just started. A couple of weeks ago."

"But you don't have children?"

"What?"

Harry managed to speak through his smile. "The way you looked at that girl."

For one yearning moment, I wanted to clutch Harry's fingers to my belly, but a woman ran past in a yellow dress, startling us both. She was sprinting barefoot. A baby was scooped in

151

one arm, her shoes dangling from her hand. She was calling out: "Emily!" Birds flocked into the sky, panicked.

Harry began to move, saying he might be able to help. He apologised for leaving then told me to be careful crossing the road.

Wait.

But I didn't say it out loud.

The bathwater is cold. Chloe has reread the same pages endlessly, tears stinging her eyes. She pulls herself back to the present, listens for Jonah, but there is only the silence of the night.

The next diary entry is a few days later.

16 September

The little girl's picture is in the newspaper. Next to a photo of her mum. That yellow dress — its brightness looks wrong.

I told the police everything I saw — Emily Richards by the beech, by Temperate House, the woman with the bob. What a terrible and enchanting afternoon. I don't know what haunts me more: Harry's gaze . . . or a missing girl.

Chloe runs the hot tap, paces the room, stubbornly sniffling, then tests the temperature and steps in. Submerging her head underwater, she holds one date in her mind: that thirteenth of September.

She had just split up with Simon and was struggling financially to commit to her final year at art college. Crashing on a friend's floor in Chiswick, she was wondering how best to explore origami in her graduation project. It was one of those fluke warm

September days that shouldn't be wasted inside, so she packed a satchel of paper to fold in the botanical gardens. She had visited with Simon a month before, so her return was nostalgic. Not knowing the Gardens, she clutched a map with the air of a tourist.

Beyond the lake, she stumbled over something that made her gasp: the surprise of a huge plot of sunflowers. The block of colour made her ache. She gazed up at the midday sun, the metal glint of an aeroplane, the blueness of the sky.

An hour later, Chloe entered an intricate glass structure, labelled on the map as Temperate House. She studied the date palm, the camellias, the chillies, then stopped to read about the cinchona tree that provides quinine. As she left, she saw a weeping child at the bottom of the steps, clutching a dwarf sunflower. Chloe looked around for the girl's parents, hoping to make this none of her business, but the child seemed inconsolable.

"Excuse me, do you need help?"

"I've killed it!"

"What?"

"I tried to pick it, but the stem was thick and the flower started screaming. Once it was torn I had to keep ripping and ripping." The girl held out the broken proof of her crime.

"I'm sure it's fine."

"But Mum's going to murder me. I'm only allowed to collect weeds!" The girl pulled at her clothes as if she could hide the flower under her T-shirt. "I get it wrong all the time . . ."

"I'm sure you don't." Chloe looked around for assistance, but she was the only adult nearby. Squatting down, she pulled some paper from her rucksack. "Perhaps there's something here that will cheer you up. What things do you like?"

The child thought for a moment, then her face reddened, as if the excitement was a rash. "Ice cream. Fireworks. Oh, I know . . ." Her eyes widened. "Really loud storms . . ."

"It was pretty blustery yesterday."

"The wind almost blew my face off!"

Chloe laughed. "We could make a bird, a plane, or a boat? What do you reckon?"

It was the most basic origami. The girl was attentive as she copied each fold, her brow creased in concentration. The end result was wonky but the child seemed pleased with herself.

"Now we should sail it!"

"I don't think that's a good idea."

"Why not? Every boat needs water."

Chloe wasn't sure how to explain the fundamental physics. She futilely tried to tuck her bob behind her ears. "Where are your parents?"

"Mum's changing Daniel's nappy, then she's getting some drinks. I didn't want to go to the loo, and I'm old enough to play on my own. She said she'd meet me here at half-past."

Bloody parents. The girl was looking at her with complete trust.

"Can we go sailing? Please, miss . . ."

154

Don't they say that kids learn from experience? Chloe checked her watch.

"OK, let's have a scientific experiment. We need to make sure you're back in time for your mum."

It was an awkward alliance. Leaving the sunflower on the ground, they picked up their paper boats and walked down Pagoda Vista. The girl reached for Chloe's hand.

Once they were at the lake, Chloe didn't know whether to warn her.

"Are you sure you don't want to keep it?"

But the girl was already teetering on the edge. She placed her boat on the surface as carefully as if she were releasing an insect. As the washi paper dropped into the water, a duck swam towards them hoping that the offering was bread. Then the boat began to disintegrate. It was a quiet shipwreck, the tiny vessel dissolving into pulp and reaching its watery grave in fragments.

There was a deathly silence.

"It sunk," the child said.

"Paper does that."

Explaining the molecular properties of paper suddenly seemed pointless. Chloe had expected more adventure — the child to revel in the downfall of a pirate ship — but the experience had only depressed her.

"Do you know how to get back? Your mum will be waiting."

When the girl pointed in the right direction, Chloe told herself she had been charitable enough. The kid smiled then walked away. Chloe took in her serious shoulders, her boyish determination; then the bow-legged child disappeared behind the trees.

Twenty minutes later, Chloe was folding an elaborate peacock among the sunflowers.

"MILLY!"

A woman in a yellow dress was running barefoot. She was juggling a baby and a bag, from which a juice box fell out.

"Emily! Where are you?"

Chloe jumped up, but the woman was already out of earshot. The day dimmed, the weather turning around them. Glancing back towards the sunflowers, Chloe saw the petals, as bright as a rape field. The yellow seared across the bruised grey sky. When Chloe turned back, the woman had vanished.

Two days later there was a photograph of the girl in the newspaper.

LOST IN KEW
Emily Richards
Last seen 13/09/03 in Kew Gardens
If you have seen her please call . . .

Chloe recognised the pigtails, the jaunty, thin limbs. She phoned the police, and went to their offices in Richmond. Her story corroborated another statement that detailed seeing a woman with a bob. Chloe asked if the child had been kidnapped.

"We did have a sighting of her running away from the Ruined Arch — but the witness was unstable." The officer flicked through his papers. "Dementia, apparently. Her son called to say she makes things up. Flights of fancy . . ."

"I'm sorry. I should have made sure she found her mum."

"Yes." The officer gave her no consolation. "We'll be in touch, Miss Adams, if we need anything."

"Of course."

Chloe stayed in Kew that day, in the futile hope of stumbling over the girl. She wanted to explain to anyone who would listen that she hadn't meant to be neglectful. It was just that she'd never spent much time with a child. Posters of Emily Richards were on every lamppost by the station. Many people said they had seen her. They talked in the supermarket, the butcher's and the post office of how they had watched a child collecting twigs, or was it flowers . . .? How they had noticed the sky, what a blue sky there was that day. Chloe remembers her walking through the trees, the branches growing bigger until she couldn't see her any more. A child had been lost and Kew would never be the same.

Chloe doesn't want to think about what happened next. She cannot hold it. On the morning that Milly's fate was splashed across the newspapers, Chloe shaved off her hair. Even when it itchily grew back, she drew pictures of the girl, and visited the Gardens regularly, growing to love each edge and corner, every pond and dell. When she applied for the Kew commission she hoped that if she created something beautiful enough she might be able to make peace with herself. On the night she met Jonah, she had gone to the lake to float paper birds and watch them sink. Now she is shocked to find herself in her dead rival's diary, and cast as the witch.

Chloe rises from the bathwater and wraps herself in a towel. Sinking down on the floor, she chews a fingernail and listens to Jonah in the kitchen, pouring a glass of water. When his bedroom door closes, Chloe's hands cast shadows across the diary, like butterflies hovering over an abyss of secrets.

She slams it shut, then stashes the yellow book in her bag — just for now, just for a while. Like a practised thief, she brushes her teeth as if nothing has happened. When she walks into the bedroom, Jonah's breathing fills the darkness. She slips quietly under the sheets, trying not to disturb him.

He rubs his eyes violently, so Chloe takes his hands until he sighs and softens. His arms wrestle with nothing until he finds Chloe's body. He smiles in his sleep. But, slowly, his wife feels wedged between them. Chloe can't compete with Audrey's curves, her hips.

She is surprised that Jonah is sleeping; then she notices the jar of contraband pills. Her own head is buzzing with stories: a little girl, a depressed wife, and a stranger's hands covered in soil.

Part III

*What We're Looking For Lies
in the Space Between Us*

Wake up you sleepy head
Put on some clothes, shake up your bed

"Oh! You Pretty Things", David Bowie

Chess

It didn't matter how often he told her to go, Milly refused to budge from the ever-darkening garden. Harry even pushed her down the path but on the other side of the Ruined Arch, she sat down, her protest cementing. He looked up at the heavens.

"What the hell do you want me to do?" he yelled.

Trying his best to stay calm, he explained the situation, but she couldn't put faces to "Mum" or "Dad", or even understand the concept of parents. It was as if she was suffering from concussion. She kept changing the subject, asking him where she should sleep, then complaining she was hungry. Harry was unaccustomed to the anxieties of children. But as the September evening chilled, he couldn't stride past his conscience as if it were a beggar, jangling a cup of petty change.

It was terrible timing. The Gardens had just endured a terrible drought. Many heritage trees were showing signs of stress and Harry was spending most of his time on irrigation. Gate receipts were up because of the glorious weather and Kew's new World Heritage status; it was now officially a wonder, sitting next to the Grand

Canyon and the pyramids. But the Gardens were tired; and so was he.

At first he tended to her like a seedling, making sure she had enough fresh air and sleep; then he tried to keep her up with maths and reading. By October, over a million bulbs needed planting, so he enlisted her help. He showed her the sacks in the potting shed, explaining the difference between the snakes-head fritillary and the pale-skinned bulbs of the narcissus, then he would take her to check on his favourite trees post-drought.

Her amnesia was a gift. She forgot about the mornings when Harry was too quiet, or didn't hear her well. They muddled along, their friendship built on him cleaning the cut on her head, or her surprising him by knowing the difference between the whistle of a wood pigeon and a chaffinch. One evening when he was putting her to bed, she called him Daddy. He pulled back as if she had burnt his skin.

"OK," she submitted. "How about Papa or Dad?"

"No, luv . . ."

"What if I take the 'd' off? Da." She rolled the word around her mouth as if it were a sweet. "That's a good idea. Do you like it?"

He ran his fingers through his hair, trying to think of a palatable explanation; but if this little fairy tale of hers helped, he might as well go along with it. What he didn't realise was how this one small word would reshape him. His days became chiselled by what would surprise her, or what she might need — and soon they learnt new pastimes, such as playing chess.

They found the board in a charity shop in Richmond. Missing nine pieces, they soon found replacements: light or dark stones for pawns, a pinecone for a bishop. The original maple and ivory was intricately carved and polished. After Audrey's death they often played the game, as a way of spending time without conversation. Harry relished the focus.

On a scorching June day, they sit cross-legged on the bleached-out grass, the board between them.

"I've counted." Milly nudges her acorn along two squares. "It's been fifty-four days. Why doesn't Jonah come play with me?"

"He's busy, luv. He's a grown-up."

Harry drums his fingers against the board then looks up to see a passer-by watching them. The man is clearly drunk, tottering from one oak to another.

"Afternoon." Harry doffs his cap. "Blistering weather . . ."

The guy sways. It's not clear if he's nodding or shaking his head and Harry worries about him vomiting in the flowers; then Jonah appears in his work clothes, walking up the mount towards them. Milly, focused on the game, doesn't notice. But Harry watches as the teacher enters the Temple of Bellona then bends down to read the bench's inscription. After gazing up at the columns, he continues walking, but the day is too hot to be searching for one bench among thousands.

23 September 2003

I was surprised to find "Mademoiselle J'Attendrai" by the

pagoda. When I sat down on the side where Harry had been, I could almost feel him.

I wanted to find out whether he'd caught up with Emily's mum, how the Kew staff were coping . . .

I sat there again the next day and the next. Listening to the still autumn air, my cigarette twitched between my fingers like a hornet.

10 October
I wring the light out of each day waiting for him. I wish my face could be free from the want of it: the nicotine, a peculiar man . . . And just now, Joe had another rant at me for smoking. The best place to be is in the bathroom.

Jonah can call all he wants: "What are you doing?" I don't want to join him in the lounge and curl up in an armchair. He'll offer me a cup of tea . . . wrap me up in cotton wool. Then he'll kiss me on the neck, and it will remain on my skin — like a trespass.

Be a good wife, Au, entice him with lingerie and laughter. But on the few occasions when we do have sex we kiss without patience. We don't give ourselves the time to see each other.

20 October
I dreamt about my daughter. She was walking along the edge of a swimming pool; then, all of a sudden, she jumped in without her armbands. The lifeguard didn't hear my screams — there were too many kids. I ran beside the pool, my feet slipping. I couldn't get there fast enough, then time tripped.

166

I clasped her body, as if I could warm the life hack into her. But there was nothing in my arms. On the bottom of the pool lay a two-year-old girl. Lifeless.

21 October

Every morning, the shower. Scouring out my tears. Adverts jangling on the radio.

I dress, careful to button up each inch of my grief.

I don't recognise myself in the mirror, but hopefully there's something good there — in the mask of my work face, or when I find Jonah in the kitchen and touch him. Always when dressed and only in passing, but I try, all the same.

Audrey was always huddled around a cigarette, as if it might warm her. As soon as she left, Harry would sit on the same bench, humming the war torch song, "J'Attendrai". He sat with his hat in his hands, to feel her presence, to smell her perfume lingering in the air. He relished the view she'd just gazed at, and as some ants carried away the crumbs from her sandwich, he felt the echo of having been touched.

He told himself he mustn't interfere, but each day he found himself hiding behind a cedar. As soon as Audrey left he would replace her exact position on the bench. All around him was the sore beauty, the "what if".

He kept himself busy by forking the formal beds, treading down the soil; but one October day, he let his guard down. Concorde was being withdrawn from service and he gazed up, waiting for the last three flights to fly at low altitude before landing at Heathrow. When they finally arrived over Syon Vista, he felt a nudging sensation, the feeling of being watched. He turned away from the sky to see Audrey standing in front of Dalí's clock. It was already too late; she was waving, and Harry began to prickle with joy. From balls to bone he knew he should have turned away but instead he began walking down the sun-soaked, tree-lined avenue. When he reached her, Dalí's sculpture was melted at six o'clock.

24 October
The benches behind the Palm House always catch the last sun of the day. As I stood by the bronzed sagging clock, I noticed a figure walking down Syon Vista, the sunlight shining around his head.

We talked about the planes then walked towards the Secluded Garden. There were poems about the five senses, a stream, and a sturdy wooden seat next to a sign that said "Hearing". We admired the Phyllostachys; a genus of bamboo, he explained. He asked me to sit down and close my eyes: I listened to the rustling leaves. The water. The thump of my heart.

25 October
When I returned home, every muscle was pulsing. I led Jonah to the bedroom and unbuttoned his shirt, but he pressed his hand against mine and said, "Perhaps we should wait. Use contraception."

29 October
Today we planted shrubs in the garden. With a knife that had seen better days, Harry took some cuttings from the

168

mock-orange, about a foot long. I removed the lower leaves then put them in the soil. There was mud under my nails, in my hair, and suddenly it felt like I could BREATHE again. I was laughing.

The way he looked at me made me feel like the only woman in the world. When H talked about his love of planting things, of watching them grow, I almost believed that something new could be born.

After a few meetings, Harry, tentatively, began to think that Audrey was his reward for getting through all these lonely years, but his better self knew it was holy madness. He still couldn't believe that she was paying any attention to him. On that first day he'd wondered if she was some kind of celestial being. But it didn't take him long to realise that she was human and lovely, flawed and engrossed in her own difficulties.

During the day, they would admire the blazing red of the maples, or a spider's web laced with dew. Often they sat by the pagoda, talking about Harry's work. Sharing the things he loved about the garden, he weighed each sentence on his tongue. Maybe after a minute, or five, but always in his own exquisite timing, he released them with the lightness of someone who knew he was right. She listened.

When it was her turn to speak, she often talked about her faults. Whenever she asked about the missing girl, he felt at a loss. This woman craved authenticity and yet he lied to her daily. He was being called upon to do something for both her and Milly; he just didn't know what.

At night, he stole into the gravelled forecourt around Audrey's building and tended to the flowers on her windowsills. As he watered the winter pansies, he told himself that this had nothing to do with courtship; he only hoped that the stubbornness of their colour would encourage Audrey to thrive. Cramped in the thin alley between the fence and the building, he passed her bathroom, carrying a pocketful of seeds and some rosemary cuttings to ward off insects. He pictured the first time she opened the window, the scent a surprise. He decided that there was no harm in pruning back the shrubs where she parked. Who would notice a snip here or there? It would stop the daily scraping of her handbag as she tried to squeeze into her car.

Taking these risks was as unfamiliar as wearing another man's clothes. At night, while Milly was sleeping, he would sit under the redwoods and stare, again, at his bookmark. As he studied the last seconds of a life, a woman falling, he wondered if the photographer from the *Buffalo Courier Express* regretted not dashing up eight flights to talk to Mary Miller. Knowing what was about to happen, how could anyone stand on Main Street, checking the best angle for his camera? As Harry stared down at the grainy image, he thought about the many trees he'd held up with cables.

"Isn't it my duty to help?"

But the tumbling woman was too busy dancing to reply, her petticoat flung up in abandon.

170

5 November
All my life I've played it safe and now I want to do something selfish, even glorious. What I hate most is the sensation of stasis and here, at last, is the promise of motion. The chance to do something rebellious. But can I dare?

My day is full of routines and lists; the months stretched out in front of me — childless. But when H looks at me, it feels both BINDING and BOUNDLESS.

My days are filled with:
science
the secrets of trees . . .
the unfathomable questions of symmetry.

I don't want to return to the world outside these Gardens. All I want is to notice the dew on a leaf. The holy busyness of worms in the soil.

7 November
Every time I see a ladybird or a fallen conker, I think of him. I might as well be scratching a heart into a metal pencil case.

8 November
Poor J. He unwittingly supports my visits to the Gardens, believing I need time and space — but every time we say goodbye, it's there.

The lies inside my kiss.

It leaves an aftertaste, even when I'm halfway down the street.

Each time Harry met the redhead, he'd set Milly up under a Hungarian oak with a colouring book and say he'd be back in an hour. He probably thought she was too young for it, or that a snotty-nosed kid would cramp his style.

She would gaze up at the clouds then try to entertain herself by giving names to the squirrels; but she couldn't escape the feeling that something was missing. She ached for friends her own age, to go to school, and after a few minutes of sitting on her own she would brush the grass off her legs and run.

When Harry returned to the oak, his eyes ablaze with the surprise of how wonderful life could be, Milly would pretend that she had been too busy staring up at the winter sun on the branches . . . or that robin over there . . . to colour in the pages. But the truth was that she had followed him — past the lady on the bench reading *The Times*, the mother in her fake fur pushing a pram — and when they reached the pagoda she snuck behind a shrub. On greeting each other, Harry and Audrey never touched.

"What are you writing in your notebook?"

Harry closed it. "Just gardening stuff."

"I love how beaten-up it is." As she sat down beside him, she tentatively touched the soil-stained cover, the broken spine. "I've never understood why people get angry when someone turns down a corner. I bet some authors love to have their books underlined, doodled on — to be lived in."

Then Milly couldn't hear them for a bit. She could just see Audrey's cold breath in the air, and Harry, mesmerised by it. Eventually her voice grew stronger.

172

"The book I'm reading at the moment is crinkled with bathwater. There are coffee spills, a greasy stain — perhaps mayo —"

Chuckling, Harry tucked the notebook safely away into his back pocket. "So your own life has become part of the story?"

"Yes! You should see the novel I took to India. A squashed mosquito, dirt from a motorised rickshaw . . ."

They held each others gaze for so long that Milly began to fidget. There was something about the two of them that made her itchy. Just do it, she silently implored, scratch it.

Harry rubbed his stubble. "Do you write yourself?"

"I try. A bit of poetry — no, it's not even that." Audrey clapped her gloved hands together but they didn't make a sound. "One day I'd love to translate a novel. One of the greats: Tolstoy, Turgenev . . ."

"Why don't you write an original?"

"Christ, I couldn't do that. Come on, it's too cold to sit."

As they passed the Japanese Gateway, Milly could see them in the distance, their heads bowed together around some delicious thought. She might only be a kid, but even she could see how their bodies bent towards each other like lovers, or like questions they didn't yet dare to ask.

A Piece of String

The sky is sweating. Jonah and Chloe overheat outside a semi-detached house, trying not to listen to the shouting within.

"Graham? Can you open this damn jam jar?"

Jonah is about to ring the bell again when his friend, Kate, opens the door and greets them fondly. Two lasses or three? In the shady hallway, Chloe collides with a child in a dinosaur costume. When she enters the kitchen, she wishes she wasn't wearing cut-off jeans; the other women are in shift dresses from Boden. Chloe hands Kate a bottle of vodka but it soon becomes obvious that the main drink of the day will be tea.

On the kitchen table is an array of cakes at different stages of completion. A couple of women beat butter icing while children, anticipating sugar, hover around them. In the corner, a baby bounces in a chair, unaware that she is the day's focus.

"Hello, little monkey." Jonah squats down to meet her. "Oh, Kate, she's a beauty."

Chloe peers over his shoulder to see the rash-covered cheeks.

"Yes. Lovely."

174

Jonah stands up and gives Chloe's arm an encouraging squeeze.

"Well, I'll leave you in the safe hands of the girls." Then, as a parting joke — "Play nicely."

He walks into the conservatory, joining the men, who apparently have no part in the minutiae of creation. Liza, a chic woman with silver hair, asks Chloe if she's local.

"No. Dalston."

She tries to hold her posture as elegantly as Audrey, but in straightening herself, she knocks over a box of icing sugar with her elbow.

"Fuck me! Sorry."

A child giggles.

"That's enough, Lily."

Chloe gets down on her knees. "I'm so sorry. Here." She tries to sweep away the spill with her hands, but a crawling T. Rex is already licking his fingers.

Kate drags the boy out from under the table. "It's chaos in here!" Behind the hastily applied make-up, her face is wan, her exhausted eyes longing for adult conversation. "It's silly to be cooped up," she says, in a sing-song voice she uses with her children. "Why don't you sit outside? It's such a beautiful day. We'll be out in a minute."

On the lawn, children are amusing themselves with two footballs. There's a book of philosophy on the garden table and Chloe picks it up, estranged from the ambitions of these cake-decorating women. As she finds a seat, she leafs through the wily words and big ideas then worries that others might complain she's not helping. But perhaps they're happy making and gathering, moving from kitchen to garden as they carry out steaming pots of tea. Maybe it's only Chloe who is embarrassed that she isn't proficient at baking, or nursing a child — and did she ever hug Emily Richards? Chloe can almost feel the little hand in hers, the trusting weight of it. *Every boat needs water. Please.*

A woman walks into the garden. She has strawberry-blonde hair, a delicate nose and wide hips: a pear-shaped figure that Chloe imagines in Wellington boots, digging up vegetables. In her arms is a wriggling infant.

"Hullo," she says. "Jonah's just told me what he'll be doing this summer — teaching music at a community centre? Apparently it's all down to your contacts."

"He started two weeks ago."

"Great."

The woman shields her eyes to survey her. Chloe becomes conscious of her exposed, white legs.

"He said you give art workshops?"

"Yes."

Chloe rubs the sunburn on her arm, wondering if they've already been introduced. Should she know the woman's name?

"Apparently he's working with refugees? No, darling, stop pulling Mummy's hair. All different kinds of music. African, Baltic?"

"I thought it might be helpful to explore different clients —"

"And they're actually interested! He told me about some lady desperate to learn the piano, and he couldn't stop talking about this rapper called —"

"Diesel. His lyrics are great."

"Well," she smiles energetically, "good for you."

Chloe cocks her head. "He'll be back at school in September. It's just a holiday thing."

"But it's great to see him getting out of the flat. We all think you're good for him."

We? Who's we?

The woman juggles her toddler into another uncomfortable position. "Has he — has he found that bench of his?"

Chloe rearranges her surprise. "He's only looking for it every now and then. Kew's a big place."

The blonde scoops the infants bum up to her face, then sniffs. "Oh crap! Do you mind keeping an eye? The nappies are in the car."

Before Chloe can say anything, whatever-her-name has left her child crawling among the daisies, unaware of the danger she has put him in. Any moment the boy could crack his head on a ceramic flowerpot or pull the table leg and that scalding pot of tea will fall. If only these women knew what Chloe was capable of. She doesn't even know how to hold him.

She glances towards the conservatory for reassurance and there he is, chumming with men who look like they work in advertising. There are no children tugging at his trousers, and Chloe's stomach flips as she imagines what these gatherings must have been like for Audrey.

Behind the safety of her sunglasses, she watches Kate venture into the conservatory and stroke Jonah's elbow. Her head tilts compassionately, as if asking how he is. But he is the one to hunch down and hold her. Their stillness contrasts with the chatter around them and Chloe wonders what secrets she and their hostess hold in common. Perhaps later, as they clear up the leftover cake, she will have the courage to ask, "Who is Harry Barclay, Kate?"

Chloe has finished the diary. For two months, she's futilely tried to bridge the missing connections. For the first time in her life she has someone to protect and it makes her nervous. She crosses her legs, her denim shorts sticky with sweat. Shit. The kid is eating a clump of grass. She rushes over, yanking it out of his hand so fiercely that the toddler begins to cry. As she scoops him up, the others are coming into the garden en masse. A couple of guys have that self-satisfied smirk, as if they've just been ribbing Jonah for pulling a younger woman. Their wives have undoubtedly rolled their eyes at the predictable choice of a middle-aged man. Chloe is trying to pull out a blade of grass from the child's mouth, her finger rooting around his toothless gums. She then thrusts the bawling kid into Jonah's arms.

"My saviour," she says drolly.

Swinging the child on to his hip, Jonah leans in with a conspiratorial whisper. "What's up, Dylan? You been eating mud again?"

The boy stops crying. He turns to glower at Chloe, his face tear-tracked with dirt.

178

The relief in her shoulders is palpable. "You have the knack."

Jonah grins bashfully then strokes the boy's hair. "How are you doing?" It takes a while to realise that the question is directed at her.

Her eyes prickle, but she erases herself with a goofy shrug. "Fish. Out of water."

"Me too."

He looks pretty comfortable to her. She squints up at the sunshine, trying to delete the image of him and the toddler, but, with his spare hand, Jonah pulls her towards him. The size of him always shelters her — the smell of wool and sea — but she's in the wrong picture. Her feelings are strangely violent. They make her lie and covet, do things she never dreamt of, things that don't make her proud. Perhaps she's not so different from Audrey. As Jonah presses his mouth against her cheek, Chloe is haunted by the dead woman's words. *The lies inside my kiss.*

As Chloe helps to clear away the dirty plates, Jonah sits in a deckchair. A mum is trying to clean chocolate off a girl's face with some spit and a paper napkin. A man pushes a pram up and down the lawn to the rhythm of wailing. Jonah taps his foot, his large brown shoe hesitating as he listens out for the next line of the song, perhaps a key change. But what's the point composing something new if Audrey can't hear it?

He leans forward to watch a boy and a couple of dads play football. Then he bows his head and hunches over the edge of his deckchair. Closing his eyes, he holds the ghost of Audrey's hand. For just a moment he feels her breath on his face, the sureness of her arms.

"Watch out!"

Jonah glances up to see the football careering towards the conservatory. Chloe, carrying two teapots into the house, manages to steer away the catastrophe with her elbow.

"Oh, well done, lovely."

As two grown men applaud her, Chloe makes an awkward curtsy. Her physicality is fluid one moment, self-conscious the next; a constantly changing thing that pulls his eye, makes him want to describe it. It's a run of quavers, unexpected rests, a shift in time signature; but then she returns to the cool of the house and Jonah is left staring at some trampled daisies.

He returns to his previous position, the sun scorching his neck. Where was he? He tries to put his arms around the soft muscles of memory. Perhaps on both sides there is an attempt? He imagines Audrey and he touching through the veils, across the impossibility of physics, both of them grappling with the question of what death is; but the truth is he can only see the grass beneath his deckchair and a bit of discarded cake. Teeth marks, icing nibbled off . . . Jonah tilts back into the slump of canvas, feeling the heavy heat on his face. He's heard other people talk about it — that reaching across the divide. It's visceral — the weight of their head on your pillow, a touch on the underside of your arm. The sensation leaves, is rationalised away — then it happens again, as mysterious and fathomless as before.

It is easily mocked. But perhaps ridicule is easier for him to face than finally admitting that someone he touched no longer exists — is nothing, deleted. All that is left is the yearning and the echo.

On that airless evening, neither of them can sleep. All the windows are open, and, wearing only his underwear, Jonah teaches her an easy version of "Ave Maria". Sitting at the piano, she copies his hands, trying not to be distracted by the comforting solidness of his forearm. By midnight, he is showing her the basic principles of composition. Chloe is surprised that there are only twelve notes. Once she realises that music shares the restrictive principles of origami, she finds it simple to play with the patterns. She approaches chords like a mathematician, curious to stretch the limits of what is possible. As her fingers strain to reach a key she notices a burn on the creamy surface and asks, "What is this?"

"An F."

"No, I meant . . ."

"Audrey used to sit here when she was on the phone. I'd point out the length of her ash, but . . ." He shrugs. "There wasn't much music then."

How can she tell him that she already knows? Look at him, now, being so patient and funny. He seems to be enjoying her clunky, amateur delight, as if there is some safety in having them both on this stool. They share the habit of making art through the night, but as she conjures up sound and nonsense, it feels strange to

181

have the immediacy of Jonah's response, to not create alone.

As he shows her how to play a different inversion, she can sense that he, too, is wondering how much he can trust this . . . their relationship . . . his music. She finds herself listening to his glances, the things he doesn't say; then she listens to his kisses, an entire language in itself.

An afternoon in Victoria Park, reading. The words in Jonah's novel begin to blur and he has to use all his willpower to stop his shoulders heaving. But still the tears come. When he looks up, Chloe is staring at him, over the top of her book, her own eyes welling up.

"What's the matter?" they ask in sync.

"Nothing," she shrugs. "You felt suddenly heavy. I couldn't see your face but I knew you were upset. What were you reading?"

"It's not important."

She rubs her eyes with the heel of her hand, grinning. "I just felt what you were feeling, that's all."

In music, he would call it resonance. Or something only a wife can do. As she holds his gaze, he can feel a mesh of empathy thickening the air, but what is he getting himself into? He turns his book face-down, embarrassed that he has been so sentimental. Not now. Not in public.

"I need to piss," he says and goes off to find the nearest toilet.

When he locks himself inside the grubby cubicle, he expects the catharsis of sobbing over the death of a fictional dog. But instead he sits very still, wondering how he's forgotten what it feels like to have someone know his feelings before he does.

Chloe sits on a stool in a man's suit. Her naked toes are painted in aquamarine, and a large paper bird pokes out of her breast pocket like a handkerchief. In front of her is a mirror. As she draws her self-portrait in charcoal, the oversized clothes look clown-like, as does her red-crayoned mouth. It is stuffed full of secrets.

It is a humid afternoon, the streets full of fumes and overheated motorists. The large sash windows are misted with dirt and there's the noise of sewing machines spewing thread, a baby crying, a lovers' tiff upstairs. She wonders if this couple also heard her yelling during her final night with Claude. They had gone out for sushi. As always she enjoyed the mystical elements of Japanese cuisine, the intricate folding of food. But at the end of an evening that was blander than the rice, she refused sex, saying she had her period.

"You gave the same excuse last week." Claude lifted his chin. "Perhaps you're spent from all your time with Jonas."

"Jonah."

"I mean — what are we doing here?" He had already started putting on his jacket. With one arm in, the other out, he gestured towards her walls. "Looking at this, anyone would think you were broody."

"God, no!"

"No, you take the pill religiously every morning. But, for Christ's sake, when are you going to grow up? You reckon you're this modern, independent woman, that as long as all your lovers know about each other it's cool. But that Jack guy . . ."

"Joe."

"Well, he's leading you on, and in the meantime I've . . ."

"Got Natalie."

"She's my sister."

"Oh."

His reddening, freckled complexion made Chloe think of a little boy, in tears, running off a football pitch. She really didn't want to spend the night alone, but still she said, "I can't, Claude. I'm sorry."

"Goodbye, Chlo."

She stops drawing and tears out an empty page from her sketchbook. After making a phoenix, she unfolds it and begins an orchid, but the paper resists, the original pleats stubborn. The creases remind her that Jonah's body has been used, that someone has already travelled the terrain of him and left her mark, ruining him for anyone else. Chloe's only defence is to make cities of paper, build castles of pulp. She rolls her neck, hoping to find the motivation to work.

The week before, she had visited the vast chilled room in Kew's Economic Botany archives. The drawers were filled with four hundred specimens of paper brought back from Japan in the mid-nineteenth century by a British diplomat. Some of the paper had been treated with a paste made from a plant root called *kon-niaku-no-dama* that produced a durable, waterproof cloth. Chloe studied the shoes that looked like leather, the hats and umbrellas, the woven ribbons that felt like silk. Many of the products were made from the inner bark of the mulberry tree and Chloe considers the patterns in its leaf . . . then the spirals of a shell. Her own thumbprint.

She watches the movement of her hands across the paper, wondering if the real magic of origami is in the doing rather than the end product. How can she translate this into her work for the Gardens? It's easy to fold the sails of a boat; but can she learn how to represent the creases in life, the words unsaid, the people that are missing? She hitches up her trousers and searches the warehouse for a ball of string. Once she has found it, she takes a wooden frame that has been propped up against the wall, empty for a year. Tying the end of the string around the wood, she begins to weave a web. She studies the holes between the mesh.

How to Not Say I Love You

Milly asked Harry if he was falling in love.

"We're friends. That's all."

It was night, February 2004, and they were lying among the redwoods, listening to *The Young Person's Guide to the Orchestra* on an old CD Walkman. Harry, intimidated by Jonah's musical knowledge, wanted to impress Audrey. Having spent hours in Richmond Library, he had chosen to start with Baroque: three collections of Vivaldi, and this. Under a canopy of branches, Benjamin Britten broke down Purcell's *Abdelazer Suite* into different sections: the woodwind, the brass and strings. The narrator explained about the fugue and its variations, the restating of the theme.

"But I want to know about Audrey."

Harry peeled off his headphones and explained how the bark they were leaning on, as red as Audrey's hair, was steeped in history.

"Everyone thought the Metasequoia was extinct. There were only fossil records —"

"Not another bedtime story . . ."

"But in the forties, the Chinese found a specimen."

186

Milly wanted to remind him that she was only a kid. Most of their time was spent discussing nature, Shakespeare or music; what about fairy tales, or learning how to skip?

"Of course, we were the first to cultivate it once it came to Britain. This dawn redwood was planted in 1949. It now measures over fifty-two feet."

Milly gawped up.

"Did you know there's a giant sequoia that's three and a half thousand years old? The largest is as tall as St Paul's Cathedral. Can you imagine that?"

Milly didn't even know where St Paul's was. She sat up and reached for her flower press — turning the screws loose, tightening them again. But it was impossible to sulk in the dark. If Harry and Audrey were together, perhaps she could have a mum. Go out to the movies, or the shops . . .

"You should tell her how you feel," she blurted.

But Harry had already put his headphones back on and was nodding his head in time. As Milly, too, gazed up at the sky, she wondered what was stopping these star-crossed lovers. She rubbed the soreness in her wrist, as if it were a magic lamp that could tell the future.

Jonah stands at Mademoiselle J'Attendrai's bench, reading the inscription about the mezzo-soprano voice that entertained troops during the Second World War. He moves on.

Her footprint on my heart and these gardens forever

He thought that when he finally found it he would fall to his knees with relief. Instead he wipes his face, exhausted. He looks up at the pagoda to get his bearings, then lies down on the bench as if Audrey's arms might wrap around him.

"So you found what you're looking for?"

Jonah sits up to see a girl half-hidden behind a bush. It takes him a while to realise that he's seen her before — her dad's a gardener. "How did you know it was missing?"

"You've been looking for . . ." She counts on her fingers. "June, July, August . . ."

"You've been spying on me?"

"Not really." She saunters out from her hiding place and perches on the arm of the bench. Jonah isn't sure how he feels about this.

"I've no idea how it got here," he mutters. "The staff swore no one moved it."

"Why's it so important?"

Jonah feels a fishhook in his chest, tugging. "It's my wife's bench."

"Oh." Milly leans across to peer at the inscription then whips away as if stung by a bee. "Her name was Audrey? What colour was her hair?"

"Red."

"But — how? How long ago did she . . ." She turns back to look at the dates.

"Where's your dad — is he busy?"

188

"You're Audrey's husband?"

"Yes. Really."

Milly rubs her wrist. Two ponytail bands are wrapped around her arm, leaving an angry imprint. Jonah remembers how, at her age, summer holidays feel like a lifetime. Kew isn't a bad place to be a latchkey kid, but still . . . he wonders if she has a mum. He tries to formulate the question sensitively, but the child seems upset.

"I don't understand," she mumbles. "What about the woman I've seen you with?"

"You *have* been spying!"

"Is she your girlfriend?"

"What?"

He can't help but smile at her persistence; but her question stumps him. Last night, he'd suggested going back to Chloe's, but she had refused, saying his flat was "better". It had left him intrigued, shut out. Jonah stares up at the pagoda.

"I think you'd like her. She could make art out of a bus ride . . ." He snorts. "You're better than my shrink."

"I'm big for my age!"

"You're a short-arse. And the problem is, short-arse, I'm still in love with Audrey."

Milly wipes her nose on her sleeve, leaving a trail of snot.

"What are you so frightened of?"

It's the kind of brazen question only a child can ask. Jonah rubs his eyes, trying to focus. Ever since the bench went missing, his insomnia has been winning.

But maybe this kid's right. He's scared of letting another woman down, of failing. When he thinks back to reading with Chloe in Vicky Park, he wonders how so many females know what he's thinking.

"I need to talk to the office," he says abruptly. "There's no way I can carry this bench."

"Can I come too? Perhaps afterwards I could show you the fish."

"I don't think so . . ."

She's already pulling him away from the pagoda. Jonah notices a hat lying next to the white flowers of the philadelphus. The flat cap is worn thin, as though the fabric has been worried by nervous fingers.

"I should take that to Lost Property."

"Nah, it's my dad's." Milly scoops up the cap and plops it on her head.

"Is he nearby? It would be good to have a chat."

The hat has slid down past Milly's nose. "He prefers talking to plants."

"Really?"

As she nods, the cap bounces up and down. She talks without stopping for breath, with no awareness of whether he's even listening.

"Sometimes, when he's on his own, he laughs. It's usually cause something's surprised him — a plant, a squirrel, a cloud." She lifts up the peak, then thumps him on the arm. "You're It!"

As she runs away, Jonah decides that he'll take her to Victoria Gate; the staff there will know her. But first of all, he has to catch up.

190

In the basement of the Palm House, a marine display shows examples of habitats: mangrove swamps, salt marshes and coral reefs. As Jonah rushes down the stairs he finds Milly staring at a tank full of kelp ribbons.

She turns to him, cheekily, then points at a hairy file fish. "It looks like a swimming hedgehog."

Jonah is still trying to catch his breath. "Why didn't you stop for me?"

An old couple stand by one of the displays, the man taking photographs of a seahorse.

"They're like hobby horses, Marge. I don't believe it!"

"Come on, luv, you've been standing there for fifteen minutes."

Climbing on to a footstool, Milly presses her face against the glass of a cylindrical tank. "Did you know that lots of fish only have a two-second memory? I learnt that at school."

"So that coral is a surprise each time?"

She squeals as a large fish swims towards her. It makes Jonah laugh. He takes out his phone, but just as he clicks, she ducks away from the gaping mouth, and he only captures the blur of her elbow. When he glances up from the photo, he realises that the old couple are staring. He's desperate to tell them that he's not a pervert who gets his kicks from hanging out with minors, but Milly has climbed off the stool and is tugging on his trousers. Hoping that he looks like a responsible parent, Jonah squats down to meet her at eye level.

"Thank you for joining me." She solemnly gives him a kiss on the cheek.

"C'mon, let's get going."

As he stands up, the couple are still gawping. Her kiss remains like a stamp on his skin.

Upstairs in the ground floor of the Palm House a Victorian glass structure is elegantly curved with wrought iron. The large sheets of glass are dripping with condensation. They walk through the moist heat, taking in the giant bamboo and sugar cane, her hot little hand in his. In the North Wing are plants from Asia, Australasia and the Pacific, and Milly points out the jackfruit and the pepper plant as if she were an ancient explorer. They move on through the Americas, past parrot flowers and Mexican yam, then Jonah stops at the entrance where the glass doors are steamed up.

"It's time I was going. Let me drop you off."

"Can't we stay for a bit?"

"Perhaps we'll bump into each other again . . ."

"With Chloe?"

"How did you know her name?"

"You said it."

It's so hot in here that even the blazing sun outside will be a relief; at least there'll be a breeze. There's the sound of heels clicking against the lattice grating, and Jonah looks around for the culprit. There are signs warning visitors against wearing heels. Psht, psht; the sprinklers spray water from the mains. Jonah squints through the mist to see a woman climbing up the spiral steps. Up, up into the foliage, her elegant figure is framed by sunlight, glass and leaves. She wears a tailored skirt with a single back pleat, and it reminds him of a Hitchcock heroine, of Audrey. The shapely legs disappear.

When he turns back, Milly has gone. He is tired of her tricks but still he searches — past the rubber trees, the ginger, the frangipani. Suddenly there is commotion by the entrance, people shrieking then laughing. Through the Palm House a blackbird flies across the view like someone caught in the background of a photo.

14 November 2003

Upstairs in the Palm House, there are hot pipes stretching the length of the balcony. If you perch on them, they warm your bum. On rainy days it's almost as good as a sauna.

The humidity has ravaged the wrought-iron arches, the white paint peeling. Birds' bottoms sit on the glass roof, orange feet splayed. A flock of gulls fly over, screeing and squalling. Underneath us are different continents of flora.

The plaques say:

Sacred fig — tree under which Buddha meditated

Fishtail palm — flowers itself to death (consumed by its beauty?)

Attalea palm — huge shuttlecock leaves (so high I can touch them).

I love the woody scent, the intermittent sprays of mist. Tiny red spider mites run along the pipes . . . one nips me. A drop of water falls on my back, as if the glasshouse is sweating. Through the iron railings, I glimpse Africa.

But he's not in the South Wing. He's ten minutes late. My mouth feels empty. In here, I can't light a cigarette.

. . .

I thought I saw him on the ground floor, but when I blinked he was gone. Was there a shadow behind the sugar cane, over there, under the coconut palm? I thought I saw a man climbing the spiral stairs but wasn't sure. Then he was walking towards me. He was smiling as if his estimate of what I would look like that day had come true. But he didn't touch me.

As we leant over the balcony, Harry explained that the technology used to build this glasshouse had been borrowed from nineteenth-century shipbuilding, the curved ribs resembling an upturned hull. He described it as if it were Noah's ark, saving a cargo of plants. With the rain clattering against the windows, I imagined this glass boat sinking to the bottom of a lush, overgrown world. A place where lost things are held.

He talked about the cycads that grew when dinosaurs roamed the earth, the strangling fig, the cacao and the stag-horn fern. His passion was infectious but I was curious about the storyteller himself.

When I asked, he said his dad had "kicked the bucket" before he was born. A couple of decades later, his mother and brother died in the same year — then Harry began describing the African oil palm. Did these losses make him hide in this garden, tending to the small things of the earth? I looked into his eyes and thought, let me learn. Let me learn to be brave enough to kiss you.

20 November
This is a romance without kisses. Today we strolled along Kew Road and he insisted on walking on the outside edge of

194

the pavement. He is thought and restraint and yearning. Or maybe that's me.

24 November
As we passed the waterlily pond, I thought I saw a little girl but she disappeared behind the trees. When Harry made a joke I heard her laughter. My lost children still haunt me.

15 December
J has agreed to start trying again. But I've had enough of vitamins and ovulation tests. There's too much damage. The only way I can fix things is through my absence.

25 December
When I went outside to bin the wrapping paper, I found the most beautiful wreath on the front door. Among the ivy and berries were tiny flowers that looked like snow. J thought that another tenant had put it there, but no one else could have made it. Only H would understand that today all I think about are my kids.

10 January 2004
Tonight I told Jonah about a funny thing I was translating for work. It felt like the past — the two of us finishing each other's sentences and giggling at the world, as if there were nothing to believe in but our feelings for each other.

But the laughter began to hurt. I chose J because he's everything my dad was not. Loyal. Idealistic. But it doesn't matter what we do; perhaps we're still fated to repeat our parents' footsteps.

20 January

Yesterday, the glint in his gaze unclothed me.

Do all wives wonder what it's like to have a different body inside them, to feel a different skin? I fantasise about H lying beside me, his eyes crinkling at the edges when he grins.

21 January

This love, or whatever you want to call it, is as peculiar as smoke. It's there but we can't hold it. Standing under the redwoods it felt like H couldn't make up his mind whether to kiss me or not. Even his hesitation was attractive.

He seemed as startled as I, both of us affronted by unfamiliar emotions, shapeshifting, daring, wilting. Oh God. This is a strange endurance.

Jonah opens his front door.

"I found the bench," he says, simply.

When Chloe holds him, she realises how much he needs to be held.

"I'm so tired," he says. "I've had enough of searching."

She tries to embrace the depth and breadth of him, his yielding. It calls for honesty so she opens her mouth to tell him everything.

"Thanks for sticking around," he adds. "I know it's not always been easy."

Chloe has lost her bearings. He is pulling up the hem of her skirt. This is the laying on of hands — the laying down and the lying.

Jonah reacquaints himself with her rebellious, tattooed body. She is naked apart from a skirt that falls in scarlet

196

folds from her waist. Her cropped hair reminds him of an animal pelt; the wolf wrapped up in Red Riding Hood's cape.

She lies down on the bed. Sitting back, he can view her like a painting, each dent and ellipse of her pale torso. Can all of this seem new to him, unopened? With his eyes, he traces the sincerity of her contours. His fingers then sketch the idea of sex into her muscles. He finds the place that he likes best. Pressing his palm against her coccyx, she curves towards him.

They are as naked as dawn, their sweat like dewdrops. She delves down into the many layers of being, drilling down into bliss, and the trick, she thinks, is for them to remember this. She lets herself be reshaped like origami.

"I want you inside every part of me."

This is the guitar of her body plucked and plucked again until there is a song spilling from her limbs; a symphony. She is so moved that when she comes, a tear spills, and this, this is a kiss. This is being touched to the very quick.

His hands are covered with her juices and the smell of spring and piss.

As Jonah sleeps, light streams through the open windows. Chloe watches the dreams flicker across his face. Her thighs throb, awakened.

Funny how well she knows his hands and feet. In return he knows little of her and she wants to write a letter on his back: a confession. Because it's these ribs she wants to press against for the rest of her life; it's these legs, these arms. He is the most real thing she has.

How to not say "I love you". The words buckle and strain in her chest, the silence painful. She dams up the words, her throat wanting. Don't breathe, you'll gasp; don't sigh, you'll scream. Keep it buttoned down, bite your lip. I love you. She can think of no other words in the English language. She stands up.

Chloe dresses in yesterday's clothes and leaves without saying goodbye, as if he were any other man she has tangoed with; she is skilled at closing doors without sound. But as she walks down the street, the sky looks strange, perhaps the blue a little deeper, or brighter, and when she sits on the train back east, the daylight stuns.

Even the patterns on the seats are vibrant. Chloe notices a lollipop stain around a boy's lips, a man doodling next to his crossword, a dead ladybird lying on its back on the floor. Each detail is unexpected. As she presses her face against the pane, she feels like a child taking her first train trip. A thousand views rush past the window.

The entire world has been rearranged — or she rearranged within it. But what has changed? Chloe remembers the night before and freezes that frame. When Jonah had gazed at her, she had noticed her reflection in his pupils. But now she feels like a newborn calf trying to stand on her legs. Unlike the serene pictures of Audrey, Chloe feels a mess. Her red

198

skirt is stained with him. She studies her face in the window — a snapshot of herself, midsummer. There she is, more naked than she has ever been.

The Wounded Angel

As usual, they sat on Mademoiselle J'Attendrai's bench by the pagoda. Harry was quietly watching the view, anticipating nothing but each moment as it passed him. He could feel Audrey struggling against it like a curbed horse. They sat in a cloud of smoke, until eventually he said, "The orchid display is on. Would you like to go?"

"Yes."

"They're such tricky, wonderful bastards. I remember when . . ."

13 February 2004

I wanted to know the thoughts he had in his silences, the sentences he never finished. The guessing is one of the things that kept me there, that kept me fascinated.

He explained how the orchids were tied on to the display with ladies' tights — something about their stretchiness being kind to the stems — but I was tired of talking. I wanted to be kissed for the longest time. I noticed the tape holding his bootlaces together and was about to ask why he wore the same suit. But Harry lit another Montecristo then joked about killing himself in style.

I want to get pregnant.

I don't know where it came from, this quiet statement, but he looked into my eyes with a compassion I've not seen before. I didn't know how to explain the ache for my faceless daughter, my faceless son. I didn't have to. I asked him what he thought had happened to them, if there was a place for lost souls, but he didn't know. I told him everything — how sometimes I glimpse a child's shape in the doorway, or feel a tug on my fingers when I walk down the street. I know I'm imagining it, but . . .

I mentioned the girl we saw in the garden, but I couldn't remember her name. Was it Emily? I confessed that sometimes I see her. It's an echo, a whisper . . . but he just dug his chin into his chest and said it was a nice dream. He edged away a little, his mind elsewhere. Perhaps Harry Barclay just pities me.

The sides of their thighs touching made Harry euphoric, aware of each place of contact, each thousandth of an inch. But each time he considered the risks they were taking, he felt seasick.

There were many things he loved about Audrey: the winter sun shining on her freckles, her hair tied back, her lips chafed with wind. Nose blushed with cold, she looked no older than seventeen. Trying to keep his mind off her mouth, he said that the weather reminded him of the Allegro in Vivaldi's *Winter*. Audrey replied that Jonah never talked about such things.

"That's not true," she added. "He used to."

Harry did consider Jonah during those winter months, but mostly he was worried about worse things than breaking up a marriage. Jonah was the man he wanted to be — young enough to have the ever-present possibility of becoming happy. And why wasn't he? Harry would give anything to wake up to Audrey's hair brushing against his face, the soft pad of her fingertip against his lips. But Audrey and he had no future. If Harry touched her the way he wanted to, she might disappear for ever.

The *Wounded Angel* has a cracked face. Only his head stands on the plinth, his hair stretched out behind him like a wing. Carved from marble, he has a Roman nose, a plaintive eyebrow and a feminine curve of the neck. He's not like the cherubim that clutter churches; instead, he feels heavily human. The left side of his face is unmade, trapped inside the stone as if smashed against a pavement, damaged by his long fall down to earth. But his right side is handsomely slanted as if in sleep. As the dew lays itself on the ground, the light streams on to his smooth, aristocratic cheek. Harry would give anything to have such nobility, such strength.

The gates aren't open yet. The early-morning light stands between them, glimmering innocently.

"Audrey was Jonah's wife, wasn't she?"

"No."

They listen to his lie again. The dawn sky reverberates with it.

"How could you?" Milly shouts.

Harry flounders. Since Audrey's death, Milly has been his only companion. He realises how quiet she was last night, silently stewing. As he looks at the scar on her temple, he can't believe what he's saying.

"I'm sorry, luv. We need a plan. Perhaps we can work out how you can leave . . ."

"Leave what?"

"Me. The garden . . . everything."

Her eyes immediately brim with tears. "But, Da, I like it here."

As if that makes any difference.

Harry walks around the statue. As he wrestles with doubt, the sky brightens. He has always loved the smell of a new day, when the soil has slept, and is now richer from the night's tossing and turning. Everything is bristling, fresh. He understands all too well why Milly wants to stay. Without her, he would have nothing.

"If you're worried about me telling Jonah, you needn't."

"It's not that." Or is it? Perhaps he's just trying to save his own bacon.

"But we've got to help him. I could just —"

"You can't."

She takes a step back, as if he might strike her. He hadn't meant to be fierce, but how can he explain about the rules he has broken — the rules she wants to break now?

"I want to be friends with Jonah," she pleads. "He's the only one who talks to me. He's been asking about my school, if I have any mates, and . . ."

Her chin is quivering. She's never asked these things before. Perhaps she knew her mind couldn't tolerate the truth, and Harry never wanted to tell it.

"Why are you pretending to be earthbound?" It is a simple question.

She shakes her head in frustration. "What do you mean?"

"Do you see any other children in this garden? Stranded? Homeless?"

"I just want someone to play with. Its —"

"Too dangerous, luv. You could cause havoc" He squats down and holds her petulant shoulders. "We mustn't interfere."

"You did."

As he smarts, one lonely teardrop falls from her chin.

"You and Audrey . . . you made a mistake?"

Harry thinks of a thousand excuses. "Yes."

As she studies him, it feels like he is sitting naked on an uncomfortable stool. People in a classroom are drawing him and he's shrinking under their gaze. But when he looks up, he sees kindness.

"We're going to make it better," she says.

"How?"

It feels like a hair is caught in Harry's throat. However hard he tries, he can't find it. He knows that the last thing they should do is meddle. But something happened to them all, that particular day in September. Perhaps he should trust the mysterious scheming of the stars. Maybe some good can come of this. That's what he prays for: redemption, or at least a way out.

The sound of screeing. The time of the birds. As the waterfowl gather for breakfast, Harry brushes off the redwood debris from his arms.

"Why don't you help feed the birds?"

He watches her walk towards the lake, where the fine morning will greet her. Once she has disappeared, Harry looks up, hoping that something will guide him. The Bird Keeper whistles and the sky darkens with wings. As two geese fly through Harry's body, their feathers don't slice his skin.

Part IV

A Difficult Art

Look out my window, what do I see?
A crack in the sky and a hand reaching down to me.
All the nightmares came today
And it looks as though they're here to stay.

"Oh! You Pretty Things", David Bowie

The Garden of Eden

Kew is in holiday mood. The sky, a devastating blue, has swept the people out of their front doors, for a walk, a kiss, a day beyond expectation. As they leave their homes, they hold their hands to their eyes, blinded by the sunlight.

In the Gardens by the Minka House, a young couple bang on the giant xylophone that stands amid the bamboo. A sprinkler catches the girl and she squeals and hops until she stands before the boy, wet through. A little way along, a solitary old man is snoring. As he sleeps on Edith Parkers bench, anyone could take his book and carefully packed lunch, but they don't. The inscription reads "One of Nature's Children".

Above Harry is a deep Rocky Mountain blue, as if the splendour of a foreign sky has trespassed over the quiet suburb. Parents juggle children and sticky cartons of juice. Harry jots down notes about a drunken bee flying between the blowsy hydrangeas, another digging around in a giant thistle. A French family is feeding bread to the ducks; then Harry notices Audrey's bench, back behind the purple petals of the great willowherb. Jonah is reading some paperwork and Harry aches to tell him the truth: his wife never sat here. But what can he do? If Harry took the bench again, Jonah would find it at the pagoda and they would go onwith this tug-of-war, pulling and pushing the bench to its rightful place for ever.

Harry closes his eyes and remembers — Audrey in the spring of 2004. That April was a time for catching, for catching each other. The daffodils were still out, and who could feel guilty on days like that? Even their petals were quaking with happiness.

"What do you believe in, Hal? Are you religious? Agnostic?"

"This garden is my church," he replied. "Trees like steeples. And the sunlight through the leaves is like stained-glass windows. Can you feel it?"

She put her hand on his chest. "I feel it here."

That was the most wonderful thing anyone ever said to him. She was like a flower growing towards the sky, feeling the encouragement of light against its being. She pressed her cheek against his, then pulled back laughing.

"I'm going mad."

It didn't sound funny. She looked at him as if he could understand each of her whims and terrors. Then, under the sun-ripped leaves, she started to weep. He held her in his arms, taking in the scent of her neck. How could he resist? She was the sun to him, the redwoods made flesh.

She began talking about her attempts to conceive. It snagged Harry's heart and yet he said, "Jonah will make a good father."

212

"Yes. Yes, he will. But that's not what I mean."

She wiped her nose then looked up, red-eyed, hopeful. "You do something I can't, Hal. You grow things, create life —"

"Only in the right conditions."

"You would make a great dad."

"I doubt that."

How could he explain? As he searched her eyes, he still didn't know why they had met. On that first day, Audrey was a little bleached out, perhaps vibrating at a similar wan frequency. But the people who usually noticed him were children, not yet addled with civilisation and logic. Or insomniacs, addicts and drunks, the kind who slipped between the cracks, but Audrey wasn't the usual hapless character chatting to herself on a park bench.

She had every weather and season inside her. Perhaps Audrey was there to show him what he had missed out on: a woman's love, the comfort of company. Perhaps he was still here because he wasn't finished, not yet. As they embraced under the sunlit trees he forgot that death was around him. The miracle was that she could feel him. He began to hope that she could give him gravity and weight, that if she assumed him to be real then he was. But it wasn't Harry changing frequency; it was Audrey becoming lighter. And lighter still.

All he wanted was to make her happy, but his logic was thwarted. He was overwhelmed by her lips brushing against his earlobe. In that moment, he didn't worry about God. The only thing he could lay claim to, that he knew for certain, was something existed called love.

Audrey drew back. "Look, Hal. I've brought you a gift."

From her bag, she pulled out an orange scarf. As he wrapped it around his hand to admire the soft muslin, he knew it was a binding of their affair, a promise. The tassels were the same colour as Audrey's hair. He held her gaze until she blushed, then she smiled too brightly. Elegantly changing the subject was one of her talents. She began talking about Vivaldi. *Gloria in D Major* was Harry's latest recommendation, but while they discussed music, their minds were elsewhere. They were giving their agreement time to settle. As Harry tried to remember terms such as "harmonic motion", their potential future was shaping itself, between them.

Harry hums the *Gloria* as the heron flies over the lake, its long neck unwieldy. The August day is turning into a sun-soaked evening. People are beating out picnic blankets, scattering crumbs and empty crisp packets. Others are closing their dog-eared novels and sauntering towards the exits. But today there is a rebellion at sunset.

It is past closing time, but various groups turn to look back at the Palm House, the light hitting their foreheads. Even the birds pause. They stand there — the visitors, the ghosts and gulls — all of them asking for one more minute with this day, with life itself. A plane flies overhead while a goose opens and closes its

214

mouth to the setting sun. The Kew constable chivvies people along.

"Time's up."

Among the dawdlers, Harry spots Milly. "We need to talk, luv."

Pretending not to see him, she crosses the road to the ice-cream van, where a dozen people are queuing. James Hopkins is at his tricks again, his skateboard wheels screeing along the pavement.

Milly calls out, "Can you teach me?"

The hooded boy continues down the road, his hands sulking in his pockets.

"Hello?" she shouts.

The constable nudges the stragglers. "Come along, I don't have all day."

Jonah is being shooed out of the Gardens.

"I'm sorry!" Harry yells.

But Jonah doesn't hear him. He walks jauntily down the pavement, his shadow trailing behind him like an uninvited friend.

In this house there are peculiar dreams.

Audrey walks through a forest. "You and I will be everything you could have imagined and more."

"And more?" he asks.

"Yes."

Jonah lays her down on a bed of nettles, glimpsing the areola of her nipple. In her mouth there is a purple flower, but there's no gap between her teeth. The white of her collarbone, her raven hair, those inquisitive eyes as bright and blue as forget-me-nots; Chloe winks.

Jonah wakes to his heart beating a degenerate rhythm. His skin smells of violets and sweat. The room is heavy with sex, the mattress still wet. He lies awake, listening to the creaking of the night, and is struck by how odd it still is, to not have his wife in the bed; to feel a different weight beside him.

He thinks about her bench at the lake. Its triumphant return was strangely hollow. Its not the same as before, as if another man once visited daily. This morning it had felt like meeting up with an ex. There was familiarity but also the sense of being mismatched, outgrown, and yet . . . it was engrained in him to sit there.

Chloe is holding his hand as she sleeps. The severity of her cropped hair has grown out and is more charming now in its slackness of shape. As he leans in closer, she wakes. A moment's confusion; then she reaches out to stroke his head.

They talk until it is light. Through the lattice window of their entwined fingers they whisper in a way that only bed sheets and confessionals witness. As he wipes the sleep from her eyes, neither of them says it, but they both feel like foreigners here, in a place they don't understand. Intimacy is a difficult art. To invest in something again; to say yes . . .

"Joe, honey, I've got work today."

"Yes, sleep. Sleep."

As she yawns and rolls away, he studies the small of her back, the etchings of her elaborate tattoo. He then pulls her towards him so they are lying in the shape of spoons. Lacing her fingers through his, she shows him

216

the shapes their hands can make against the wall: a rabbit, a bird, a crocodile. When she falls asleep Jonah begins to cry. But he isn't sure if he is happy or sad. Perhaps there doesn't have to be a reason. Not wanting her shoulder to get wet, he pushes his face against the pillow

Chloe sits on a chair and creases light. Her hands may be ugly, her cuticles torn, but when folding paper she is immaculate in her passion. Outside is an Indian summer, the sunlight streaming in through the large sash windows. All through August, Chloe dreamt of measurements, her sleep filled with millimetres and compasses; exact geometric imaginings. She commuted to various offices where she photocopied and filed, but lunchtimes were her sanctuary. In cafés, she fiddled with napkins, making fragile things among the spills of ketchup and salt. There are paper cuts on her fingers.

Endless folds and hours. Innocent, it looks, this art, this subtle pastime, but really she is pulling together hell and heaven. She has the power to choose what is next to happen. Putting down her work, she walks to the centre of her studio, where an enormous hoop of entwined bamboo hangs from the ceiling. String has been threaded across the circle, creating a web with a hole in its centre. The string is dyed in different tones of blue and hanging from it are tiny birds made from tracing paper. Chloe studies the gaps in the mesh, how the sun plays against the colour.

Origami is the art of economy. Why shout when you can whisper? She closes her eyes and thinks about

Jonah; surely if he knew about her deceit, he would leave her. Chloe knows too well how lives are cluttered with careless creations. Returning to her desk, she lays out a blank sheet of paper.

She begins to write, but the truth feels difficult to find; from here it looks so different from how it looked over there, as if truth is a trick of the light. She tries to explain why she didn't tell him earlier, but when she realises she has written "sorry" seven times, she rips the paper. Holding her head in her hands, she fantasises about a series of birds with messages wrapped inside them. Jonah could unfold each one to crack his fortune open.

She picks up a square of tracing paper and writes:

It is a movement and a rest, you and I.

She can't believe she is going to compose her first love letter. She can hardly bear the exposure, as if her body is a photographic film spooling into sunlight and everything is too bright, too vulnerable, the moments in the film now lost for ever. But this tracing paper intrigues her. It has a ghostly quality, translucent but hardy, impervious to water. As she folds it, the letters become faint under the layers but they are still there, as if the words are both the sound and the echo.

Focusing on technique gives her the nerve to do it. For this to work, she will need to write back-to-front, so that when the creature is folded, the words can be read the right way up. She practises for hours, until it is night, and then she starts creating not a dove of peace,

218

but a message-carrying pigeon. A bird that knows the way home. Chloe unfolds it, remembering where the wing, tail and beak once were, then, holding a pen, she tries to muster her courage. The paper awaits the footprints of letters. For now there is perfect quiet on the wing. Destiny, as always, is silent.

It is a methodical act, writing the words in their mirror image on the correct part of the birds anatomy. During this intricate calligraphy, the silence in the studio holds her spaciously. The hours widen until time is forgotten, but, by three in the morning, the ink is drying. Once she is sure the words have set, she folds the bird back into its original shape. Chloe's final act is to breathe it into life, so she brings her mouth up to the hole in the bird's underbelly. As she exhales, the body inflates. She pulls the wings out to full stretch, and there it is, a pigeon tattooed with black ink. Chloe finds a red box and puts the tracing paper in its nest. She plans to leave it in Jonah's flat, but can she dare? Everything is wrapped inside it.

26 April 2004
A normal Monday morning, sitting at the table, watching Jonah eat toast. He stood at the counter, scanning the sports page, while I thought of the dream I had woken from — of Harry and I making love.

An orange scarf was draped around us. It trailed across the white linen, the room overexposed with sunlight. It blurred our skin, bleaching out my freckles, evaporating even the feeling of pleasure, until there was nothing but white. Brightness.

As I passed Joe the milk, I couldn't believe I once thought his burgundy polo neck was charmingly retro. Everything he did annoyed me: him swilling his coffee as if it were mouthwash, or humming "Oh! You Pretty Things" — I've heard it one too many times.

It's unfair to make him wrong, but I'm not used to being the villain. When Joe was touring, I was paranoid about him having affairs but now I am the one doing the betraying. I have inherited my parents' genes — and now I know that each day holds more than one possibility. I can choose to be, or not to be, vicious, malcontent, or even happy.

While Jonah swallowed a large piece of toast, I glanced at the door. Could I walk through it?

I said I had to go. When he asked what I was up to, I told him the truth. I was going to the Gardens. I blathered on about having an hour before I needed to be in Baker Street. He looked up expectantly for his morning kiss. I picked up my coat and pecked him on the cheek.

This was the thrill of the heart, the rush, my guilty footsteps clanging against the pavement. When I reached the Ruined Arch, there were three choices. I took the right tunnel and entered darkness.

Harry's voice was welcoming. He told me about the architect who had built the arch to remind people of the passing of time. But I wasn't in the mood for visitor information. I asked if we could talk.

He held out the crook of his arm and led me into the sunlight. I knew my love for him was indefendable but still I stood there, trying to find the words.

"If we can't talk about it to each other, then who can we talk to?"

"I don't understand."

"Then you're a liar."

He looked so beautiful then; a man surprised by an insult. His arm reached out then hung in the air like a question. The blue sky of his eyes, the light — I tried to get my bearings. I focused on the stone slab behind Harry. A woman with wings, a bearded man . . .

"There is so much I have to tell you, Audrey."

But I stopped him talking and brought my mouth to his. In one gesture everything changed. We kissed.

The garden seemed to shapeshift. The atmosphere thinned, the texture of the air so shallow I couldn't breathe. My world was being sucked away.

I stepped back, uncertain. Harry stood limp, his mouth forming a shocked "O". His eyes were still closed.

"I'm sorry," I said.

"Audrey, let me explain."

"Please don't."

He tasted of smoke, but I had felt no heat or pressure. It was like kissing someone who didn't exist. I smiled through my tears and joked, "The wind is making my eyes weep."

Each part of his lips had been kissed. Harry had inhaled her breath until he could have called it his. But then he'd felt the weight of her soul in his arms, the sensation of falling. When she stepped back, they were both still standing together. Surprised.

He wanted to sink to his knees and pray for forgiveness. How stupid he'd been to believe that she was some kind of gift. He should have trusted his first instinct. If they crossed the physical boundary between them, she wouldn't live.

Audrey was smiling and crying, but he could still feel the warmth of her body, the faint taste of her caffeine-coated saliva on his tongue. They were trapped inside an awful joke. As her face grew paler, he wanted to reassure her in that ruined place, to whisper, "Au, you have taught me so much — how to risk, how to hope." But she said she was late for a meeting. She walked away looking uncomfortably breezy, as if she had just won a dare that hadn't gone to plan. He loved her for that. He heard the swish of her coat, her footsteps ringing out against the concrete path; then she disappeared around the corner, leaving behind the quiet.

Staring up at the sky, Harry measured the light and his absurdity. He made his decision, a soundless vow. The morning became god-stung, leaving a bittersweet taste in his mouth.

Homing Pigeon

This was life in his hands, the heat of a woman, and yet. Harry threw it away. On the twenty-eighth of April 2004, Audrey and he sat on Mademoiselle J'Attendrai's bench by the pagoda. She had bought a plastic cup of coffee and was warming her hands around it. There was a fine mist that day, as if the sun was still sleepy.

It had been two days since the kiss. Both were expectantly awkward, their greetings full of exclamation marks. But when she smoothed down her skirt, he saw it clearly. While he had been seduced by the reality of her, she was flirting with something diaphanous.

He took a deep breath. "Do you think that I might be becoming — a distraction?"

She pulled out a cigarette. "From what?"

"Your husband."

"I thought you liked spending time with me?" Behind the haze of smoke, her face was self-conscious, twitchy.

"I do. But . . . how would Jonah feel?"

She tapped some ash, straining for composure. "Don't you see, Hal? You're something that's just mine."

"This can't amount to anything. It's not . . . sustainable." Then he finally said it. "I don't trust why you're here."

"In this garden?" She stopped to breathe it all in, as if she could smell what wonderful smelt like. "At first I was trying to find something to believe in. Then I found you."

As Audrey stared up at the white sky, her eyes were veilless, open. Only then did he realise how much she'd been appreciating the sun on her skin, the light shining on a fence, the drenching wonder of a rainstorm. She was facing each day with the vivid intensity of someone dying. Perhaps it was her yearning for her children that had brought them together; her kiss a death wish. Or maybe she had confused this luminosity for something else. Either way, she had become too close. Harry was baffled. How had he and death become so synonymous? He'd always preferred to grow things.

"I'm not who you think," was all he managed to say.

"You are." And there it was, her smile.

The sun was getting warmer. What right did it have to shine that day and what right did she have to look so good? The trees were wallflowers in comparison. He doubted whether she had been rejected before. The disenchantment suited her. It was as if the shell of her had cracked, and inside was the yolk, the real essence of her.

"I could leave Jonah."

"What?"

"I've been thinking for a while that I should let him go. He could still become a father." She went on to

224

explain that he had come home late the night before and she had fantasised about him sleeping with the English teacher. "She's young, idealistic. Legs up to here."

"You're being paranoid, Au."

"I just want to see him happy. She's —"

"Not what he wants."

Audrey scooped up her glorious hair and tied it back in a bun. Her face looked younger without this halo, as if she had just taken off her make-up.

"We could always go back to how it was before," she said. "Before — the arch . . ."

"I'm sorry, Au. I don't think we should see each other."

"You're kidding."

When he didn't answer, she started to gather her belongings, as if she didn't leave now she would start crying. How could he shame her? There was an ache in the pit of his stomach — not now, just a few minutes longer — shall I tell you that I love you?

"Wait," he said. "Let's have one more smoke."

She hesitated from snapping the clasp of her bag. Inside was a book covered in yellow fabric. Her fingers hovered over its spine then she reached for her Silk Cut and lit a fag.

As he wondered how to say goodbye, they were shy of each other, fidgeting. Maybe he should wait until this day had lengthened into tomorrow, or until the next days tomorrow had passed into the past, but it didn't matter. They lived in a bruising. More than anything he wanted to say, "I'll stay with you. Let us trick time . . . trip up the hours."

They sipped the silence of the morning, Audrey drinking her breath from the now empty cup.

"Well, if we're not going to see each other, can you tell me the best way to propagate my primroses? They've been so lovely on my windowsills . . ." She laughed.

"Early summer."

He felt foolish that she knew about his clandestine planting, but as he continued his gardening tips, the energy between them still sparked and rubbed. They held on to their words a little too long: nonsense about the seeds drying out. Audrey smoked her cigarette down to the stub.

"Sometimes I think we have to do the thing we're most frightened of to get what we want."

She challenged him directly, her hand on his thigh, and there was nothing more he wanted than to kiss her. He would love her, devour her, until there was nothing left.

"You will be OK, Au, I promise."

She had the expression of someone witnessing an accident — looking on, helpless.

"But I'm only OK when I'm with you, Hal."

She looked across to the pagoda, her face slashed with light.

"I'm being childish. Sorry."

"I should be saying that."

He still wanted to kiss her. As they stood, unsure of their final gesture, they were fully dressed yet this was

226

the nudity of being. He was doing all this to keep her alive; but between his reticence and her pride, the conversation ended. Neither of them knew, as they awkwardly clasped hands, and he felt the warmth of her fingers for the last time, that in less than a month she would be dead.

If this were our last week together, what would I say?
I would want to make sure there was no inch of you unkissed,
the country of you left untraced.

If I could learn to love like this,
You would be the place where I discover
Limitlessness.

Beside a bowl of untouched cereal, the red box is open on the kitchen counter. Jonah is warily holding the pigeon in his palm, as if it were an extraordinary, unknown creature. Mesmerised by its translucent angles, he turns the three-dimensional poem this way and that, admiring the tip of the beak, the curve of the tail. Tiny writing runs along one of the edges. He remembers that Audrey had a magnifying glass, so he walks to her office, carrying the bird with him. Rummaging through drawers, he finds what he is looking for and holds it up to the wing.

Sometimes I realise that forever is now
You, beside me, unblinking.

227

And what I learn is this:
Hope is a rhythm.

His stomach flips. It takes him back to singing onstage, then being a child in the wings: his first school play. He peeked beyond the drapes, catching glimpses of velour costumes, the wobbling spotlight; then, stretching out his neck further, it hit him: the darkness, the many-headed beast. He listened to the communal breathing, a cough, the rustle of sweets, and more than anything he wanted to impress. But as he tried to remember his lines, he became hot and sticky. He was going to fluff it.

As he looks down now, the paper bird feels too fragile, his hands apish. How can he not crush it? By stating her position, Chloe has allowed him no movement of his own; at least, nothing that's worthy. How can he match it? He had been travelling towards her at his own steady pace, taking his time . . . shit! He's late.

Shoving the red box into his satchel, he rushes out of the house to the tube. The bird sits in his bag while he teaches the beginnings of rock 'n' roll. At lunchtime he eats a dry tuna sandwich in the canteen and fumbles with his phone. "What a surprise!" he texts. "What a thoughtful gift! Thank you!" He removes the exclamation marks then deletes the message.

In the afternoon Jonah teaches the musical terms for repeated patterns of notes. He plays some examples, comparing the ostinato of *Carmina Burana* to the guitar riff on "Le Freak".

"You see? It's the same technique."

Chloe has arranged to meet him after school. He takes some paracetamol for his headache, collects a pile of essays, and for once walks away wishing he could stay at work. If he were a braver man, he would write Chloe a song. The least he could do is take her to an expensive restaurant, buy her flowers or a necklace, but what would they talk about . . . their future?

Chloe sees him sitting in a café off Carnaby Street. From this distance, Jonah looks uncomfortable, as if he is waiting for a blind date. As she enters, he stands up, but his hand doesn't feel like his hand, his eyes don't see her, and there is a nervous pushing towards her as they greet.

"Did you have a good day?" he asks.

She puts her bag on the table. "Another office, another boss . . ."

"Thank you for the present. It was lovely."

She sits down and busies herself, tidying the pepper and salt. "Great."

He is already studying the menu. "Do you want cake?"

They tell the waiter their choices. Once they are alone, their unspoken words pull taut between them like a tripwire. He doesn't seem to understand how much she has risked. Through the cacophony of the coffee machine, the customers who "needed-to-be-somewhere-five-minutes-ago", there is the bark of a small dog. Jonah is describing a terrible essay on the evolution of music, but it's hard to hear. His mouth dries up.

His smile is like a shrug. When he glances up at the ceiling, she wonders if he's thinking about Audrey. He always looks beautiful when he considers her, his gaze glistening.

She stands up, irritated. "It's getting late. Shall we?"

"But we've just —"

"Screw the tea. Let's go home and drink gin."

His chair scrapes back. "Your gift . . . I really want to say thank you."

He kisses her, one wary peck on the cheek. It is an insult.

Back in the flat she explains how she created the bird, giving him the sacred opportunity to be more than he was at the start of the evening. But neither of them sleeps happily. He grinds his teeth while she twitches like a child hurt. Eventually she sits up and stares out of the window. It is a sullied night. A blackbird flies away from the dirty street into the serenity of the Gardens.

This is Audrey's bench, and here is a bucketful of questions. Here is the moon looking down on Milly, and in the dark, all she has to hug are her knees. What did Harry mean? But the sky is too vast to answer her silly questions. It just watches her.

Why are you pretending to be earthbound?

Harry's words; she can't get rid of them. She should ask why no one notices her, or why she sleeps in the Redwood Grove, but she isn't sure if she wants to know. She can't even decide if this glinting moon is magical or sinister.

Some people see her: the lady who reads the newspaper, that mum with the fake-fur coat. Then there's the photographer who waved, his shirtsleeves rolled up. Once, an old lady had pinched Milly's cheek, as if she could snatch her childhood between her fingers and thumb, through that little shake of her wrist. Her breath stank of sickness and boiled sweets.

Milly has no watch, but soon, she hopes, the sky will brighten. Perhaps tomorrow is the day that Jonah will see her. But she's been waiting for weeks. The moon is rising, and look, there's the shadow of the bushes, the bench. She twists around as if someone has tweaked her T-shirt. Peering from different angles, she searches for the silhouette of her uncombed hair, her scrawny shoulders. But there's only a shadowless girl, and a lake under moonlight. The throbbing begins, the usual drumming under her temple.

Her disbelief flutters. It's like a moth bashing against a light bulb, and in that glowing, electrical sphere she sees a yellow dress. Milly leans into the soft cushion of this woman's belly. But she is jolted away from the warmth, and now there's a fridge magnet of an elephant, smeared with fingerprints and something white, like dried yoghurt. But the stain becomes the milky moon and Milly is back on the cold bench, hugging her shoulders. Her mouth opens, silently at first, until the sound is shaped into a scream. It rebounds off the stars, her "no" getting lost in the immensity of the night.

231

A Game of Conkers

The trees are still clothed, but Chloe notices the lack of light in the evenings, the summer felled. With Jonah, there have been no arguments, no truth-telling; just a catastrophic, mild harmony that prevents her from leaving.

On one October evening, they sit in a seductively lit pub, full of nearly fashionable people. Kate asks Chloe if she wants children.

"Christ, no! I love my freedom."

Jonah shifts forward on the leather banquette. "You never told me that."

The silence curdles.

"But who would want that responsibility?" she begins. "All those accidents, waiting to happen . . ."

Chloe stops. Her scarlet polo neck feels too tight around her neck. But Kate is unaware and tipsy, intoxicated by a rare night out.

She flirtatiously picks a stray thread from Jonah's arm. "Well, we all know you'd make a good dad. Do you still want that?"

"Well, yes. One day, sure — with the right person."

When the group turns towards Chloe, she flashes her brightest smile. She feels the urge to flee, to fly, but imagines falling instead, the cold pavement smashing against her face, her wrists futilely flapping. She claps her hands, hoping to herald a new conversation. Kate's husband is so embarrassed he offers to buy the next round. Chloe cuddles up to Jonah, pretending they are a couple that know each other, that everything is "just fine".

Later at the bus stop, Chloe circles the pavement.

"What do you want, Chlo?"

"For the bus to come."

Jonah sits down, deflated. He is too big for the red plastic bench. "Why are you so angry? Are you pissed off about what I said back there?"

"I didn't realise I was a stepping stone."

"That's not fair. What were you expecting, Chlo? We never said this was about forever."

"I wrote you a frigging letter."

She rocks back and forth on the edge of the kerb, as if teetering over a long drop. How many times has she wished she could take that damn bird back?

"Talk about mixed signals," he deflects. "You won't even let me come to your flat."

Chloe sees her walls, covered in Milly. It never mattered what Claude thought, but with Jonah it is different. She pictures the eyelashes, painstakingly drawn, but Jonah blocks her view — of the empty street, the non-existent bus. He is wearing an orange fisherman's jacket: sturdy toggles, a sheepskin-lined hood.

She stuffs her hands into her pockets. "Where is that bloody bus?"

"Don't change the subject. How are we supposed to get to know each other, Chlo?"

"I'm right here."

"But I had no idea you didn't want to be a mum, that we want different . . ."

Her laughter is an attack. "From the start, you've been telling me we have no future. And now there's kids in it?" Her voice is higher than she wants it. "If you're hoping for someone like Kate, you're barking up the wrong tree. I don't even bake."

"I don't give a shit about your cooking."

"Is it that bad?" A beat. She desperately wants to make a joke of it, but Jonah's eyes are glassy from drinking three gins.

"Audrey and I, we tried to have kids —"

"But this wasn't in our agreement."

"Neither was your letter."

"What?"

"That's not what I mean. It wasn't until what you said in the pub that I realised I'd begun to imagine more . . . I mean, your poem suggested . . ." He stops. "I just don't understand who we are any more."

"That makes two of us."

It feels like they're playing a game of conkers, their horse-chestnut hearts skewered on to string. *Take a swing, darling. Missed?* Chloe tightens the string around her knuckles, but the bus arrives when she no longer wants it. As she stares out of the window, she sees the back of a young girl with pigtails, standing at the bus stop.

234

Chloe can't explain that she lost a child, not to someone who wanted to be a dad. That night when he is unable to sleep, she lies in bed wishing she could change her shape into a piano. She could lay herself out under his fingers and tell her story: in the striking of the felt hammers, the change to a minor key. As Jonah plays in the next room, she turns on to her belly. Putting her head under the pillow, she wrestles with her assumptions of what she is capable of. Surely if Jonah were serious, he'd talk about smaller commitments; they could go on holiday together, get a dog. She's not even sure if he wants her, or just someone to bear kids. His wife's photos are still staring down at him.

Over the next week, they watch each other lessen. She hates their cowardice to not revolt against this deadening, this dampening of light. She promises to split up with him, but on Sunday morning they are lying in bed and his calf in the autumn sunlight is so touchable she doesn't know how to break the habit of him. His body still reminds her of Achilles — tussle-haired, wounded — but she knows that, to survive, she has to put him in a different frame. One evening she sleeps with Claude, and when Jonah asks where she was, she replies that she had dinner with an ex. It is Jonah who smiles apologetically.

"Well, we're free to do what we want."

Their nights are blue. Chloe is on her knees, her head rammed into the pillow; but she is the one who has put herself there, as if wanting to be punished. There are always three in the bed, entangled in knots of red hair. When Jonah lasses her neck, she feels suffocated by secrets. Perhaps she should return the diary to the flat; somewhere he will find it.

Once Jonah is asleep, he dribbles on to her breast while she stares up at the ceiling. She contemplates how the flat has become a battleground between two women. But Audrey never steals the duvet, leaves the toothpaste lid off or nags about the stale milk. On the fridge door, there's a photo of their wedding day; the outstretched arm making it apparent that Jonah took the picture. The angle is wonky but they are laughing at the joke of a selfie on such an auspicious occasion. He's wearing a purple velvet suit and she's in a white shift decorated with rosebuds, and it doesn't matter where Chloe looks, there are always the beautiful imperfections of a marriage.

He hasn't seen Chloe for a week; nor has she answered his calls, only sending him a perfunctory text saying she would ring soon. He can't bear the thought of her sleeping with another man. But perhaps this is healthier: to disappear into the simplicity of solitude.

Wearing a frayed navy dressing gown, Jonah plays in a dim, dawn-lit room, his knees crammed under the piano. He begins composing, but each idea retreats until he inexplicably plays the *Minute Waltz*. For years, Audrey has been his muse, but now he forces himself to explore the possibilities in the present; the choice between one note and the next. He tries to form a chord around Chloe's body. But all he can think about is her desire to not have kids. He'd always assumed he'd be a father; but does he really want to risk the heartbreak of trying again? He pictures Chloe in a hospital corridor, crying.

"I'm not Audrey," she once said. The last time he saw her, she was standing in his kitchen, her skinny jumper and flat pumps reminding him of a Beatnik poet. All that was missing was a Gauloise. "I react differently. Want different things."

She stared out of the window. As she bit her nails, he wanted to ask what had hurt her, to tell her that she was lovelier than she could imagine. He yearned to speak of fragile things, to open up the space for candour, but instead he put on a CD hoping that the music would speak for him.

As he sits at the piano, he loves her, surely. Because he has noticed her habits — the way she props her elbows up on the table and smiles through her hands, or always blows her nose when sitting on the lav. Or perhaps that's just familiarity. Perhaps only another man can make her happy.

Above him, is a photo of Audrey walking through a Cornwall meadow. He takes it off the wall and polishes the glass with his towelling elbow. As he studies it, he realises that, with both women, there were parts he was never allowed to become acquainted with, as if he were a boy shut out of an adult conversation. But if he gave Chloe enough room, what would happen?

Jonah feels the grief of leaving a place. It's like the last day on holiday, or packing up his student digs for the final time, a glance back at the Blu-Tack on the walls. Jonah walks around dazed, taking down photo after photo. Speeding up, he begins to snatch, as if quickly ripping off a plaster; but he hesitates at Audrey sunbathing in Sicily, wearing a pink, floppy hat. Her arms are hiding her naked breasts, her face turned towards the camera. That one stays, as does the photo by his bed.

When Jonah returns to the lounge, his skin is vibrating, as if he is high and hallucinating. Above the piano, the wall looks stark and unforgiving. Jonah's fingers tune the air before searching his laptop for a replacement. He hasn't taken a single photo of his girlfriend but grins when he finds a picture of a bright blue fish, the edge of Milly caught in the foreground. There's just a blur of mousy hair, a wisp of motion, but the majority of the image is of the fish and clear water. He prints it out and puts it in the frame. But when he hangs it up, he feels queasy. He stares at the picture for a long time, the stupid fish gaping at him; then he staggers to the bathroom and retches.

Chloe stands in front of a gravestone in Mortlake Cemetery, trying not to read the initials as "rip". When she turns away from Emily Richards's name, she sees the little girl several rows away, framed between the graves. The same ragged pigtails, the stripy top . . . Chloe blinks back the blurry flecks in her eyes and looks again. Nothing.

She hurries towards the place where the girl was, navigating her way past mounds and stone angels, but her attention is pulled to a flicker of colour behind a tree, the crunch of footsteps against gravel. She jumps at a barking dog, the glimpse of a blackbird. A dark figure moves behind the graves — but it is only a Greek woman dressed in mourning. The sky is bleak and quiet.

A couple of hours later, Chloe is in her studio, folding birds of paradise. She is trying out new designs using layered colours but is becoming increasingly frustrated with the limitations of a square. Surrounding her is an array of tiny models that will be scaled up for the botanical gardens — miscarried objects, all of them. She sweeps the origami off the table then holds her head in her hands, hoping that Jonah is feeling her absence. Staying away is a tactic.

As she begins her third attempt to fold a heron, Chloe grapples with magic, rage, and the need for freedom. She notices her pale skin in the window, as translucent as paper. Her reflection tells her that nothing she touches survives. Even her work will decay. It will yellow, curl, disintegrate.

Milly has followed her from the graveyard and is standing in the corner, surrounded by scrunched-up balls of paper. She has been trying to work out how they know each other, but these walls confront her. Her own face peers back. The room is covered in her smiles and tears. What is she doing here, duplicated and scribbled out a hundred times over?

The woman at the desk is caressing the nape of her neck, her fingers squeezing an invisible ache. Then she stands up and opens the large sash window. As Milly walks over, her eyes prickle. It hurts to not be seen. Chloe puts the heron on the sill, then flicks it off, the bird falling three storeys into the gutter. They both lean over the ledge to see the paper turning to mush in a puddle.

19 May 2004
I remember the moment when I realised I wanted to have sex with H. Because I had found out all I could by talking and now needed to rely on touch and sense. Because the only way to get to know him better was to see what it felt like to have him inside me. And to know what it would feel like afterwards, listening to him breathe.

How could I have been so foolish? I was sure that Harry wanted it too — but now I daren't look at myself in the bathroom mirror. After a couple of glasses of wine, I can see my mother. She's etched into my face, the turn of my chin. It quietly disgusts me, my need for approval. Why did H — ?

The flowers are dead on the sills. It's been three weeks since I heard his feet on the gravel. Sometimes, I daydream that he's here at the window. Tonight, I drew a heart on the steamed-up glass, then the name of one of my children. As I pressed my forehead against the pane, our eyes met. I saw him through the "o" of Violet. But then he was gone.

"We'll have to pretend it's sunny," Jonah mutters.

The October sky is full of rain that isn't quite falling. A pigeon stands in the middle of the road watching them make their way to Victoria Gate. They are wrapped up in hats and coats.

"Lets not pretend anything." Chloe wrestles Jonah's arm from his pocket. "Let's walk under grey skies, hand in hand, together."

240

Despite her apparent calmness, she thinks back to earlier. Jonah had been excited to show her his empty walls, the thrill of a new photo.

"Was that when we were at the aquarium?"

"Er — no."

"Whose shoulder is it?"

"Just a girl who happened to be there. No one special." As he studied the distrust in her eyes, he seemed deflated. "I'm trying," he said. "I promise."

A rainstorm is coming. At Temperate House the windows are ajar, and everything feels clouded: the sky, the glass, them. They walk to keep warm while coughing out a conversation. Dog-tags jangle in the trees.

The land is weather-beaten. She leans into Jonah as if leaning into the wind.

"I wish I could make you happy. You might notice all this beauty then. Like that oak over there, I wonder how old . . ."

"You're such an artist, Chlo. You see beauty and then what?"

"It makes me feel less ugly."

"How can *you* not feel beautiful?"

"That's easy."

As a plane flies overhead, they look at each other, confused. The wind is in Chloe's ears, muffling her thoughts. Forcing herself to step away, she notices an object on a nearby bench. It is square and wooden. The garden lurches. The decorative carvings are ridged with dirt, the press overstuffed with flowers — but the wood is a different shade from the little girls. Jonah calls.

"We'll be sheltered from the wind in here. C'mon."

They pick their way through the Redwood Grove until they find a path that leads them to the garden behind Queen Charlotte's Cottage. They sit on a bench, occasionally stretching out an ache in their necks, or rotating an ankle. Chloe rolls the sentence along her tongue. *Yesterday I found a diary; I haven't read it, but I thought you should know.* She imagines reaching into her bag and handing him the yellow book, but her lies press her hand flat.

Jonah stands up and stamps off the chill. "I'm sorry, but — can we sit somewhere else?"

"Don't tell me. Something happened here? Say, under that birch?"

"No. Well, yes." He shakes his head, defeated. "I proposed."

Chloe fantasises about the insults she would like to throw. They are familiar enough to hurt each other with ease; they know the words that cannot be taken back, the best ways to humiliate. She stands up and walks away without waiting. When he catches up, she collapses to the ground, just for the hell of it.

"What are you doing, Chlo? It's freezing."

On the muddy grass, she splays her body out into a star shape. Her new perspective is refreshing, this direct contact with the clouds, but Jonah is not so cavalier; he squats down, protecting his trousers.

"Are you OK?"

"No. No, I'm not."

The wind is laced with light, a fragile shining. She squints up at him with one eye open, the other blinded.

242

"I know you've been unhappy," he begins, "but I think, we could —"

"Actually I think we should split up." She delivers it like a statement, but really it was a call for his passionate, appalled response. When he is silent, she sits up and frowns. This is not how the story goes.

He is slack with uncertainty. "I was hoping we could work things out. I dunno, maybe you're right — I'm not that great at —"

"That's decided, then."

"Don't be dramatic. Let's go home."

"Home? Where's that?"

The debris of their relationship is on the shelves: CDs and books, a sketchpad, her underwear. It seems an effort to sever the two lives that have been knitted together, and yet, everything is frayed. Still wearing her hat and coat, Chloe stands in the middle of the room like a child who has forgotten her lines in a school play.

Jonah keeps an honourable distance. "What can I get you?"

"Nothing." She shifts her weight to the other hip, smiles weakly. "Everything?"

"Can I hold you?"

"No." She stares at the floorboards. "It hurts."

"Where?"

She gestures to her chest. Jonah walks over and places his hand there. It is solace; a quintessent pause. She wants to say this: loving you is like learning a foreign language. Instead he wipes a tear from her cheek, and his finger, now moist, ventures beneath her skirt. They push at the edges of intimacy. Does this hurt? Does this hold?

As Audrey circled the pagoda, she seemed upset. Milly ached to take her by the hand and lead her to Harry. He was squatting in the exotic bed where they tested the hardiness of certain plants. He would be fretting over the ornamental bananas or the gingers, but she was pretty sure he'd stop for this. Audrey began walking towards the exit.

Out on the street, Milly grabbed her hand.

"Are you looking for Hal? He's in Duke's Garden —"

It was like Audrey was wearing someone else's skin. She looked older, her face taut with a determination that wouldn't stop for a gawky girl who was all elbows and tied-tongues. She was too closed off to see; but a few paces on she hesitated, as if she could feel the tugging of a child's hand.

"Audrey?"

After a pause, the elegant woman continued her journey. Milly's left wrist hurt as she yanked on Audrey's arm, her plimsolls trying to find their grip on the pavement.

"He loves you!" she yelled. "You've got to listen."

Audrey cut down a side road then stopped in front of a Georgian terrace. On a polished black door was a plaque stating that this was an office of the Royal Botanic Gardens.

When they entered the small, carpeted reception, the house felt like a quiet hive of activity. Milly hung back, waiting.

244

Calming herself to the building's pace, Audrey laid her hands on the desk. "Excuse me, I'm trying to track down an employee named Harry Barclay."

The elderly woman wore a mauve cardigan and a brooch of a four-leaf clover. Milly knew that was lucky.

"I've been here for twenty years, dear, and I don't know anyone with that name. You say Barclay?"

"Yes. Can you check?"

Her nametag said she was Miss Edith Bronwyn. She tapped into the computer then said, "He stopped working in the sixties."

"The sixties?"

"Yes."

"Perhaps there's another Harry Barclay? Or he had a son — a Harry junior maybe?"

"I'm not going to find that in these records. These are very simple archives . . ."

"His address?"

"I'm sorry, dear, that's confidential."

"Of course." Audrey pushed her hair back from her face then took a deep breath. "I'm thinking of buying a commemorative bench for my daughter. She died recently."

The receptionist touched the crucifix nestled against her neck. "Yes. Of course, dear. Yes."

This bereavement was a shock to Milly. As Edith Bronwyn knelt down to reach under the desk, she tiptoed across the once-plush carpet. She glanced at the computer screen at the same time as Audrey.

BARCLAY H. 1A EARL ROAD, MORTLAKE, SURREY

When Miss Bronwyn stood, she didn't notice a girl's fingers gripping the counter. Instead she held out a glossy brochure describing the options of commemorative gifts, from planting trees to sponsoring spring bulbs. She passed the information to Audrey delicately.

"I'm sorry to hear about your daughter. What a terrible loss."

"How kind of you. I'll be in touch."

Harry was still in Duke's Garden.

Milly rushed over to the bed. "I tried to stop her."

"Slow down, luv. Breathe."

"Audrey found an address, but it's not where you live. I tried to tell her, but, Hal, she couldn't see me . . ."

"What?"

"She looked straight through me."

Harry began muttering to himself. Something about a couple of days ago. At Audrey's house.

"I just wanted to check she was all right. Christ! Why couldn't I stay away?"

He threw down his gardening gloves and half-ran, half-stumbled towards the exit. Milly looked down at where he had been working. Next to the lavender was a small pile of cigar ash, but the wind soon took it.

246

Interludes in Late October

It is a masochistic passion: autumn. It leaves Harry with an ache as deep as a broken bone. With the expectancy of loss there's always a better appreciation of life. He writes in his notebook about burnished days and falling light.

Photographers cluster around the chittamwood, as if the scarlet leaves were starlets.

An unusually quiet school trip. The teacher gestures in sign language.

An old lady feeds a squirrel the crust of her sandwich . . .

"C'mon, Hal, you promised."

"All right, I'm ready."

They are sitting under the *Wounded Angel*, Harry's back resting against the plinth. When they start the chess game it's obvious that Milly's mind is elsewhere but it takes her twenty minutes to ask how old she is.

Harry splutters. "What do you think?"

"I'm eight," she says.

"You're ten. And don't ask how old I am. I've lost count."

She fiddles with the pinecone that is her bishop. "But someday I'll grow up?"

Harry lifts his palms.

"Not even when I'm forty-five or ninety-two?"

"I'm sorry, luv."

Neither of them can bear to say it, but the truth sits between them. If passers-by came close, they would think it was a discarded chessboard, but then they would notice a pawn disappear and reappear an inch from its original place. Once it leaves Harry's grip, it becomes visible again, like the trail of his cigar smoke wafting in the air. He tries to explain that they are subject to the squint of another person, like a shaft of light picking up dust; the particles are still there in pitch black.

"I don't believe you." Milly's stare melts into tears, but her eyes refuse to release them.

"Why doesn't that skateboarding lad see you? The Bird Keeper ignores you. Everyone does."

"Some pay attention. A baby. That guy yesterday . . ."

"He was drunk."

Milly refuses to look at him. Her jaw is locked, resisting. "But Jonah can . . ."

"He's an insomniac. And now that he's getting more sleep . . ."

"We haven't talked for months."

"Exactly." Harry takes off his hat. "I'm sorry, luv."

She covers her ears. "I don't want to know. Shut up."

"After a while Jonah won't feel your hand in his."

"But I'll feel him?"

"Yes."

"You're lying."

How can he explain that when the world's memory of her fades, her impact will evaporate? That's when the dying really happens. Harry kissed Audrey and she felt nothing.

The sun highlights the curves of Harry's black queen. As Milly stares at it, he wonders how many boys she was supposed to date. Is there someone out there who was destined to be her husband? Which exams did she never pass, what countries won't she visit? Would she have been happy and full, fat with life . . . lucky?

He mustn't break. "There's nothing here for you, luv."

"There is."

"But if you leave you might be able to grow up."

Her eyes remain locked on the chess piece. "I'm scared."

"Of what?"

"That my memories will disappear."

He doesn't know how to tell her that what she's really frightened of is remembering everything she has lost.

"Please don't," she whispers.

The plinth of the *Wounded Angel* is hurting his back. As Harry stretches out his spine, a joint cracks.

"I've no idea how you can leave. Perhaps you have to accept what happened."

"But I don't remember anything."

"Then you're not ready yet."

He thinks back to the Ruined Arch and its crumbling promise. Then he looks up at the sky and takes a breath. He tells Milly about the time when the bluebells were out. He was pulling out the giant hogweed, the yellow perfoliate alexander, then a tourist looked him dead in the eye.

"He was Japanese. Sober. Not the sort who usually sees us. So I followed him through the woods. A few minutes later, the man clutched his arm."

Harry remembers the sound of him falling into the flowers. He had known what this stranger was feeling: the irregular rhythm of this unexpected hour. While the tourist's wife screamed in a language he didn't understand, Harry crouched down and squeezed the man's fingers. When his breath stopped, the day settled into a sense of rightness.

The ambulance men came for the body while Harry and the stranger went for a stroll around the Japanese Gateway. Harry talked about his years of waiting, but as they walked under the Ruined Arch, his companion disappeared mid-sentence. Even his words seemed to disintegrate.

Harry stared at the Ruined Arch for a long time. He was, perhaps, there for days. The man had taken the central tunnel, not the left like Harry. He had assumed that there was only one opportunity to leave this place, and for all eternity he would be huddled around that missed chance. But now that he was given a choice, he hesitated. He peered through the middle arch. Should

250

he do it on hope alone, or curiosity? To walk into the unknown . . . he daren't do it.

"I've dedicated my life to this place. After the war, luv, I found myself again — in the soil, the Victoria, the arboretum."

He picks at some mud on his trousers, wondering how to explain this to a kid.

"I've planted so many of these trees, watched them grow. Who in their right mind would want to leave?" He puts on his hat and tips the peak. "I'm exactly where I want to be."

Milly's forehead puckers. "But you've walked through it. All the time you . . ."

"Never the middle one."

"But I have."

"'Fraid so. I don't know why it doesn't work, Milly. It should be as simple as walking through . . ."

He pushes back the hair from her face, but it sticks to her cheek, glued down by her salty, snotty weeping.

"There were others," he tries. "Every few years. I'd be minding my own business, then someone would look at me. I'd check they weren't crazy, then I followed them."

"And . . ."

"They died."

There was no leveraging of their fragile souls from their bodies. It would just be Harry sitting next to a corpse, surrounded by crying.

"So what was different about that bluebell guy?"

"God knows. I was thumping his chest like an idiot. A similar thing happened with you. I got all heroic . . ."

"And why are you still here?"

"Because I chose it."

Harry notices the one button left on his jacket; it is hanging by a thread.

She looks at him squarely. "I don't want to leave this garden."

Yes. That's the rub.

The world sighs . . . or that's what it feels like; the last breath before winter sets in. Harry looks up at the trees, wearing their dying glory, then spots Jonah in the distance. He remembers how he relished his time with Audrey and tentatively says, "He's waving." Milly looks over her shoulder. She hesitates for only a moment, glancing back for Harry's blessing, then she runs off, leaving the discarded chess game. Jonah greets her fondly and off they go, Milly trotting to keep up. They gaze at the Turkish hazels, savouring autumn's pleasures and flavours, and Harry realises he has sympathy for them all: the living, the dead, and the beauty.

"So, tell me about the guy you were playing with. Was that your dad?"

"Yup."

Jonah had only seen him from a distance, wearing a scarf and hat. He knows he should go back and talk to him, but Milly is pulling him down Pagoda Vista. Besides, he's too exhausted to be a responsible adult. He's still trying to work out why Chloe doesn't want kids. She never had a father, so maybe . . . Milly is

252

rattling on about a game that involves racing around the pagoda.

"You do it three times. Then you run around the other way. Backwards."

He thinks back to the moment when Chloe's tears had moved him, when the two of them standing in that room had felt significant. But it was like putting a plaster on a broken bone. It was stupid. Stupid. Exasperated, he glances down at Milly.

"God, you're shivering." He squats down to rub her arms, her nose in need of a tissue. "You should bring your coat."

She is always wearing the same clothes. Jonah thinks how different it would be if he were her father. They stare at each other, unflinching, then Milly pulls on his beard, making him roar like a lion. He snatches her body up high, her legs flailing.

The sky is the bluest Milly has ever seen. Her feet dangle in this bluest of blue; then she glances down beyond her toes and sees a woman placing flowers on a nearby bench. Wriggling out of Jonah's grip, she drops down, her feet jarring against the suddenly close pavement. She scratches that soft bit on the inside of her elbow, unsure why this woman makes her nervous.

She looks scooped out, her torso concave. She's wearing a yellow coat, the colour of daffodils, and there's a toddler beside her who is leaning over to watch something in the grass, an ant maybe. Milly moves closer. The woman's eyes are stung, as if all the stories she believed in have gone. There are only atoms and chance.

Milly can almost remember . . . a life glimmers in the distance. She can feel dry hands on her brow, the hum of a lullaby, then the memory wavers. This woman is a stranger; yet Milly knows exactly what she smells like, of flowers, coffee and newspapers. She knows what tunes she sings when she's washing up supper . . . or when she's drying up a plastic red mug. It had a daisy on it.

"He's much older," Milly mutters.

"Who? That little boy?"

A cloud of whiteness. A tissue is thrust in her face, her nose wiped roughly.

"That's better."

Jonah scans her up and down then grabs her hand. As he pulls her along the path, Milly glances back.

For the rest of the afternoon, she can't settle. While they sit under an oak, her remembering slips away — then nudges her like a playground bully.

"These leaves must look forward to autumn, don't you think?"

"But they die."

"They've been sitting up there for ages," whispers Milly. "Then they get to do the perfect sky-dive."

They squint up at the leaves waving precariously above them, hanging on to the twigs for just a moment longer.

"I wouldn't want to be a leaf 'cause I'm nervous of heights," jokes Jonah. "Are you all right?"

254

"I was thinking of a photo that my dad showed me. It was of a lady falling from a building."

"Really?"

"Yes."

She stands up over Jonah's legs, her arms outstretched like an aeroplane. As she looks down, she feels like that woman tumbling through the air. She can see the pavement, but she never reaches it. She just keeps falling. She's not in one place or another, but in between, and there's no end to it. There's just the wind whooshing by and the sight of the looming pavement and a couple of bystanders forever screaming.

HB. 29.10.05 Redwood Grove

As you die, you remember all the times someone's mouth has touched yours.

Illicit kisses,
rushed kisses,
lost or stolen.

At bus stops,
in a hallway,
at the front of an aisle.

Harry doodles some flowers and wonders what Milly remembered. The scratchy kiss from her grandmother, the kind that kids shirk from? Or the way her legs ached in kiss chase, her thighs flushed hot from running? Maybe one day she'll recall a smoky kiss on her forehead at bedtime. But when it came to Harry's time, he saw nothing.

He never sought them out; the deaths he witnessed were rare. But in those last moments, he met their gaze and saw, in their mind's eye, a lifetime of kisses. Some were propositions or a reconnaissance. Others an apology or a question. Then there was the girl with mousy hair. She was in her early twenties, slowly starving herself. He first noticed her being pushed around the Gardens in a wheelchair. When she raised her chin to watch him, he could see what she ached for: the purity of being. She wanted to rid herself of the blubber of sex, the stress of success, to find a simplicity that cut things to the bone. Such clean angles: to be air itself.

Harry followed her for days, watching her weaken. In her final moments she turned to him as if he could tell her the secrets of God. Perhaps she thought she would see a tunnel of light or an angelic choir. But the only thing she saw was every kiss she had ever experienced — and she realised she was where she wanted to be all along.

The Stillbirth of Anything that Craves to be Born

23 May 2004

Jonah has bought tulips. Yellow, like sunshine on our table. But there's another brightness, just a few streets away. Don't be stupid. If you DO go to Harry's house, be angry, self-righteous. But the truth is I want to see him.

On the next page is a simple drawing of the sun.

Doesn't everything ache and bend towards it?

It is the penultimate entry, but it doesn't matter how many times Chloe has read it: she is no wiser about what happened at the T-junction. A few pages earlier, there's a scribbled address and Chloe has walked the ten-minute route to the ominous brick wall and beyond; the journey that Audrey never completed. When Chloe finally arrived at Earl Road, the couple in 1A had never heard of Harry Barclay, or a redhead named Mrs Wilson. The diary, like Audrey's life, runs out.

Chloe now faces a different kind of crash. Jonah is pumping away inside her but she can no longer feel him; their lasses mistimed, his touches misplaced. She focuses on the sound of the creaking bed. When he stops moving, Chloe's muscles tense. She hovers above the statue of his body, then she lies down, breathing on to his chest. Sweat slips from his armpit on to her neck and she stays very still, hoping she can hide from this. But a few minutes later he fidgets, making it clear he no longer wants her weight. She rolls over and they lie like two corpses in a shrine. The silence drips from the ceiling and lands on to her brow. She wipes it off and sits up. Then she reaches for her knickers and pulls them on.

His hand on the small of her back. A beat. She waits for him to speak, then, tired of waiting, she rips away from his grip.

"I think I should spend the night at home."

He flops his weight back against the mattress. A thousand clichés swarm through her head while he just lies there, contemplating the ceiling. She searches for her bra then struggles with the clasp. Ridiculously, Jonah gets up to help, but she pushes him away.

"Don't touch me. Don't."

The carpet seems more interesting to him than her face.

"Shouldn't I be the one who's offended here? I'm sorry I couldn't keep it up. It's the insomnia —"

"That's not what this is about. I'm going home. I've got to work."

258

"Work?" He bats away her words. "Because that's so important — more important than talking about us? Folding bits of paper is hardly earth-changing stuff."

"What about you?" she yells. "A failed musician, a failed husband. Even your wife was bored with you."

"What?"

She can smell the damage. Audrey's photo sits on the bedside table, her smile warping the film with light.

Chloe feels too drained to compete. She can't even remember who she is lying for.

"She wrote a diary," she says evenly.

"Who?"

"Your wife."

There are so many words she wants to say; they clog up the bottleneck of her throat, stopping the telling until not a single word can escape.

His expression is strangely courteous, his body rigid. "That's not possible," he says. "I looked."

"I found it in her office but . . . you might not want to read it." Enough excuses. "I'm sorry, Joe. She met someone else."

She always thought he would win their game of conkers, but now this sound will echo through her nights. The splintering of his heart.

His gaze is frayed at the edges. It is a stare that wants to hurt her, but it's his eyes that are smarting — with fury, loss. Disbelief. He turns away.

"You're lying," he whispers.

Her thoughts collapse like clothes without a body. "I'm not."

Jonah begins to sway. It is making her seasick then his hands slam against the wall.

"How could you? When did . . .?"

"It's in my flat. I can give it to you when —"

"Your flat?" He lurches.

"I'm sure Audrey —"

"Don't say her name. You didn't know her. Get out!"

It looks like he's about to hit her, but instead he pushes beyond her, slamming the door. She pulls on the rest of her clothes, as if this will stop her guts falling from her stomach; she leaves without saying a word.

Harry sits by the lake, watching Chloe on the other side of the water. Perched on Audrey's bench, she is clutching a yellow book that is horribly familiar. He aches to go over there and read it. It would be like hearing Audrey's smoky voice again; but he has stolen enough.

He thinks about the different versions of a story crashing into each other; the battle over who is right and who is wrong. Both sides portray themselves as victims; both accuse the other of perpetrating. The intrepid adventure becomes a tale of pity. The page in Harry's notebook is smudged with rubbings out.

We covet happy endings. So why do we end up the authors of our own failings?

Harry's hands are blotchy with cold. His eyes scratch with tears as he thinks of the many lives he has wrecked — not just Audrey's, but Jonah's, her parents'. He's even hurt this young woman who is nervously glancing back towards the dogwood. She wipes her nose then hunches down deeper into her coat. Harry can no longer feel the pencil stub between his fingers.

When did this tale, this little death, begin? When Audrey miscarried, or when she met me? But I am too biased to tell this story honestly. Forgive me.

It is a bleak November day, the Gardens so empty of visitors that even the birds seem lonely. The water is on the verge of freezing and Chloe thinks back to a little girl's boat on the lake, the paper sinking. Hands stuffed in her pockets, Chloe stares down at the eyelets on her hobnail boots. The wind is making her eyes water and she blinks, angry that Jonah suggested they meet here: a perverse joke.

Across the lake, Chloe notices a trail of smoke. It's a strange place for the gardeners to light a fire. It dissipates, then she sees it again, a couple of metres away — some kind of mist or fog. Jonah walks around the corner. He stands stock-still by the red osier dogwood.

She speaks quickly before he can accuse her. "I'm sorry, Joe. I made a mistake."

He still doesn't move. His chest is visibly rising and falling, as if he's having to focus on pushing out the air. "You've been laughing at me."

"I haven't."

"All this time you knew . . ."

"I didn't know what to do."

"Tell the truth."

They stare at each other like strangers, who thought from a distance they recognised each other, but now feel foolish.

The conversation is like chewing gristle.

"I wanted to protect you."

"How kind of you!"

His sarcasm makes him step on to the deck, his large arms emphasising his point. As Chloe shrinks back, he forces himself to stop. He takes a breath, digs his hands in his pockets.

"I trusted you."

"If you want me to feel shame, that's simple."

She can wholeheartedly admit to what she has done, but can't yet bring herself to agree to the consequences. She wants to ask, who hasn't been broken? Who isn't also beautiful? But Jonah holds the savageness of a man fighting for survival.

"Who was it? A friend of ours? Who did she sleep with?"

"I don't know him. I'm not even sure they had sex."

Jonah reminds her of a wounded animal, moving around the deck, then he pulls up his trouser legs and sits down on the bench. But even with him beside her, she misses him. There is only the absence of comfort.

They both gaze across the lake. A goose is waddling on to one of the islands, its honk reverberating around the empty garden. A heron is perched on a small rowing boat. Watching it, Jonah rubs his knuckles.

"We knew each other so well. At least — I thought we did."

262

She wants to ask if he means her or Audrey, but anything she says will be a disappointment. I will disappoint you if I speak; I will disappoint myself.

"I'm sure she loved you. Perhaps, after the miscarriage . . ." She keeps talking, in the hope that she will find the right words, but none of them make the appropriate sound. Her voice feels fake, as it often does when she is honest. "Jonah, she loved you."

She hands him the artefact that is about to annihilate his past. He flicks through the pages, then stops, recoiling from Audrey's handwriting, the familiar loops and dots.

"It's getting cold," says Chloe. "Why don't we walk for a bit, to warm up?"

As he stands, she glimpses the magnitude of his grief. He glares at the dogwood, the clouds, his shoes — anywhere but where she is.

"You betrayed me. You both did."

Under a blistered sky, she tries to help Jonah breathe. She apologises again, tries to touch him, but his pride is deaf to it.

"I should go."

Stay. Just a bit longer. We could circle the lake? Visit the pagoda? But wherever they go they won't be able to walk away the damage.

She places herself between Jonah and the path that leads to the exit.

"Do you think there's a chance we can work it out?"

But the only "us" is Jonah and Audrey. He even looks confused by her need to ask. It is a calm violence. This is just a love song of what could have been, and is not. He tucks the diary under his arm.

"Goodbye, Chloe."

"Bye."

The sight of him walking away bruises her eyes. She turns and tosses a small pebble into the lake. As she watches the ripples she mourns the stillbirth of anything that craves to be born. It doesn't have to be a child. It can be an artwork, an idea, or a miscarried love.

Part V

The Flower Press

Just when we are safest, there's a sunset touch,
A fancy from a flower-bell, someone's death,
. . .
The grand Perhaps!

"Bishop Blougram's Apology", Robert Browning

The Dreamcatcher

The Gardens are quiet, the land asleep, as if dreaming of summer days when it throbbed with flora and tourists. A retired couple brace themselves against the weather. As they bend into the wind like twigs, it looks like the sky could snap them in an instant. A gardener is pushing an empty wheelchair along Syon Vista, as if a ghost is being given a guided tour. But the chair is only being returned to the entrance. Staff sit at Victoria Gate, idly chewing their nails.

Around the lake, peacocks perch on benches to keep warm, replacing the visitors who usually sit here. The regal birds stare at the large, lone man hunched on the other side of the water. Wearing thick gloves, he struggles to turn the pages of a book. His eyes, hidden under a woollen hat, would make the peacocks wary.

Jonah has become a witness to his life from a different perspective, his past rewritten by a different author. It makes him a stranger to himself, as if these last ten years have been a pantomime of gestures. All roads lead to Audrey. Jonah has visited many places in the diary: the Palm House, the Ruined Arch and Mademoiselle J'Attendrai's bench by the pagoda. But

269

he has never met the woman who walked through these pages. He recalls Audrey's many trips to Kew, how her smile had felt like a secret. Jonah had been blind. He looks up at the charred, grey sky and thinks, you let go of my hand.

A peacock shifts its weight while Jonah folds down a corner on one page, his fingers clumsy. The figure of Harry Barclay haunts him like an out-of-reach itch on his shoulder. Audrey's description matches up with the stranger at the funeral: a misty figure. But whenever Jonah tries to picture what he encountered among the gravestones, all he sees are masks and shadows.

He knows he should go home and mark that pile of essays. He has been turning up late to school, unwashed, and only yesterday he came close to slapping a child. It frightens him how easily he could have done it. He is no longer able to measure himself against others' expectations; instead he is remembering that final morning, how Audrey put on a darker shade of lipstick than usual. She had rubbed her nose against his as a goodbye, not wanting to get the lipstick on his cheek — or that's what he thought at the time.

A shriek. Jonah turns around to see a splash, a struggling in the water. Two birds chase each other, their wings viciously flapping. The heron, poised on the bank, closes its eyelids. Jonah wants to throw gravel at its tatty plumage . . . to yell, "Did you see them together?" Instead he makes a sound, somewhere between a scream and a shoo, but the heron doesn't move. Its bruised wings stand out against the apple-green reeds, the smudged sky promising rain.

270

The two birds plunge into the lake then surface, all feathers and beaks. When they dive down again, Jonah stands up, trying to spot them. He looks over the calm water then glances behind him.

Her footprint on my heart and these gardens forever

He urges himself to sit down again but it would be like embracing the woman who has cheated on him. It would make him a fool in front of Harry Barclay. Perhaps he should take an axe to the bench, burn it. But that would make his wife truly dead and he cannot bear that either. There is little he can endure, but this cold, this greyness. He beats his arms for warmth, his breath steaming in the air. As he follows the path around the lake, circling the bench, he realises that he is waiting for a man in an orange scarf to turn up and unwrap a Montecristo.

Not yet. Be patient. In winter everything seems frigid but underneath the surface, creation is seeding. Under this frost, miracles are waiting for their precise moment to happen.

Harry waits. Along the Holly Walk, the trees are one hundred and thirty-five years old, and among them is a sparrow of a woman in a tweed coat. She has just fondled a sprig of berries and turned to smile at him, her eyes hazy. It's inevitable, this second where she knows, but, mistrusting herself, she turns back, berating her imagination. As she makes her way to the exit,

Harry is unsure what to do. There's a chance that this woman can show him how to help Milly. He follows her past the Temple of Bellona. As they leave the gates, Harry braces himself for the chaos of civilisation.

Outside Kew Gardens station, mistletoe hangs wistfully, but the couple nearby don't notice it. Harry waits as the old lady ventures into the bookshop. People queue outside the butcher's, stamping against the chill of the pavement, while two children are snarled up in so many layers they can't move their arms freely. They peer at a stall selling mince pies and homemade pickles. Items are crossed off lists, dogs are yanked away from hung, plucked fowl, and pigeons scour the paving stones for crumbs.

When the tweed lady comes out of the bookshop, Harry extinguishes his cigar and follows her on to a train. She leads him through the maze of the Underground, and when they finally surface Harry is faced with Oxford Street, both its grime and magic.

The road is jammed with buses and gaudy lights, festive rage and aggressive anticipation. The harassed, the overexcited and the overegged limp towards the finishing line of Christmas. The old lady enters a store and Harry flinches at the fluorescent strip lighting, the reek of plastic and money. As the woman joins the queue, she glances doubtfully at the CD she's holding, then checks her list to see if it's what her granddaughter wanted. As she feels her heart knock, once, then twice, she turns to look at Harry, her lips slightly parted. Her fall to the ground is strangely graceful. Harry feels helpless. He strokes her brow while someone calls for an ambulance.

On Christmas Eve, Harry walks down Richmond's busy, tinselly streets. He is desperate to understand how people leave. He purposefully shoves into the frantic crowd of shoppers, daring someone to make eye contact; but no one notices him. He stands forlornly outside WHSmith then takes the bus back to Kew. A man, struggling with several rolls of wrapping paper, sits down beside him. He jokes with Harry about leaving things until the last minute.

On the big day Jonah drags himself to Surbiton for lunch with his dad: a quiet affair with two presents and a turkey crown eaten in front of the telly. Neither mentions the soggy sprouts or the inedible stuffing, and Jonah doesn't speak about Audrey's diary. Their dead wives are present, however, in the empty chairs. Especially when Jonah remembers Audrey giving his dad a kiss on the cheek. It always made the old man blush pinker than the strawberry wrapping in the Quality Street.

Harry sits in an unfamiliar armchair in a house in East Sheen. The last-minute shopper is having yet another roast potato; his eldest child is asking for watered-down wine while the youngest's wide eyes suggest she's overdosed on chocolate. A little while later, the dad is reading out paper-thin jokes, his wife passes him a jug of cream, and Harry counts how many hours he has been waiting. He's heard that Christmas Day is often busy for A&E: people hold on until the last moment to see the opening of presents, or that there are enough crackers under the stairs for the uninvited neighbours. Or they wait so they can please their wife one last time by swallowing that mouthful of her Christmas pudding. The penny gets stuck in the man's gullet. As his eldest son slaps him on the back, he falls into Harry's arms willingly as if the gardener is a long-lost lover, or salvation from the chore of eating the Boxing Day leftovers. But when he looks at his wife he grabs Harry's elbow and says, "Not yet." But there's nothing Harry can do about it.

As he stares into the man's eyes, he sees a kiss he has already witnessed. Last night the man and his wife had been hurriedly wrapping gifts. When they both reached for the Sellotape, his elbow crashed into her forehead. They shouted — then they kissed, a kiss full of love and mess and "Where did you put the scissors?"

The paramedics arrive. They struggle to carry the stretcher past the table laden with half-eaten pudding, while a shocked, still-drunk wife tries to reassure her children. Harry sits on the bottom of the stairs, remembering the deaths he witnessed in the desert of El Alamein. He wishes he could go back and be with those soldiers in their last moments, or hold his mother's hand as she lay under the rubble, her house bombed in the Blitz. Then he thinks about Audrey — how scared she must have been.

He leaves the house quickly. As he pounds down the pavement, he needs to help someone, anyone, but the streets are empty. Everyone is still eating lunch, or sleeping it off, or watching telly. Then he has an idea. He takes a bus to Kingston Hospital and wanders the corridors until he finds a room that doesn't have visitors. He enters, bobbing his head in greeting, then sits down and takes the gnarled hands of an old woman. She wears a paper hat, her cheeks strangely sunken because no one has remembered to put her teeth in. She seems glad to see him. But he can't think of the right words to help, he can't fix his face into a beatific glow; his expression is pockmarked with anxiety, he stinks of cigar smoke. He uselessly strokes her bony fingers, trying not to knock out the drip from the back of her hand. He doesn't know whether to rage at God, or to rage at the lack of His existence. But before he can decide, the woman dies, leaving a sigh that lingers in the room long after her pulse has stopped beating.

Christmas night is spent on the roads. As the drunken drivers swerve they see a man in a buttonless coat leaning against a parked car, or nonchalantly dodging traffic. Harry is on the streets again on Boxing Day morning, at the precise moment a six-year-old girl forgets to look both ways. How light she is in his arms, how noisy her mother's screams. But she doesn't stay.

HB. 26.12.05. Potting Shed
Sitting opposite her mum in the bath — a kiss on the lips, full of soapsuds.

Her mum's kiss again, her back crawling with chicken pox.

Her mum soothing a scrape on her knee. The smell of BBQ and suntan lotion.

Kissing the belly of her toy rabbit.

On December the twenty-seventh Jonah goes to 1A Earl Road, obsessed with the mystery his wife was trying to solve. Having taken some pills, he's had a full night's sleep, but he's still not sure if he's resourced to do this. At least, now, he has someone to blame. His anger since Audrey's death sharpens into focus, drilling down into this street, the house with the navy door, the bell: Jonah rings it. A man of similar age greets him. A toddler is wrapped around his hips, the boy's face smeared with chocolate.

When Jonah asks about the previous owners he is told about the Banerjee family, but nothing else about the house's history. When pushed, the man explains he has never heard of Audrey or a Harold or a Harry.

"A woman with red hair didn't come? A few years ago?"

"What is this? Last month, I had some chick ask the same thing."

Jonah winces.

"Is everything OK, honey?" A voice from the kitchen.

Harry peers past the front door and sees they've covered his wallpaper with ghastly peppermint paint.

The old place still smells the same, though, of gravy, must and soil, and there's a bit of his carpet cut out as the doormat. That makes him feel welcome.

Wary of what Jonah might discover, Harry has followed him all morning.

"My missus is calling."

"Yes. Of course." Jonah steps away. "Just one more thing. Harry Barclay. Do you know if he had a son or any other family?"

The man is exasperated. "I don't know what you're talking about, mate."

He glances back towards his cocoon of turkey sandwiches and festive films, blind to the ease of his good fortune. Harry fights the urge to spook him; but Jonah takes the hint and walks away, calling out a lacklustre "Happy New Year" as he reaches the pavement.

A few days later, Jonah visits the Kew office, but receives even less information than Audrey. He then ventures to the National Archives, just a short walk from the Gardens. Trawling through press cuttings, he flicks past a story about a girl who was lost in Kew, but doesn't recognise her pigtails. Then Jonah does something his wife didn't think of: he walks to Victoria Gate and trawls the acres, looking for staff that might have known Barclay. Most of them are too young, but there is one, the Bird Keeper, who remembers.

Peter Trestley has the dignity of a sixty-year-old man who has held the same, beloved job for decades. He prides himself in telling Jonah that he knows these birds as well as the weight of his balls in his hand. While he scatters grain, Jonah listens.

"I was a whippersnapper back then."

Two swans float by like sheets of ice. Pete has the cough of a man who spends too much winter outside; he doesn't even notice he's doing it.

"Ask Hal about any species — he had the answer and then some. He was obsessed with his seedlings. No woman got a look in. They all thought he looked like a matinée idol; what was the name of the guy in that film — the one about outlaws? Anyway, who wants to know?"

"My names Jonah."

Pete ignores the extended hand and throws a fistful of grain. "He served in the war but never talked about it. He worked with the Victoria. But everything excited him — the first sighting of blossom, the magnolias. They got blight one year — you should have seen him: devastated."

"But did he have family?"

"Don't think so. If I remember rightly they died in the Blitz." Pete sniffs deeply; a nasal mark of respect. "He was in the Berberis Dell when he keeled over. Heart attack, they said. That's the way he would have liked it, the sky staring down at him."

Both men look out over the lake.

"He had this potting shed but no one could find the damned key. Would have expected someone to break down the door, or knock the thing to smithereens. But it's not in the way . . ." Pete becomes distracted by the antics of a couple of geese. "Bloody teenagers! Why do you ask, Mr . . .?"

"Wilson. I'm trying to track down another Harry Barclay. I thought he might be a descendant."

"Sorry, guv. That's it."

"Thing is, there's no record of another Barclay that worked here."

Pete rubs his hands vigorously. "Maybe someone's using a false identity; you know, an alias. Perhaps someone's stolen poor Harry's name to get up to mischief."

"Perhaps."

A few days later, fireworks scatter the sky. As the world enters 2006, Pete sits by the darkened lake, clutching a flask of whisky and a packet of digestives, while in a flat on Kew Road Jonah watches a television overflowing with streamers. As he listens to the swaying notes of "Auld Lang Syne", he doesn't know what he should remember about his wife.

It is a bright, white Saturday in January. By 11 a.m. Jonah is still in bed, mesmerised by the mix of sun and snow outside his window. After an hour he gets up and peers down the street. A boy is trying to skateboard along the pavement while Milly is leaning against the garden wall, shivering in a T-shirt. Why doesn't her dad ensure she is better dressed? Jonah decides to meet him, play the concerned teacher, then goes for a piss. After making some coffee he returns to the window to the same scene. The slush is drenching the boy's jeans and Milly is trying to engage with him. Jonah bangs on the window but the girl is too far away. He presses his palm against the pane.

The next day there is a fresh fall of snow, and Milly is wearing a red duffel coat. After thanking Jonah several times, she stretches out her arms to admire herself.

"We should show your dad."

"He's in the nurseries today. You're not allowed."

"What time does he finish?"

She pulls a face. "Dunno."

As they walk towards Temperate House, Milly talks earnestly about what she has learnt about the politics of birds.

"They move about in tribes. If you look carefully you can tell who the leaders are . . . who are the look-outs or guards."

They stop at a temporary ice rink, packed with people nudging their weight forward with nothing more than air, or each other, to hold on to. When one youth throws himself into a grandiose spin, there is the muted sound of gloved applause.

Milly and Jonah circle back towards the lake, where the ducks are also slipping on frozen water to reach freshly thrown grain.

The Bird Keeper raises his arm. "Mr Wilson."

"Pete."

Jonah steers Milly in the opposite direction, hoping to ward off conversation.

She tugs on his sleeve. "What's wrong?"

"Nothing."

He pauses. This white sky is good for him. He enjoys the fact that he can't feel his fingers. He raises his shoulders then drops them, testing the frozen ache of his muscles.

The child is still peering up at him, worried.

"I'm fine, sweetheart, really. You're too young to . . ."

She runs off, tripping up over the snow. Berating himself, Jonah watches her become smaller; then her weight buckles. He breaks into a trot, worried she has fallen. By the time he reaches her, she is lying on her back, moving her limbs to push the snow away, creating miniature mountains and avalanches.

"Come on, Joe. Join me!"

"There's no way I'm lying in that."

Her legs move fervently, her determined face blushed with cold. At least she's not sulking. Resignedly, he drops his bag and lies down. The damp soaks into his back, his buttocks, then he feels something touch his face, as ephemeral as feathers, like the ghosts of Audrey's fingers. Opening his eyes, he sees flakes falling from a vast, light sky. It feels like he is upside down in a snow globe. He opens and closes his legs, his wet jeans chafing his groin.

After a minute of Jonah gritting his teeth and forgetting to flap his arms, Milly shouts, "Time out." They haul themselves off the ground, him dusting the ice off his arse; then they gaze down at Jonah's snow angel — a six-foot creature with feeble wings and a wide skirt. He squints at the place where Milly lay but struggles to find the imprint.

"The new snow must be covering your tracks."

Milly's cheeks are flushed.

"Why don't you try again? Sweetheart?"

They stand together in their loneliness. Physically they are close, but the distance between them feels impassable, as if the snow is creating radio interference. The wide horizon tempts Jonah to melt into this whiteness . . . like the final page of Audrey's diary.

"At school I learnt about the water cycle," says Milly. "Do you know how it goes?"

"Try me."

"It rains. Then the puddles evaporate and become clouds again. Round and round it goes. It got me thinking how nice it must be for a raindrop to become a snowflake. For months you're just rain and everyone hates you. But then one winter the weather gets chilly and you become a snowflake with its own shape and pattern. And you're the only one of your kind of snowflake and everyone loves you. I reckon snow must be God's gift to the raindrop."

"That's a great idea, Mils. I love it." Jonah considers the ceaseless cycle of a raindrop, the losing and gathering of itself.

"I hope," says Milly, "that when I leave for good, I'll become snow."

"Right." Jonah has no idea what she's talking about. He searches the white sky. "I reckon we're going to have to deal with being raindrops for now. Accept our humble lot."

On the eleventh of February Jonah goes to Tesco Express near Kew Gardens station and is inundated with window displays full of Valentine cards and teddy bears. Clutching a plastic bag containing a loaf and several tins of soup, he hovers outside the bookshop where a couple are peering into a volume of poems. She is obviously whispering something funny and seductive in his ear, and Jonah can't help it. He taps on the window.

"Excuse me, did you know that St Valentine was the saint of epilepsy?"

The startled couple gesture that they can't hear him.

"Love is an illness," he mouths. "Comes in fits and spasms."

The couple edge away, leaving him to stare at his own tired reflection. Jonah presses his nose against the pane but no longer recognises the man in the shop window; the one who has started to smile and cry at the same time, the carrier bag digging violent red marks into the joints of his fingers.

Half an hour later he has dropped off the shopping and walked to the Gardens. It has begun to rain, so he makes his way to the Princess of Wales Conservatory, and as soon as he opens the glass doors he can smell the orchids. Beyond the dry tropics and beds of cacti, he enters the annual display. From floor to ceiling, orchids are interwoven through wire structures, their potting hidden by clumps of moss. Flowers hang from immense voluptuous bowls, the glasshouse bedecked with petals. It doesn't matter how many times Jonah has seen them; he remains overwhelmed by their lush beauty. Brightly coloured bromeliads are speared through the orchids, and carnivorous, glossy anthuriums bustle for space among delicately spotted petals. The vividness of scarlet and tangerine wars with lilac, pink and velvety purple. Jonah reads the labels with their hint of eroticism: slipper orchids or Paphiopedilum; the Enycylia, the speckled moth. He walks through a tunnel of Vandas shining brighter than the sun and each flower is curiously alluring, their petals unfurling like labia. Among them, phallus-shaped spadices are erect or malformed and perhaps this is why Jonah loves them; they hold the idiosyncratic flaws that make the human body so tantalising. If flowers could have tongues and lips, lust and talons, these would be it. He likes that he doesn't trust them.

Once he has drunk in this paradise of enchantments, he walks through a set of doors and enters the Zone 2 display. At the rear of this glasshouse stands an immense circular structure, almost as wide and high as the room. Inside a huge hoop of willow, string has been threaded into an enormous Native American dreamcatcher. Hanging from this web are origami birds folded in an array of colours. But some of the wings are crumpled, the beaks torn.

Jonah had forgotten about Chloe's artwork. He looks around, concerned he'll bump into her, but of course she's not there; the exhibition is a month long. He walks towards the stand and reads the title.

A PLACE FOR LOST THINGS

He can't believe Chloe remembered his whimsical idea. He turns around, taking it in. Trestle tables stand along

284

one side of the room, and next to them are two large buckets. Both are filled with sheets of paper: the first, titled LOST, holds green, grey and blue squares, while the second bucket, FOUND, contains the warmer end of the spectrum; reds, pinks, oranges and yellows. On the wall above is a set of instructions. WHAT HAVE YOU LOST? WHAT HAVE YOU FOUND? People are invited to write on the paper, and, intrigued, Jonah peers over strangers' shoulders. *My rite glove*, writes a child on sky-blue paper. *I found my husband*, scrawled on joyful red by his mum. *Missing for years — or perhaps it was me that was lost*. Further down, an old man sucks on the end of his biro. Eventually he lists names under the heading "Dead Friends"; then he writes about jokes he has stumbled upon and used as his own. On another sheet he describes the ring his wife lost down the sink, and the love of his dog, Agnes.

There are clear diagrams, describing how to fold the paper into a crane. Each step is followed carefully, the mother using her wedding ring to flatten down a stubborn crease. Once the birds are complete, two Kew volunteers are there to help. The first uses a needle to thread the paper, and the second climbs a ladder to hang each bird. The colours are no longer separated, but intermingle so the web is as vivid as a rainbow. Hopes, celebrations and griefs entwine, as if this dreamcatcher is salvaging wishes, stopping them from blowing away in the wind to be forgotten by time.

As Jonah reads fragments of folded words he discovers what people have found in Kew Gardens: the time to breathe, or the name of a particular tree that

285

has bothered them for years. Friends have been reunited, the pagoda a focal point in a sprawling London. Jonah tries to find something equally positive, but ends up snatching a handful of the "lost paper" and, on a grey page, he writes TRUST. Then he crumples it up. Starting again, he writes a series of random musical notes on a stave then folds so hurriedly that the bird is mangled. He slams the creature into the assistant's hand then walks out of the conservatory. The landscape is sodden.

Jonah didn't see her among the stupid orchid-gazers, but for once Milly doesn't care. Everything is blurring, her tears turning paper birds and people to mush. A woman pushes past, her handbag bashing through Milly's chest, and it hurts, the leather and studs. It feels like her legs won't hold her. Yet she remains motionless, staring up at the dreamcatcher.

Birds hang from the strings, and in the holes of the netting there's something sparkly, like dewdrops on a web. As Milly blinks, these drops become seeds that spiral in, until they form the centre of a sunflower.

The stem is in Milly's hands, her grip tight. She is trying to pick the flower but it won't let go of the soil. Now she's broken only half the stem so she has to keep on ripping and ripping, and the flower is screaming — it's like bludgeoning something to death that won't die. She was only trying to rescue it, to keep it safe, but now there's a woman with black hair. It's cut into a bob, but it's definitely Chloe — crouched beside her, worried.

286

Milly's eyes are misty; she can't see. There's a paper boat sinking, but the lake is full of dust and weeds. She blinks away the dank water then studies the words that triggered her memory. At the bottom of the dreamcatcher is a plaque.

For Emily Richards
1995–2003
FOUND in my heart, always

Jonah walks without direction, gulping down the fresh, wet air. He sees signs of Chloe everywhere. Exotic paper birds perch in the trees, and he stops to watch the rain falling from their wings. He doesn't understand what the birds are made of to resist this weather, but he continues to stumble over Chloe's creativity, the evocative and sensual. Vivid flowers float in the lake; then, among the reeds, he spots an origami heron. It is exquisitely crafted, each fold not just creating the limbs of the bird, but the poise of patient waiting.

Jonah wipes the rain from his beard then sees Milly, in her red coat, running down Syon Vista. She looks upset. He starts to follow then loses sight of her among the holm oaks. He sees her again a little further away. After fifteen minutes of chasing her, Jonah loses his bearings.

He is near the main gate, an area of the Gardens he doesn't know intimately, but he can't piece the landmarks together. He walks along a path of sentinel stones that leads to a gigantic woman made of clay and moss. She is lying on her side, her eyelids closed. Her arm is crooked around a breast made of dirt.

"I don't know if she's sleeping or dead."

He whips around to see Milly, her eyes puffy.

"Sshh," she says. "She's dreaming."

Not for the first time, Jonah ponders her strangeness. He wonders if his insomnia is denting his reality, or if he's drinking too much; then he focuses his attention back on Mother Earth, her knees bent in towards her turfed stomach. Her pose is both sensual and foetal, but the soil around her mouth is dripping. Milly reaches out to touch the rain damage. With her other hand, she presses her fingers down on the pulse of Jonah's wrist, as if worried that a hug might hurt him. They stay like that for a minute, a statue of friendship.

"Can you feel it?" she whispers.

"What?"

"Me."

He is about to say yes then stops to pay attention. "Must be a dead arm or something."

As he squats down to match her height, he notices the sign with W.B. Yeats's poem: "The Stolen Child". Jonah feels dizzy. Perhaps it's the way he's crouched in the rain, or he's too unfit for running. It doesn't feel right being in such a secluded place with Milly. In an attempt to straighten himself out, he pushes back her messy fringe, then notices a scar on her temple. She starts talking very quickly — something about a paper boat. A flower press.

"Chloe told me to keep away."

"From the flower press?"

"No. It was my mistake."

"You're not making any sense."

"It's why Chloe's got all those pictures on her walls."

There's no logic to this conversation . . . or the lack of sensation in his face. He can't even feel her muddy palm on his cheek.

He can see her trying to articulate, but all she can say is one word.

"Please."

The Ruined Arch

HB. 31.03.06 Broad Walk
Be still. Let every sense
quiver with awareness . . .
in the tiny hairs on your arms,
the nape of your neck.
First there is the breaking through
of the green, hopeful tip.
What audacity to nudge its way up,
its soul aching for sunlight.
There it is, pushing through the soil —
the very first crocus.

1. *Prune the roses*
2. *Mulch the herbaceous beds*

Over 100,000 daffodils have bloomed.
They're like sunlight in a jar . . .

The flowers glimmer as day turns to dusk, the evening as tender as a lover. Harry tucks his notebook inside his breast pocket and strolls towards the lake. A breeze sets free a haze of pollen. He is drawn towards the *Tsuga*

290

canadensis, a coniferous dome with overhanging branches. Its other name is the weeping eastern hemlock and Harry is surprised to hear crying emanating from its leafy cave. When the sobbing becomes louder its as if the leaves are shuddering with tears. Pushing back its branches, he discovers Milly huddled on a bench.

"There's no need for that."

She hugs her knees tighter as if trying to make herself disappear. Harry stoops under the tree then sits beside her, his eyes trying to acclimatise to the darkness.

He rubs her hand, waiting for her to speak. He knows this bench well: "Wherever in the world we are, this is a piece of our love that we built in England". He wonders if the couple are still together or bitter with recrimination.

"I went to see Chloe," the child splutters. "Three times I've been to her studio, but she never listens."

"She's a well-adjusted, rational woman. She can't hear you —"

"But it wasn't her fault."

The light through the leaves scatters the darkness, highlighting patches of her expression, her naivety. Harry leans forward.

"Do you remember what happened?"

"Bits." She wipes her nose on her arm, her snot leaving a silvery trail. "But how can I help her? You told me that everything will fade away, that I can't make a difference." She stands up, frustrated. "I don't want to be useless. I love these plants, but I want real friends, I want —"

"But, Milly, don't you realise? If you're remembering, you might be able to leave."

He can only see her silhouette under the branches. Her voice is so quiet he can hardly hear.

"And then what?"

Harry won't survive it. "I'm sure there'll be kids to play with . . ."

Look at him, pretending he knows what will become of her, but he's just flailing around in the darkness like everyone else.

Milly reluctantly returns to the bench. She searches his face for what frightens her, but all she finds there is a friend. She's remembering the million things she has lost and can never fetch back; she's beginning to realise the world is unfair.

Harry squeezes her hand. "You remember all of it? You have to piece it together bit by bit. What colour was the sky that day, what were you doing . . ."

"Mum had to change a nappy. Then we agreed to meet at half-past."

"Where?"

"A glasshouse."

"Which one? Come on, Milly, you need to remember. Relive it. And this time I won't interfere."

"Will you come with me?"

"Don't be soft." He knows if he glances up, her hope will break him. His callused hands become fascinating. "We don't even know if this will work. I could ruin your chances . . ."

292

She looks at him squarely. "But you'll help?"

"Of course." His ancient eyes are full of tears. "How did it start?"

She shrugs. "With a blank sheet of paper."

Milly says goodbye to the bookshop, the plastic dog outside the butcher's, and the fish with their glassy eyes, lying in beds of ice in the fishmonger's window. She even waves goodbye to a couple of flies circling above the mackerel. But how can she say goodbye to every house and tree, each cat skulking along the pavement, every passing car full of people? So Milly stops trying and dawdles on the street, peering into a doorway where a man is cutting a key. A few minutes later she strolls to the main road, where the skateboarder performs his usual tricks.

"See ya, James." As she reaches the pedestrian crossing, she yells, "I always liked your trainers, by the way."

After entering the Gardens, she is ambushed by a memory: her dad wrapping a towel around her dripping shoulders and giving her a squeeze. She remembers the smell of his ironed shirts, how his cheek scratched against hers; the way he sang along to Simon and Garfunkel and said, "Mini Milly, I love you a million." She can recall the daily noises of the kitchen, toast popping up, her mother calling from upstairs, "Have you got your cardy?" Now she's walking towards Temperate House hoping that her mum doesn't only come on the thirteenth of each month, but on the ninth of April.

The mother is sitting on the bench dedicated to Milly. Her knees are pressed together, a bouquet by her feet. She is holding the empty cellophane in her soap-dried fist. Today is her daughter's eleventh birthday. But there's no point in Milly shouting, or waving her arms. She sits down, her fingers touching the back of her mum's hand. Too late, she recognises the Russian wedding ring, the white moons on her nails that was something to do with calcium, but she stops herself remembering further. She cannot hold it. Her mum is focused on a passing peacock.

"Pretty, ain't it?"

The woman doesn't answer. Her fingers twitch in response to an imaginary ant wandering along her hand, then she smooths down her skirt as if brushing away crumbs. Once she has tidied the yellow flowers, she walks away, leaving Milly alone with the grass and the sky.

Her nails dig into her palms but still she squeezes tighter. She walks to the Japanese Gateway, then all the way to Queen Charlotte's Cottage; she walks so far her hip sockets ache. As she passes through the Redwood Grove she studies the colossal trees that have been her four-poster bed, the dead leaves her mattress. Harry always props himself up against a trunk, waiting for her to sleep. Each night, she still fakes slumber so she can feel his goodnight kiss. This is what has rooted her here — the shy tenderness of a man who will never be a dad. But she doesn't want to be like him, forever haunting these Gardens. She has given up hope of changing anything that matters. As she makes her way to the

Wounded Angel, her eyes well up at the magnolias in full flower.

The marble angel has a noble face, his hair stretched back into a stony plume of feathers. Harry's muddy boots peek out from behind the plinth then he takes a step forward and hands Milly a white square of paper. Now all she has to remember is the art of origami.

Under Harry's watchful gaze, she kneels down on the grass. She creases the paper like Chloe showed her, folding this way and that, until she's tucking the paper backwards into the base of the hull. She tries really hard to fit the pieces together: what happened that day, and in what order. Then she folds one of the triangles into the main sail and it finally looks like a boat. She checks she's done everything correctly, then glances up — Harry has gone. Her throat feels like she's just swallowed a gobstopper. She is alone and the scene is set. This is how it was.

Milly picks up the boat and squeezes the flower press into her trouser pocket. Once she reaches the lake she sits down and swings her legs back and forth over the edge. A couple of grebes are mirroring each other in a graceful duet. Milly looks beyond the sunlit surface to the huge clumps of blanketweed; then Jonah arrives on the other side of the water. It takes all her willpower not to run over to the safe haven of his chest. She dithers, unsure if she should go ahead. But Jonah hasn't seen her. He's drumming his fingers against Audrey's bench, tapping along to a tune that no one else can hear — and look, the sky is a seamless blue, just like last time.

Milly grazes her elbow as she leans over the brink of the lake. Carefully launching the boat, she watches it float for a few seconds, then sink. After saying goodbye to Chloe, she'd returned to the water. Now she's balancing her weight over the edge, further and further, just like before, until the flower press drops from her pocket. A slow-motion fall. All those things saved from dying, all those months of collecting, lost. She remembers reaching, the flower press bobbing precariously on the surface. She lowers her body down into the lake, her muscles bracing.

Jonah hears splashing. He pulls his gaze from Audrey's bench and sees Milly wading into the lake. It looks like she is trying to reach something, perhaps a large piece of bread.

"What are you doing? Get out of there!"

She doesn't listen. She goes deeper then loses her footing. Her head plunges under, and all that is left are ripples that vanish. Jonah tears off his shoes then throws off his jacket. When the spluttering child surfaces, something dark drips from her forehead.

"Milly!"

Her strokes are uneven. She sinks, comes up for breath, then is pulled down again. Jonah looks around for help, but there are only a few coots by Audrey's bench. He wrenches off his jumper and wades in.

The lake is shallow, reaching his calves, his knees, but then there is a drop, the cold flooding his groin until Jonah is swimming in water greasy with weeds. The

296

ducks leave noisily, appalled by the intrusion of hectic, human limbs.

"Milly! Sweetheart!"

He ventures underwater, but the blanketweed is blinding. His jeans are so heavy he struggles to surface.

"Someone's drowning. A little girl. Please!"

Jonah refuses to lose this child. Not this one. As he dives down again he thinks about his children, how he would have done anything to save them. But then he glimpses Milly through the cloudy water. She is walking serenely across the bottom of the lake. This must be a dream. Jonah feels an intense pressure in his chest. He reaches up for air, his mouth full of algae and bewilderment; then he glimpses a man in a suit standing on the island in the middle of the lake. The stranger from Audrey's funeral. How did he get there? Why won't he help? Perhaps these visions are the thoughts of a man losing oxygen to his brain. Jonah submerges again, his eyes groping through the stirred water. The weeds entangle his limbs, a rising panic. Searching for Milly, his arms flail.

Be calm. Think.

Jonah becomes still. Suspended in the rippling light, everything is muffled. But he hears a voice ask: *Why not let go?* Its audacity shines brightly in the water. Could he follow his wife anywhere? He closes his eyes and the questions cease pounding. This is the silence when your head is underwater, the soundlessness of sleep. The world stops moving.

In the absence of time there is only pause, a faith uncomplicated. Jonah looks up at the sky above the water, the sunlight dancing, and his thoughts feel crystalline, fluid. This is a strange kind of drowning. He thought he would remember his past, but what he sees are the endless possibilities of the future. He is clutching a newborn child, holding the exact weight of hope in his arms.

As the impulse to survive surges through his waterlogged body, the distress hits; the crushing of his lungs, his ribs crying out like a dam breaking. He looks up to see the man standing on the islands edge, shimmering above him. Next to Harry Barclay is Milly, soaked and shivering. Both are shaking their heads.

Jonah surrenders: not a giving in, but a giving upwards, to something greater than him. It powers his muscles to wrench free from the weeds, it pulls his body to the surface; he splutters green spit. Milly is gulping down tears.

As the man leads her away, Jonah scrambles through the water.

"Wait!"

Pulling himself on to the island, Jonah staggers to standing. Half-running, half-falling through the copse, there is no one to be seen. He lurches around an empty island with just a swan for company, then comes the crushing realisation of his mistake. Perhaps she is still underwater, drowning. He squints at the surface of the lake; then notices a couple by the edge.

"Did you see a child with me? In the water?"

The couple cock their heads. He can see what they're thinking: who is this crazy idiot marooned on an island?

298

"You just dived in, screaming," the guy shouts. "Are you OK?"

Bile rises in Jonah's throat until he vomits weeds and water.

It doesn't take long for a crowd to gather. They stare at the big, soaked man, doubled over. A woman makes a phone call, while another turns her children away, pulling their heads to her soft belly. *We are the lucky ones. Safe.*

The Bird Keeper waves. "Don't worry, sir. I'm coming to get you."

Jonah's legs convulse then give way. It is only now, when he drops to the muddy ground, that he feels the glacial temperature of his clothes, his skin developing a rash from the water.

When the rowing boat arrives, the Bird Keeper wraps him in a tartan blanket and helps him into the hull. As he is rowed back to the mainland, Jonah notices the heron standing in the reeds, and feels just as detached; a mere witness. He becomes aware of his skin lying loosely over his bones, his used muscles. He listens to the creak of the oar, the paddle tearing free from the blanketweed. He feels the bobbing of the boat, as soothing as a cradle; then he sees the pity scratched into the Bird Keeper's brow.

The flower press still sits on the bottom of the lake. When Milly reached for it, her hand became wedged between two rocks. She fought to free herself, but eventually she was suspended in a calm grave.

The drought that summer had clogged the water with weeds. Growing three feet each day, they hid her body. But, a few days later, her decomposing corpse ballooned with gases, the pressure dislodging her broken wrist. When she floated to the surface, the Bird Keeper discovered the girl riddled with insects. Her polyester T-shirt was still wrapped around her ribs, and her plimsolls, covered in algae, were straining at the seams. She had bloated feet.

When Harry had seen her mother panic, he had instinctively run to the lake. It was natural to help; he was full of bravado from his first encounter with Audrey. Carried away with the belief that he could save people, he waded in. Underneath was a murky haze. As he yanked the girl's trapped hand, he could feel the bones in her wrist snapping. Her kicking legs stilled, then, with one last wrench, he set her free. Holding her, he felt triumphant; then he saw her body beneath him. The girl in his arms opened her eyes and gave a bemused, wet grin.

Christ. He felt sick. He carried her to land then stumbled towards the Ruined Arch. If he did it quickly enough she might not notice. As he placed her feet down on the path, she was disorientated. He guided her into the central tunnel, shooing her along as if he were encouraging a baby bird, but she walked out the other side.

"You're not supposed to be here," he gasped.

He tried to persuade her to walk through again. Holding her wriggling arm as tenderly as possible, he knew she was scared of him. Who wouldn't be? She kicked him in the shin.

Running away, she found a barefoot woman.

"Emily!"

Her mother looked through the soaked, bedraggled girl then continued her frantic run across the diagonal of the Gardens. Milly didn't know who she was or what she was supposed to be doing; she turned back to see Harry standing in a puddle, his suit dripping. She didn't have much choice but to trust him. She was delighted when, a few weeks later, he gave her a new flower press. That was the first time she hugged him.

As the seasons passed, the sight of her mother would stir her, like a prod on the back, or suddenly remembering she'd left her glove on a bus. But for her mum, it was different. All that remained was a book of stickers, a much-loved bear, and the awful shock of seeing Milly's fingerprints left behind on the kitchen window.

"I almost killed him," she says.

Harry's jacket is draped around Milly's shoulders.

"Jonah's fine," he comforts. "It was a scare, but . . ."

"You were right. We can only cause trouble."

Her skin is goose-pimpled, her corduroys muddy and drenched.

"I'm sorry," he says. "I think I trapped you here. I was so carried away by saving Audrey . . ."

Her hair drips on to the page. Harry tries to dry her arms with his jumper, but it is scratchy, useless.

★ ★ ★

The image is clear on Jonah's computer screen: a school photo of Emily Richards accompanying a newspaper report of her drowning. Her hair is combed, her red cardigan neatly buttoned. Her smile is cheeky.

Jonah must be imagining things, but the truth stares at him, mocking. He turns to the photo above the piano, but Milly's blurred elbow could easily be his thumbprint. He even remembers Audrey talking about the tragedy. There were posters of a missing child outside the station. His subconscious must have been playing tricks on him: the delusions of a man who never allowed himself to say how much he had let himself love his children.

Jonah doesn't believe in ghosts. He refuses to accept his experience, but at night he dreams of a child's corpse on an autopsy table, her tiny frame pale. Her fingernails are lined with mud. Under a hallowed light, her mouth is prised open. From her throat grow leaves and buds, and on her tongue is a pressed flower: a primrose.

Jonah believes it is he who has drowned. Like Audrey, he lingers in a liminal space: a threshold. He calls in sick at work, and, over the next few days, reads everything he can about Milly. The photograph of her father looks nothing like Harry. Thirty years old, the papers said — a cabbie. But Jonah's convinced he saw the two of them playing chess; only now does he place the orange scarf, the tweed cap. He trawls the Gardens, hoping to glimpse Milly. Instead he finds her bench near Temperate House, sitting between an ash and a maple.

302

On the thirteenth of April, Jonah watches a family ritual. Her father is skinny, his elbows so threadbare that they seem to have been dipped in talcum powder. Underneath his cheap suit is the suffocation of a man who looks after everyone else's sorrow. While he tends to a little boy, his wife arranges the flowers then warily raises her chin at the watching stranger. Jonah tries to stop swaying. He leans towards the tilt of the sky, worried that gravity won't hold him.

As they walk towards the crumbling folly, Milly is chatty.

"Miss Tanner told us about Jesus and Allah — and an elephant god I can't remember the name of — but I'm sure they know I was naughty. Mum told me not to touch the flowers. Or talk to strangers." She is pulling on Harry's sleeve. "Do you know what happens next? Where I go, do you?"

He shakes his head. "I've never been there."

He expects Milly to falter, but the only sign of anxiety is her holding his hand too tightly. It is Harry who is nervous.

"Will you be OK?" asks Milly.

"Of course. Once you're there, you'll wonder why you stayed. There'll be comfy beds and hammocks. Loads of gardens . . ."

"Please come with me."

They stop walking. As he turns to face her, her eyes are smarting with tears. He knows he should chaperone her — to where, to what? Nothing? He can't exchange that for the redwoods, the Lucombe.

"This is where I belong. Everything I love is here . . ."

"Everything?"

"Of course not." He squats down to her level. "You will be OK, I promise."

Once they arrive at the Arch, the only thing alive is the ivy. Milly becomes jittery and Harry prays that she's going somewhere even more beautiful than this garden. He clasps her tightly, taking in the scent of her hair, the pressure of her limpet grip around his neck. Every part of him wants to say, don't go, don't leave me. But when she frees herself she barely looks at him. She is pouring her strength elsewhere.

As she stands before the three arches, her tiny back is determined. She has a child's simple acceptance of what has happened: all it took was a pocket too small.

The folly waits, its bricks pretending to crumble. As Milly steps into the central arch, her leg becomes fainter, like a sketch fading on paper. Her hips grow paler, then her torso; a rubbing out. What must it be like to become undone, just particles of dust?

Time stands still. Even the breeze stops. And this is the devastating gap where someone once was. Harry is left alone with the scattered wind, his exhilaration and loss. All that remains on the ground is a flower press. Harry already misses her dirty kneecaps, the dried snot on the back other hand. He hasn't a clue where Milly is, or how something can become nothing. He just remembers all the lies he told her about her destination, as if he were someone wise.

Part VI

A Song in Q

We do not remember days, we remember moments.

Cesare Pavese, found on a bench in Kew Gardens

A Misfit

Jonah wanders down the A307, unable to find a place that brings rest. He is still on sick leave, his sleep slashed with nightmares of bones, flowers and murky water. He thinks about the aquarium and the old couple staring; was he talking to thin air about fish? The truth is indigestible. Jonah has returned to his therapist who logically explained that the insomniac, unable to dream, hallucinates.

"Did you see the girl when you were most exhausted? And only then?"

"Yes."

Paul Ridley's blond eyelashes quivered. The hypothesis was simple: what Jonah's subconscious knew about Milly's death became bound with his grief. He only imagined this child and the man by the lake. It was a manifestation of his recent obsessions. But this doesn't explain the mysteries surrounding Audrey's stranger. It's impossible for an intelligent man to fathom.

His loyalty to Audrey still feels misplaced, but something jars him. Harry was at Audrey's grave, on the island with Milly, as if he were some kind of angel of death. Jonah feels as crazy as the strays he sees on the tube, digging their fingers in their ears to poke out the voices that chant and curse; a chorus of derangement. He recalls, again, the man wearing Audrey's scarf, then evidence of Milly's existence: her smacking her lips together to imitate a clownfish, or scratching her earlobe when she was thinking.

Jonah can't help it; he turns into the Gardens. At the lake, damselflies skirt between the nettles, and a pond skater walks across the surface, not caring that it's performing a miracle. Nature hums and buzzes. Putting on his headphones, Jonah listens to Bach's *Concerto for Two Violins in D Minor*, but the strings' cries feel distant. What he needs is the warmth of a human being. Finding Chloe's number on his phone, he wants to talk about Milly but doesn't trust his memories. The dreamcatcher, which became heavy with things lost and found, has been dismantled, but he has read about Chloe's work in the newspaper, her career blossoming like the orchids. He wonders how her life has changed, and shocks himself by wishing her well.

Jonah walks away from the lake and the memories of a little girl kicking. He tries to shuffle off the sense of insanity that follows him like a headache. The dim light of the Redwood Grove gives him some comfort, so he sits on a bench and lets himself be soothed by these American giants. The only truth is his smallness.

Jonah smells smoke. The air begins to bristle with an incessant whisper. Someone is stroking his temples. It's so precise, the soothing spiralling of a finger. The aroma of tobacco . . . Audrey? Life buckles Jonah enough to surrender. As he weeps, he recalls a foetus in his palm,

310

his wife's face cut by the windscreen, the splintered glass studding her cheeks like tears. He remembers the musty smell of her diary, the yellow cover thumbed by Chloe, a woman who breathes life into paper. Then he thinks about the snow, the endless snow, and Milly leaving no footprints.

His sobbing comes in waves. When all beliefs have been smashed what is left of a man? His convictions crack and collapse until he finds himself beyond grief. He rests, worn-out, in a silence that demands nothing. It has no answers, only arms that hold him. It cradles him like a boat floating to shore. As Jonah wipes his face on his sleeve he wonders if tears are the most necessary thing of all. If there is a God perhaps it is his greatest gift.

Jonah stays for an hour, letting the feelings sway and subside, and when he feels dry enough and steady, he stands up and leaves the grove. The bench remains under the redwoods, the inscription faint from age, forgotten by most.

Harry Barclay
1918–1969
Twenty years of service to Kew

In May Chloe walks through the Gardens. She hasn't been to Kew since her work was removed, but now she returns to test her belief that she's recovered from Jonah Wilson. Almost six months ago she'd left his flat riddled with guilt, but this turned to the rage and resentment of a lonely Christmas. She ate packets of biscuits to stifle the hurt. Then, hauling up the drawbridge, she focused on work.

Huge squares of paper covered her floor. She needed assistants to pick up each corner, the paper becoming smaller as they made each fold. Despite the intricate mathematics, creases were pressed down with knees and elbows. Chloe grappled with flimsy sheets that billowed and tore. But, finally, in her studio, stood a heron, ninety centimetres tall.

After her success in Kew, Chloe was offered many new commissions, and now only temps one day a week. She walks through the Rhododendron Dell, her hair grown into a long, choppy bob, her shape a little softer from lunches with the artistic elite. But as she leaves the dell, the sunshine scuffs. A mother and child are sitting on the grass, cocooned in their private world, their hands gently clapping and parting. Between them the air vibrates with a love that knows each other's faces in detail. It leaves Chloe wanting.

A while later she is walking through the conservation area near Queen Charlotte's Cottage. A guide is talking to a school group, her voice lost under the drone of a passing plane. Chloe catches names such as fiddle dock and knotted clover.

"It's important to leave fallen trees for insects. We encourage brambles and stinging nettles. I'm sure you'll be pleased to know that, for once, it's not about being tidy."

Many of the young listeners are carrying sticks they have picked up on the way. Others are touching the bark of a nearby hawthorn. Chloe is intrigued by how they explore the world around them; then a boy viciously chases some wandering geese, and she moves away. A few minutes later, her eyes are drawn to a couple leaving the woods, looking strangely luminescent. There is a savouring to their movement. It tempts Chloe to enter the same tree-lined avenue where a corridor of sunshine is banked with hundreds of bluebells. It is wild. Lush. Ancient. Amid this sea of flowers are shafts of lime from the yellow perfoliate alexander, and white petals that smell of garlic. A few people stand gawping as if they are paused in grace, taking in one time-stretched moment.

Chloe pulls out her camera. She's so enamoured with what she wants to capture that she doesn't feel the raindrops. As she crouches down to take a close-up of the belled beauty, the storm drenches. While she rushes to protect her equipment, the others run from the woods, clutching bags or newspapers over their heads, the sky shifting to darkness. Alone, Chloe raises her arms, letting the rain soak her dress, the thin fabric clinging to her torso. Water cascades down her chin as she looks up, losing her edges. She blurs with the rain, for a moment, a year, a lifetime, then the deluge stops. The weather simmers, undecided. Once again, there is brilliant sunshine. The bluebells, now radiant, glisten with raindrops.

There is magnificent quiet. As Chloe walks through the woods there is no soul to be seen, and it feels as if the entire world is breathing in time with her, or her with it. She pauses by a splintered bench.

Set free to enjoy these flowers for ever
In loving memory of
Violet Marshall 1881–1978 and sister Daisy Slight.
Painters for many years of these bluebells

Chloe cherishes the smell of the wet earth; the way the rain has polished the petals. Then she notices a man, with his eyes closed, sitting on a bench. It is the only seat situated squarely in the light, and his face is tilted up towards the sun, like a flower craning towards what nourishes it. He doesn't seem to mind that the bench is wet, but, as Chloe moves closer, she hesitates. There is mud on his trousers, and even from here she can smell the age in his suit; autumn leaves mixed with the dankness of a charity shop.

Pulling out her camera, Chloe takes a photo but the click wakes him up. As he startles away from the lens, she tries to reassure him. It takes a while for their gaze to meet. His blue eyes have a twinkly charm; but in that glint is a sad compassion, the weight of someone who has seen too much.

"I'm sorry I disturbed you," says Chloe.

She feels dizzy, as if the world is turning too slowly, or her thoughts too fast. His ever-changing gaze is like a flock of sparrows, re-forming and gathering in the air — a murmuration. He opens his mouth, but no words come out. It's so awkward that Chloe apologises and walks away.

The sound of her feet on the gravel, her head down. Chloe tries to move as quickly as possible. Anyone could have taken his wallet, his hat. His hat — an old, tweed cap had sat beside him like a loyal lover. Chloe stops. She fumbles with her camera, finds the photo, but there's a blur in the middle. She can only see the hat, the bluebells and a sunlit bench. As she makes her way back, her heartbeat quickens.

"Harry? Mr Barclay?"

There is no one there.

"Wait!"

Chloe breaks into a run, but she doesn't find him at Queen Charlotte's Cottage or the waterlily pond. She walks back to the woods, beyond the bench he was sitting on. There is a thud behind her. She turns around to see a boot lying on the ground. Then another falls out of the air and lands on the gravel path with a clatter.

Chloe peers up into the trees; it's probably those school kids playing a trick. But there are no flickers of uniform, no muffled laughter. When she searches the beds, the bluebells shudder. She returns to the path and picks up a boot. There's Sellotape around one lace and the leather is as wrinkled as old skin, the studs caked with soil. Collecting its partner, Chloe feels a pull, as if her soul has snagged on something sharp and if she moves too fast she will unravel. She teeters back from the edge and returns to the bench where she sits down, clasping the muddy boots to her chest. If that was Harry, what did Audrey fall in love with? A fantasy? A man? Or something that felt like her own death?

Harry followed her through the bluebells. He kicked off one boot, then the other. Nothing worked. Just twenty minutes ago, in the rain and bluebells, Chloe was so vividly awake that she could see him. He silently rummaged through so many things to say and how to explain them, and when she walked away, he stumbled after her with yells. But she could no longer hear him.

She is hugging a pair of dirty boots and shivering. The sun isn't warm enough to dry her dress; her skin is goose-pimpled. As Harry sits beside her, he resists touching her cheek. Perhaps it's a good thing she can no longer see how dishevelled he is. Since Milly left, he hasn't combed his hair, and the lining of his suit is growing mildew.

He can't believe he chose these trees, these weeds, over Milly. Constant in his mind is her hope-drained face, her saying to the ground, "But, Hal, I can't make anything better." All those times he told her she mustn't interfere, but Harry is sick of watching and waiting: he has to, at least, try to help. Perhaps if he's brave enough, Chloe might listen. But he isn't sure how to let anyone know him. Even when he was alive, he poured all his love into trees and reading, things that wouldn't challenge him to show himself. It's always been safer to pretend that he is self-contained, impervious, unloving — but the only way to explain that would be to start at the beginning.

Perhaps he should tell Chloe that he was born in the year that the Great War ended — that his dad died in battle, soon after Harry was conceived. When he grew up, he almost shared his father's fate, in El Alamein. He could tell Chloe about the bombing in '42 that killed his mum in the house she'd always lived in, and that his

316

brother died in the same year, fighting in Europe. When he returned to London there was no one left. Not even a neighbour.

This garden became his salvation. Bombs had damaged many of the buildings. Plants were being replaced and the herbarium specimens returned from temporary storage. During the war, Kew had been busy finding alternatives: coconut water for saline drips, belladonna as an antidote to nerve gas, nettles to strengthen the plastic in planes. Kew was now working with the Commonwealth War Graves Commission to advise on suitable plants for the new cemeteries. Harry was part of a team that researched the impact of bomb blasts on trees. Dormant buds were suddenly growing and their resilience inspired him. He began to believe that, together, he and the plants could survive the thrall and challenges of each season.

He wonders if he should tell Chloe about the bicentenary celebrations — how he had met the Queen. But the story he really wants to share begins ten years later. On an April morning in 1969, he was digging in a remote part of the Gardens. He describes the moment when he fell to the ground, his heart clapping the strangest beat. As he looked up at the trees, it was as if a drunk was striking his chest in some euphoric devil-spun trance. Then his heart simply went kaput. Jesus, what a sky there was. Harry swears that it winked: the shutter of its heavy blue eyelid closing and opening, its lashes draped with bird wings that looked like tiny sequins. He remembers thinking of the arteries in his heart spreading like branches across his chest, the sunlight dissolving him. But he couldn't let go of the thought that a hose needed fixing. It niggled him so much that he turned away from the light, and as he made that choice he felt the ground beneath him. Then he did what he always did; he taped up the punctured hose, and tended to some pruning.

It wasn't unusual for him to spend weeks without conversation, so for a while he continued unknowing. He could still smell and taste, or, at least, he held on to the memory of these senses, but gradually he lost interest in eating and drinking. Needing the toilet became a habit like the itch of a phantom limb. People came into his home and sent his books to landfill. The Banerjee family moved in.

He continued to hope that something had happened that had scrambled his brain cells; that he was simply a missing person, alive and vagrant. But when the staff put his bench in the Redwood Grove, the dates felt definitive. Part of him was pushing up the daisies, or kicking the bucket. Somewhere in Mortlake Cemetery, his body was rotting. He'd always thought his ashes would be scattered under his favourite tree — the North American tulip — but he never got around to making a will. He set up a cautious camp in the Redwood Grove, the one place where part of him was still rooted in the earth. Lying next to his name on a plaque, he huddled under the stars with his mattress of duff. Trying to enjoy the Gardens' simple pleasures, he waited for something, or someone, to guide him.

At first he saw his predicament as proof that heaven was a figment of the world's imagination. But as the

318

months went by, he feared that he had been abandoned. Often he would gawp up at the night sky and ask, "What is this?" Looking for answers, he ventured into Richmond Library, a quaint nineteenth-century building. He read about death and the afterlife, but nothing matched his experience. He was leafing through some old *LIFE* magazines when he stumbled over the photograph of the falling woman. He became transfixed by this moment between life and death, a person frozen between heartbeats. He didn't think about her being scraped off the pavement; she was still alive enough to touch him. As Harry ripped out the page, he began to weep. It was the first time he realised he could still do that, that tears could fall from his ducts like a kid.

Harry had no road map. But as he returned to the Gardens, he realised he could either wallow in self-pity or continue root-balling plants and checking on the Victoria. The annual schedule of work gave his days a much-needed framework. He would tag a potentially dangerous branch, log it in the mess room, the staff too busy to realise that it wasn't one of their colleagues. He often worked at night, trying to save plants from dying. Each time he mended an apprentice's mistake, the minutiae of survival relaxed him.

Sometimes he explored areas that he hadn't specialised in. One night he sneaked into the herbarium and found himself walking into heaven. In a vast, triple-levelled wing was a multitude of wooden cabinets. Inside were over seven million dried plants pressed on to paper. The type specimens, in red folders, were miracles — an official discovery of a new species.

The files were oily to the touch, covered in hundreds of years of layered dust. As he struggled to read centuries-old handwriting describing family, region and genus, a museum beetle scuttled across the table. He smashed it flat with his palm. Taking in the smell of musty paper, he gazed up at this library of plants. So many lost things gathered: an ark.

Harry spent hours opening drawers full of carp — strange fruits and seeds that looked like they came from another planet. Then he found the spirit collection containing fragile items in jars. He studied the pickled orchids then stumbled over a specimen collected by Darwin. Harry was sitting inside the story of evolution. He remembered an old wives' tale about the herbarium suffering bomb damage to the ceiling. Apparently when the rain came in, some of these pressed seeds started to germinate. He pictured them now, tender green shoots pushing away from the paper, coiling out of the cabinets. Extinct species awakened.

The next morning, Harry woke up with renewed belief that he had a mission. There were times when he missed drinking hot mugs of tea, or the satisfaction of having a piss; but each day he wrote in his notebook. He wanted to preserve the passing seasons, each flower, even himself. He wrote about the altered states that allowed people to see him — the drunks and insomniacs — then there was the unblinkered innocence of the very young. He also described the deaths he'd witnessed. Each time he found himself

320

sitting next to a corpse, he wondered why he was different. If the Japanese tourist had only lingered because Harry interfered, then why was he still here? No one had struck his chest, or ripped his soul from his body. As the family of another dead person wept and wailed around him, Harry came to an uncomfortable realisation: when it came to his time, no one grieved.

Beside him, Chloe has taken out her sketchbook. He tries to explain what it's like to fidget in eternity, to be out of step with time.

"I'm a misfit, Chloe."

But she doesn't hear him. Instead, she draws the bluebells; then she writes a note to herself among the scribbled petals. *What happened to Audrey?*

Audrey didn't know what she was going to do when she saw Harry. Shout at him, or simply stand there, letting his light soak into her being. He's probably not at home, she said to herself, as she applied her lipstick, or I'll discover he's married with six children.

She kissed a tissue, picked up her keys, then remembered earlier that week, when Jonah had bought tulips. She had taken a vase from the piano then paused in the doorway. Jonah was studying his reflection in the bathroom mirror. He examined a blemish on his arm, then pulled in his stomach and grimaced. She hadn't wanted to laugh. She had yearned to hold him and whisper that she loved his flaws too. That she could learn, again, to appreciate the shorthand of a marriage. But she didn't say a word. Standing there, framed in the doorway, she could love him immaculately, without him knowing. Or either of them ruining it.

The moment had filled her with expectant happiness. She promised she would return to her husband as soon as she had confronted Harry. As Audrey climbed into her Ford Ka, she felt exuberant. But as she got closer she kept thinking about Harry's eyes, his mouth. As she drove through that blue-sky morning, she was singing along to a CD: "Oh! You pretty things, don't you know you're driving . . ."

They helter-skeltered towards their tragedy. Harry rushed down the street to get to his old house before she did; Lord knows what the Banerjee family would say. He planned to meet her on the pavement and pretend that he lived there, to steer her away from the door and the truth. But there wasn't any logic. There was just the need to be with her, the excitement scatting in his groin like some hopeless, hope-filled adolescent.

At his grandparents' house on Mortlake Road, James Hopkins was celebrating his ninth birthday. When he unwrapped the red skateboard, he begged his parents to let him go outside on the pavement. Unsteady, yet jubilant, he lifted one foot, raced forward, then lost his balance. Moving precariously down the street, he became aware of a car driving towards the T-junction. In front of him a hat appeared, falling through the air with elegance.

★   ★   ★

322

Harry was still running when Audrey's car reached the T-junction. As she looked in his direction, his hat slipped from his fingers. The boy on the skateboard wobbled to dodge it and it was those few inches that did it. He skated straight through the gardener's body. The whoosh of another's limbs careered through Harry's liver, his ribcage. He was doubled over, winded and staring at the pavement, when he heard the shriek of brakes locking. The sound of the universe screaming. His ears bleed, remembering it.

When Audrey spotted Harry, her foot hesitated, but she continued to turn the car. Then she saw a boy skating right through him. What had she seen? An accident? A trick of the light? Her vehicle pulled right, her heart pulled left . . . then there was no control, just endless panic: a never-ending second when she tried to haul herself back to safety. As the white wall loomed she felt the familiar flicker in her belly. She saw the fluttering eyelids of a child on the other side of the windscreen — then everything faded into white. Her last thought: is this what obliteration feels like?

The entire world had been crushed into a ball of glass and metal. But the car stereo was still playing the song as if nothing had happened. A woman got out of a Nissan Micra and began screaming. As more vehicles pulled up, someone called 999, and others argued about lifting Audrey from the debris.

"She just drove into the wall," said a witness, "it was so quick, I . . ."

Harry peered through the window. Splinters of glass had shredded Audrey's face, her head cocked to one side, revealing her beautiful, broken neck. She looked like a startled dreamer, her gaze wide open. If he had got there in time, perhaps he could have wrenched her free from her body — please, Lord, let her linger. But Audrey was pinned in time, her last minutes repeating like a stuck record, the scratch scratch of the same second. As her carcass lay motionless, Harry felt human for the first time in thirty-four years. Small. Useless.

While the medics worked, Harry felt the pitying gaze of heaven, then realised that the boy with the skateboard was gawping at him.

"Clumsy," he yelled. "Why didn't you look where you were going?"

Even through the spit of his shouting, he knew that the boy wasn't to blame. But Harry couldn't take the words back. As they both stared at Audrey, Harry wanted to tell him her name. He needed to confess — this woman never knew that I loved her — but all the boy could see was a crushed car and a dead person. They were both accidental perpetrators, both victims.

James didn't remember seeing the man before. The hat had been falling on to the pavement; but now this man was holding its rim in his hands and worrying it between his fingers. What had happened? This hat had tumbled through the air, then there was the sensation of skating through something that felt like blossom . . . then a clod of earth on a coffin. The scream of brakes, a silver car, the hollow of hollowest thuds, as if the earth hadn't dared echo, but held its breath, just like the boy had done. The day stuttered.

There were many people. His parents were flapping like crows, and he could see the smallness of his grandmother watching in the doorway, but that man standing there, that everyone was ignoring . . . the tears were dropping from his chin, as if he might turn into a man of rain.

"Clumsy," he was shouting to himself. "Clumsy. Clumsy . . ."

James buried his head against his mother's chest, but she held him too tightly. When he looked again, the man wasn't there. As his parents led him back to the house, James suspected with a child's instinct that his confidence would become muted, that his shine would turn into a dark shyness. Somehow he knew that he would skate each day, like clockwork, waiting for the tick-tock of time to lead him back to that man with the hat. He didn't know why or when. Perhaps it would be on his dying day, as either a nightmare, or a friend.

The sunlit tide washes over the bluebells. Harry sits on the bench, nursing his shame. If he had revealed himself to Audrey, things might be different.

Chloe stares into the blue-flowered distance. She has been drawing the belled petals, each stroke of her pencil bringing her back to the known boundaries of perspectives and colour. But perhaps it doesn't matter that she can't hear. Harry feels lighter in the telling. It might still be worth something to the trees, or the sky — and finally, this is his story, as slim as light. His confession.

The Patterns that Make Us

As Jonah gets on the train at Paddington, laughter erupts from a bunch of drunk, wide-eyed girls; he puts on his headphones and listens to *Stabat Mater*. He's been back at school for a couple of months. There is chewing gum stuck to the opposite seat, and dirt on the windows. A depressed-looking woman holds on to the rail and several cramped businessmen struggle to read the *Evening Standard*.

Having researched the newspaper articles about Emily Richards, he's discovered that Chloe was the last person to see her. It took him weeks to steel himself to ring on her doorbell, but there had been no answer. In a moment of madness, he climbed up the scaffolding around her warehouse, in case she was refusing to open the front door. Not knowing which studio was hers, he passed several windows, then came across the room. He almost fell off the scaff. There were drawings of Milly everywhere. They mapped what Chloe had lost, but in the following weeks, he was too dazed to call her. He held on to his discoveries, as she did with the diary; but now, as he sits in the carriage, all he thinks about is the anticipation of regret. The idea grows in him like a cancer.

***

Harry's shed has been wrenched open. The books he read to Milly, from Roald Dahl to Paul Gallico, have been thrown into black sacks, his tools removed, and it's no longer a safe place to hang up his suit. He sits on his bench in the Redwood Grove, the slats cracked, the wood green with mould. Nearby some children are playing hide and seek. There is noise, a count to ten, then quiet — just the caw of an invisible bird. As the Kew Explorer trundles by, a small boy waves at him through the glassless window. Breathing in the thick, moist air, Harry tries to not think about forever.

As the skies open, he notices the mildew on his trousers, the hems thick with moss. Perhaps his toes will grow roots into the earth, but he doesn't deserve to be a tree or anything good. Looking up at the dripping branches, he prays that Audrey is playing with her children; but to believe that would require a faith in heaven. Filling his lungs with smoke, he hunches under the hood of the weather. There is rain in his bones. He is shoeless, his socks sodden.

Wrapping Audrey's scarf closer, he tries to conjure up her image but all he sees is bent light, her shimmering bone. What comes into focus is Milly. Harry leans against his love for a little girl. She'd always held a faith that he had lacked: a belief in people. She yearned to participate, to help. His socks are in tatters as he runs past the lake, the Mediterranean Garden, the Temple of Bellona, until he finds himself at the London Underground. When he disembarks at Earl's Court, he finds a landslide of people, the ticket gates opening and

328

closing as if herding cattle. Using umbrellas as weapons, the passengers shove forward with their deadlines and agendas. As Harry waits for his connection, some are paralysed by indecision, while others are running so fast they have lost sight of where they are going. "Who would venture towards this life of love and loss?" he asks. "Who would choose it?"

During his journey to Paddington, he overhears a woman complaining about the weather. Harry whispers, "This here is the breath that matters." He wants her to know about the nature of time, how the years pass as slippery as quicksilver, as fleeting as sand. At Bayswater he rushes up the stairs, then crosses the bridge to get on a train going in the direction he came: the 4.19 from Paddington. But despite searching each carriage, Jonah is not there. Harry gets off at Ravenscourt Park, then waits for the next train and walks its entire length. He begins to despair as he jumps on to another train, and another — until after three more attempts, he finds Jonah slumped in a carriage.

Under the hood of his fisherman's jacket, Jonah observes the faces that watch his in the window; then the strangers glance down at their shoes, avoiding eye contact. They don't notice a man, his suit growing weeds, shuffling down the carriage. He sits next to Jonah.

"If Milly was here," he nudges, "I bet she would have ignored the dirt on the windows. She would have pointed out that woman opposite. How the wrinkled tights around her knee look like a face of smiling nylon."

As the train lurches, Harry talks about the chipped plate that remembers the kiss after a fight, the rust on a much-loved bike, or the childhood story behind a scar ... the flaws that hold the staggering beauty; then he notices Jonah's headphones. They tune out his surroundings so Jonah can't see a man looking homeless, buttonless, ancient.

It's only when Jonah smooths out the creases in his trousers that Harry's plan comes into focus. Reaching into his pocket, he takes out the visitor map of Kew Gardens and tears it roughly into a square. As he folds, he fumbles, unaccustomed to corners. He knows more about spirals: how a sunflower grows, the habits of plants — the patterns that make us.

Leaning on the rules of Fibonacci, petals eventually bloom from Harry's fingers. He drops the paper flower into Jonah's lap. The lights flicker. When Jonah looks down, the filthy train becomes licked wet with hope.

Jonah feels as if he has been drunk for years and is recovering from a hangover. Sitting in a grubby park near the Paddington comp, he holds an origami flower. He is moved by the frown of a woman reading a novel on a nearby bench, a pigeon feather in a puddle, a man's cigarette smoke becoming blue against the light. He yields to a world that is supple and changing.

He doesn't know if the origami is a message or serendipitous litter. Last night he unfolded it to discover the pale lake standing out from shades of green, but what is this map telling him? What direction should he take? He has folded the paper back into its original form, religiously following each crease and hearing Milly's words.

"It was my mistake. Jonah?"

He has a thought so fragile even to remember it is a risk. Chloe in a blue dress . . . or was it red? The low-cut back, the flexing of her shoulder blades — he can recall the feel of it, the swish, then the image fades into the distance.

Once school breaks up for summer, Jonah stares at the rain like an eternal student squandering his holiday. Paul Ridley has persuaded him to take meditation classes and every now and then he practises, becoming aware of the relaxation of his muscles. Occasionally he jogs, the flab rubbing against the waist of his tracksuit. On his fortieth birthday he goes to bed, and hears the first three chords of Purcell's *Abdelazer Suite* so clearly he becomes convinced that someone is playing his piano. He finds the living room empty, but sits down and repeats the same three chords over and over.

The next night is the same. He lies in bed, listening to the notes, then he settles himself down on the stool, where there's the faint aroma of tobacco. Jonah repeats what he has heard, then plays a new phrase that sounds like the beginning of "Space Oddity", the baroque mixing with Bowie until it grows into something battered but hopeful.

Note by note, he builds architectures of sound, that don't need applause or recognition. The more he explores the possibilities from one chord to the next, the more he remembers: Chloe's sleepy smile in the morning, the night's crust in her eyes, her face indented by the stitching on a pillow.

As July turns to August he takes a pad of paper and writes freehand, not letting the pencil stop for twenty minutes; then he rereads it and circles, in red, possible lyrics. He plays arpeggios so fast his fingers stumble into new patterns. Each time he leaves the stool, his jaw feels bloodied. But he returns the next day, hammering out chords until something breaks — and finally his body remembers how to be relaxed at the piano. He loses himself in a glorious mess of sound.

In the early hours of the morning, his memory is subtle. Chloe changes in his mind like a square of paper into a secret box, a dove, a kimono. Hands paused on the keys, Jonah remembers the small of her back . . . her scent, as discreet as dew or the juice of a melon, so delicate it must have been something he imagined.

"What's your favourite smell?" she had asked.

"Tears. Salt. Skin."

Jonah stares at the rug where she practised yoga. It was never self-conscious, but as if something was stretching her. She thought with her body, even when she sketched; yes — she would sketch, he would play the piano, and now he recognises how their bodies and habits fitted together. Her belief in him now hurts. What wonderful thing could they have become if he had really seen her? He didn't appreciate her creativity, her sense of adventure, her deceit. The thought slashes like whiplash.

He remembers an evening last September when he had caught her unguarded. She was staring out of the window towards the Gardens. Wearing only his T-shirt, her bright bravado was gone. Her body was curved, as if she was trying to embrace something he couldn't see. It was the same concave posture as Milly's mother.

The next day he clears the files from Audrey's study and paints over the names of their unborn children. From that blank wall, the world shifts. A friend from uni gets in touch, saying he's been commissioned for a documentary and needs some help. Jonah is about to say he doesn't have the time, or the chops.

"The project doesn't start until December. They only need seventeen minutes of music. It's right up your street — oceans, coral reefs. I can send you some files. C'mon, Joe, what do you say?"

"Sounds great."

In the last week of the holidays, he volunteers again at the community centre, working with sufferers of dementia. He returns home and clears the unread post off the piano then replaces it with manuscript paper. As the days go by, he is so lost in the process that he constantly forgets where he placed his pencil. By the time he returns to school, he has completed three songs and a bridge.

One Sunday in October, he is supposed to be marking essays, but begins to fold paper aeroplanes. He launches them around the kitchen, experimenting with aerodynamics, then chastises himself and settles down to a paragraph about Bach. Five minutes later he is folding again, and remembering Chloe's graduation project: a thousand cranes made out of newspaper. Jonah can see her now, eating an apple and leaning against his sink. She was describing a famous origami master.

"At the end of his days, Yoshizawa said: 'I've spent my entire existence trying to express with paper the joy of life . . . or the last thought before a man dies.'"

Chloe spat out the pips.

Tearing out a page from a Sunday magazine, he begins to fold, his mind tracing Chloe's angles and edges. But as the paper resists, he begins to doubt his chances; he's hardly a stable proposition.

"Shit!"

He cries out — a paper cut on his finger. The precise pain wakes him up to the present, and wrapped inside that moment is one word: *Yes*. There's a scrambling in his gut as he realises, with that one small syllable, how many more things there are to say yes to. They could kiss, start a family, move to the coast — but what if Chloe says no? Jonah takes some manuscript paper and writes down dots and rhythm. Everything is in the attempt after all.

The artist has become formidable. Dressed in a black polo neck and trousers, her raven hair is tied back into a severe ponytail. Chloe opens the door of her warehouse, looking civilised and cynical. The postman passes her an innocuous cardboard box, but when she climbs back up the concrete steps, she stops. Jonah's address is written on the side in black felt tip.

After the incident in the bluebell woods, Chloe has been tempted to call him, but to say what? She has convinced herself that the experience was simply her

334

imagination plus some kids mucking about, but the boots still sit on her shelf, gathering doubt and dust.

Holding a kitchen knife in her hand, Chloe makes the first cut. It takes a while to slice through the industrial tape. She levers the box open to find a large screwed-up ball of newspaper, the many sheets of the *Observer* stuck together. She turns this bundle over, then unravels each sheet, the ball becoming smaller and smaller as if she were playing pass-the-parcel. She notices the grinning politicians, the murders and passing fashions, then, on the penultimate page, red pen is slashed across the newsprint. *Because despite all this you make me want to get out of bed in the morning.* The final page is not a newspaper but a score. It has been screwed tightly into a ball. As she smooths out the wrinkles, she cannot read the music, a foreign language to her, but she understands the simple title: *Found*.

Harry has watched the routines of a solitary man; the self-doubt Jonah faces in the mirror. He has seen the widower swear when he stepped into a paint tray, but also the boy-like hope when he stared out of the window. Harry has played another man's piano, and watched Jonah sleep, and in the early-morning light he has understood what Audrey fell in love with.

He is on the train east. His old green jumper droops with longing, the wool aching for its grave. When he arrives in Dalston it begins to rain. He takes off his socks, now no more than threads and stitches, and throws them in a bin. He stands under Chloe's window and begins to sing. He knows Jonah's composition by heart. At the piano, Harry had hoped it wouldn't cause any harm. Not this morsel of compassion. Not this invisible, much-resisted love.

As it pelts down, water drips from Harry's chin. Flawed as they are, both men still have enough faith to highlight their favourite sentence in a novel, or create something in a broken world and hope it will flower. It doesn't even matter that Harry is singing off-key.

Jonah's strange love letter has been sitting on her kitchen table for several days, Chloe glances at it as she picks up her portfolio, and, glad to leave, she walks down the stairs. Striding down an autumnal street, she wonders if Jonah's playing her at her own game. "It's safe to want something you can't have," she chants under her breath. Dressed in navy, she takes the overland to Highbury and Islington, looking elegantly pale.

In Euston, she meets a man who wants to commission several paper mobiles for Great Ormond Street Hospital. As Chloe leafs through her portfolio, she remembers her habit of running away; then she discusses colour palettes and hanging space.

Chloe has lunch with a gallery owner who will be showing her work next spring. There is talk of the exhibition travelling to America, and they discuss the practicalities of transporting folded paper overseas. It is rush hour by the time Chloe returns to the station, but she doesn't get on the train. Clutching her portfolio, she watches the constellations of people gathering and departing, movement and stasis. A couple debate the best route to Piccadilly Circus. The woman jabs at the map emphatically but they are at sea amongst a maze of choices.

The Last Thought

The train moves from the tunnel into sunlight, and Chloe leans her head against the window to gaze at the stretched-out sky. It's like diving into a swimming pool. Thirty minutes later, she is standing by Dali's clock in Kew Gardens, wearing an elegant blue coat and no lipstick. She swaps her weight from right foot to left and considers Jonah's parcel. She promises to be as clear as the sky in her intention: she has only arranged to see Jonah because of a woman she has never met, because she refuses to become another ex-lover haunting his future.

She almost relaxes into this glorious, autumnal afternoon but when Jonah walks towards her, she realises she had forgotten. Now she sees it coming, the earthquake of him. She had remembered his orange fisherman's jacket, the sturdy toggles, but she had forgotten the sound of his footfall. Ten strides away. Here comes the cavalry of his smile, the arson of his charms. He takes off his woollen hat. Close enough.

"Hi there." He bats his beanie against his hand. "You look fantastic. Shall we?"

He holds out the crook of his arm, but she stuffs both hands into her pockets.

338

"Sure. Where to?"

"The pagoda?"

As they walk, she keeps one step away. Jonah celebrates her artwork.

"It was a wonderful concept. Really caught people's imaginations."

"Did you fold a bird?" Of course he did. She had unwrapped each one and catalogued the messages. She knew the grey bird was his, the one with the stave and notes scrawled inside.

"Yes," he says. "I can't remember what colour." He gestures towards a bench that stands between an ash and a maple. "Can we sit here a while?"

She wants to keep moving, but his smile is true, broken. After taking in the cool elegance of Temperate House, she perches down. The bench is warm from basking in the sun. The weather watches them, waiting.

They each have different motivations for being here, but the risk of failure and success sits equally weighted between them. When he turns towards her, it is a scuffed moment.

"This is Emily's bench we're sitting on," he says. "Emily Richards."

He is looking at her pale face and thinking of Chinese porcelain. He is picturing pagodas painted in dazzling blue, the same colour as her eyes, and how not to break this plate he holds in his hands. Her features are delicate. He doesn't know how to tell her about his months hanging out with a dead girl — his madness. His body is still registering the shock of it.

"You were the last person to see her."

Her fingers grip the bench, trying to steady herself; but it looks like the slightest breeze might take her away.

He yearns to put his hand on her knee. "I read it in a local newspaper. Why didn't you say something?"

"Because I could have stopped it. Because I thought . . ." She smiles wanly. "I thought you would hate me."

Her lips part, hesitating, then she starts from the beginning; how she once stumbled across a weeping child. She describes the broken sunflower and an origami boat. Jonah thinks of all the places he could start, but begins with the ending, in one incomprehensible burst.

"It wasn't your fault."

Chloe's forehead crinkles with confusion. He wants to stroke her face, as if it could be uncreased, unfretted, adored.

"I've been having these dreams — well — hallucinations. The doc says it happens when people haven't slept." He squirms then takes a deep breath. "I saw her, Chlo."

Her laughter mocks him. "Like some kind of visitation?"

He tries to chuckle too. "Crazy, I know. But have you ever dreamt about stuff and you can't let go of this feeling that it's trying to tell you something?" He can't stop tossing his hat from one hand to the other. "She always carried a flower press. It was full of daisies, dandelions . . ."

Chloe shakes her head. "How could you know that? You must have known her before."

"No."

Chloe stares into the middle distance. It is an uncomfortable silence. It waits, doubts and waits some more.

"Either you've gone insane, or you're making it up, trying to make me feel . . . Are you asking me to . . . surely you don't believe in ghosts?"

"No. I don't."

Silence again. She is still refusing to look at him, her eyes set on Temperate House. She hasn't let go of the edge of the bench, as if her hands are the only things keeping her here, and every other part of her wants to run.

"I left Milly on her own," he tries. "Time and time again. It could have happened to anyone."

Her jaw tightens — her shoulders, her neck. "But you said it wasn't real . . ."

"My choices were." He drops his hat, puts his hand over hers. They both stare down at her bitten nails. "I wish you had told me."

When she turns to him, the rims of her eyes are red. "I went to her funeral. But I could hardly go up to her mum and say I was the one who didn't bring back your daughter. But she knew who I was. We both knew. We both recognised each other's failure."

"You've got to stop blaming yourself."

"You can talk."

Jonah leans back, as if studying the missing pieces of a jigsaw.

"I went looking for Harry at the house on Earl Road," he nudges. "The guy said you'd been there."

341

Chloe takes her time. But finally they are sharing their seasons of spying and secrets.

"I saw him," she admits. "Harry — in the bluebell woods. He kind of vanished. But this is ridiculous. This is . . ."

"Don't you remember what you told me? All those traditions you studied when you learnt origami. You said it, remember? Some Japanese believe in ghosts like we believe in the weather."

"Jesus. Can you hear yourself?" She frantically searches his eyes. "I don't trust you."

He lets out a short laugh, then raises his arms in surrender. "So now you know how it feels."

It is said without malice. As he holds her gaze, her expression changes; a sky full of clouds and flux and the hope of light.

"I'm sorry, Chlo. I didn't treat you the way you deserved."

Her sigh scatters his words like seeds from a dandelion clock.

"I should have told you sooner."

As they recount their misdemeanours — not just remember, but honour — Jonah sees a broken-hearted splendour, a scarred loveliness.

They stare at the glasshouse where Chloe saw a girl holding a sunflower. Their postures haven't changed, yet there is a different quality in the air around them, the moment when two people witness the beauty in each other. The woman next to him is gaining more presence, more weight; she has never looked so human.

He wants to promise that everything is going to be OK, but it would be a lie masquerading as faith.

This is the last day of summer. The sky is so still, it's as if all states, all seasons, are holding their breath.

She breaks.

It starts with her body, the tiniest tremor that asks more questions than he can answer. Tears flood her face, and he knows them, he knows their smell. They are for her lost childhood, for Milly's.

As he holds her, Chloe's muscles remember what it feels like to have his body upon hers, the crushing together of their limbs and sex. Everything he has told her is surely a delusion. But stranger than a child's ghost is this, this unfamiliar surrender. Now he is resting his forehead against hers, the air dense with hesitant breath.

"Chloe, I —"

"Thought you wanted to go to the pagoda."

She wipes her face then stands up; vigorous, practical. Why would she choose to return to this haunted land, to a man who is now frighteningly available? She tries to hold on to the sound of the birds, the grass beneath her. When they arrive at the pagoda, she gawps up at the flaking paint, the large arch windows.

They skirt around each other, dwarfed by the rotting, red pillars.

"I know you think I'm insane, but I was hoping . . ." He rubs his forehead. "I am getting help," he adds. "Getting better."

"I wouldn't worry about it," she suggests.

It sounds like an unfair dismissal but she's still reeling from the impact Milly had on her life. As she looks up towards the top of the pagoda she feels her weight plummeting.

"Perhaps," says Jonah, "love is when you hold on to something and fall through the air. You don't know if you're flying or falling —"

"Until you crash," she says.

Jonah knows he will remember this day in the future. The way Chloe looks now: her coat the same blue as the pagoda.

"What do you want, Joe? Really?"

He tries to ignore her crossed arms, her impatient stance.

"Everything," he says simply. "And I know what I don't want. A lightweight life."

She looks at him quizzically.

"I'd rather have pain," he continues, "than be on the peripheries, alone, and . . ." He squints in the sunlight. "I don't want to grow up — I want to grow down, you know, grow some roots. Like having a child, or staying put."

He catches a glimpse of the finial and wonders if he is on a fairground ride, the world spinning.

"It's fine if you don't want kids. But please choose for the right reasons —"

"But —"

"When you start appreciating what you have, when you settle for what you've got, perhaps life starts sparkling."

344

"Settling for what you've got?"

His momentum is broken. "I didn't mean that."

There is her back again. Beautiful though it is, he is tired of seeing her turn away and gaze into the distance. The poise of her neck, the defiance of her chin, her young, brittle will coming up against his.

"A relationship is not a thing," she states flatly. "It's not an object you can hold or plan out on paper. It's a movement. Love is what you do."

Jonah knows this. It's listening to your wife when you're exhausted, remembering to unstack the dishwasher, or compliment her shoes. Countless little gestures, the daily attempt to see your partner anew. It's making a woman a piece of music. But Chloe mutters, "This way. C'mon."

As they stroll down Pagoda Vista, she remembers them on a beer-soaked evening, ambling through an open market — when being together was as simple as sunshine. Then she realises they are walking in time. Right foot, left. Even though they are a metre apart, a passer-by apologises for striding between them. She remembers what she wrote in her letter. Hope is a rhythm.

Once they have passed the Palm House, they stop by a bench.

Well, there we are, aren't we?
In loving memory of Dilys "Phyllis" Schub
1920–2003

As Chloe continues to stare at the inscription, she feels the beginning of a movement, just the quiver of some kind of momentum, however small. She tries to stay with it, to listen to that tiny impulse.

She can feel, without looking, that Jonah's brow has softened.

"What are you smiling at?"

"Nothing."

She turns to him. "No . . . what were you thinking?"

"Just thank you — for making these years easier. I've been . . ."

"An idiot?"

The anticipation of a kiss is almost the best part: the shyness, and the doubt. Their eyes search for agreement. When they kiss it is all the more tender for the wait. The ambiguity of words, the slip of the heart, all being surmounted by this. This kiss.

Chloe pulls away — sees the hopeful slant of his mouth.

She takes his hand. "There's something I want to show you. It's not far."

She leads him past Kew Palace to a path he has not seen before. Through the bushes is an undiscovered garden. Jonah turns around, taking it all in. On the right is a modern glasshouse, angular and curved.

"It's closed to the public," says Chloe. "But I saw a paper collection there, for work."

They walk further into a place that holds no memories for Jonah. There is a lake overhung with beauty, and a path wandering through rocks, leading to a bridge across to the Sir Joseph Banks Building. Standing near a fountain is a heron Jonah has never met before: leaner, perhaps younger, preening its feathers and catching the last hour of warmth.

The day is ending, but it feels like a beginning as Chloe ventures along the path, urging him forward as if she wants him to open a present. He follows her beyond the lake, where a wrought-iron rotunda stands on a mound. From here there is a view across to the formal garden of Kew Palace. There are clipped box hedges lined with statues and beds of herbs. To the right is the Thames, and, as Chloe stretches out her arms in appreciation, Jonah fumbles in his coat for his phone and takes a picture. It is not of the landscape. Standing under a mustard sky, half of Chloe's face is lit by the sun, the other half remains in shadow. The intensity of her blue eyes is focused on the man behind the lens and Jonah grins at the image, then at the real person, checking to see if he has captured what he wanted. He knows "5.09" will be the title: 5.09, the twenty-ninth of October.

As they stand opposite each other, Chloe balances like a tightrope walker on the middle of a wire.

"The gates are shutting. We should go."

"Stay. Just for a minute. It's quite a sunset."

As he sits on the grass, Chloe gazes down at his shoulder. A moment of indecision, then she joins him. Jonah lies out, resting his head on her stomach. She lets the sun warm her bones, feeling the encouragement of light against her being. She stares at the subtle divide, the fine line of the horizon, and wonders what they are supposed to birth together. A friendship? A child?

It seems such a distance to travel, but when she brings herself to the present she realises she is already there, his hand on her thigh. She looks up again at the dying light.

"It's different every time I turn back," she murmurs.

As the sun begins to dip beneath the horizon, they shift position. She lies down, resting her head on his chest, the simple gesture of allowing herself to be supported. She remembers him talking about silence; without this lull the beats can have no rhythm. His heartbeat against her cheek sounds like a bass line.

"We should get back," says Jonah. "The policeman at the gates . . ."

"All right."

He offers out his hand and hauls her up to standing. Not knowing the future, they walk away. This is the day British summertime ends. The clocks change.

Harry continues caretaking the benches, moving forgotten pieces of wood into the sunshine or twinning two together so a family can enjoy the view. He tends particularly to the ungrieved, those who didn't love enough, then he rests on a bench that says simply "We Miss You". Stretching out his muddy toes, he wonders if Chloe and Jonah will eventually be here, and whether their benches will stand together or alone. Later he spends the night on the street and discovers them sleeping behind an open window. A guitar leans against the wall. The wind moves the strings but neither of

348

them hears it. Harry is so overwhelmed he has to sit down on a brick wall.

In November, trucks of steaming mulch are carted across the Gardens. The giant compost heap is fuelled by fifty-two daily tonnes of manure. The rotting vegetation generates sixty-degree heat. As the mulch is tipped around the trees, the energetic spirit of the plants re-enters the roots. A little way along, a team are cleaning the Palm House glass with scouring pads taped on to poles. Algae and local traffic pollution are a constant problem. It is close to freezing outside, but these men scrub and sweat in the tropics.

In December, there is no tide of tourists washing in and out of the garden. With the sun low in the sky, Kew is a skeleton, the bare trees casting long shadows. Without the civilisation of his potting shed, Harry looks like a vagabond, his scarf knotted with bird droppings. He shuffles past the glasshouses as if they are ruins of a past romance. The garden embraces him, his toes growing mould, his trousers thickening with moss.

On a quiet and cloudy day, Harry stops at the flagpole. When the tree arrived it was three hundred and seventy years old. He helped the 23rd Field Squadron brace it with steel on the fifth of November 1959 — a Bonfire Night to remember. But the Douglas fir has been ravaged by wood-peckers and there's now talk of taking it down next summer. Its absence will make Harry feel like the last man standing. He looks in the direction of the Ruined Arch, his blistered feet itchy. Absurd that he has never taken his own advice. *Why are you pretending to be earthbound?*

It is then that he sees them. It starts with a thickening in the air, then his eyes focus on a woman sitting on a bench, filling in a crossword. He walks up to her and notices the date on *The Times:* 1953. He glances at the plaque behind her.

"Nancy? Nancy Drabble?"

"Yes?"

But her eyes glaze over. She rubs her nose then returns to the clues she will be filling in for ever.

Harry's chest twinges like a pulled muscle. He pats his pockets as if he's lost a pair of spectacles. How many people have refused to let go of this place? As he stumbles along the path, he sees a mum in a fake-fur coat, pushing a pram. She wears it in every weather. Her baby is always a baby, so what happened to them — a train crash, a fire?

Along Pagoda Vista, he spots a man in uniform sitting on Duvan Novakovic's bench; then, further along, is Vanessa Tunston, "who found peace in this garden". There's a woman in an empire-line dress, a photographer with an old-fashioned Leica; but their thoughts fidget. Their longing is like a radio frequency that bothers the air, a broken circuitry of echoes. They shake out their lives until all the missed opportunities tumble out. Too busy listing regrets, they don't notice each other.

Harry doesn't want to be the same. He doesn't want to be unable to escape the nagging feeling that somehow he missed the boat. It seems like these people felt that at forty, or at seventy, until there was no sea left. They are mumbling to themselves about why they

350

don't want to leave. They're frightened of hell, or waiting until their wife dies, or they know the results of the Cup Final — but these are excuses. They have all experienced insufficient happiness.

It knees Harry in the balls. He had thought he was too in love with life to move on, that these trees were all that mattered. He didn't even know he had regrets until he met Audrey. He's never been brave enough.

There is a foreign flickering in Harry's gut: the taste of free will. As he walks to the Ruined Arch, the fading light glimmers. He stretches out his back, then bends his knees to peer through the centre of the folly. As he stares into this endless space, he prays that Kew's plants are proof that the universe's imagination exceeds his. But still it is a gamble. His existence doesn't prove that there's anything out there. He's just a bundle of electrons, doing what they always did ... spinning around the thing that they love ...

Fiddling with the rim of his hat, he squints up at the darkening sky but no heavenly vision comes to guide him. He sits down on a nearby bench and takes out his notebook. His pencil stub is so small it chafes his fingers. He cocks his head to view the Arch from a different angle. He tries to concentrate on what might be waiting for him — the contours of his future, his freedom. He writes: *Perhaps Audrey is out there.*

At midnight he is still on the bench, as if he is waiting at a train station for a friend to arrive and wondering how much longer they will be. He'll be damned if he's going to be as scared of death as he was of living, but how can he leave? Here, in these Gardens, he needs more words for bliss. Words — that's it. He stumbles across to the Redwood Grove, where he begins to dig. He pushes back the duff with his hands, turning the soil, until he finds a corner of white plastic. He buries deeper, unearthing a dozen shopping bags; then he sits back, wiping the mud off the logos.

Inside are over five hundred brown notebooks. He plans to leave his life's work in the mess room. He switches on his torch and opens the nearest volume. But the page is empty; he can only make out an occasional outline of faded pencil. Turning over, there's a few stubborn words, a date or two, then nothing. He opens a second book and another, but only the last three journals are legible.

The night sky is laughing. Once again he feels mocked by a God that he stopped believing in when he was fighting. But Hal was never worthy. How foolish he was to presume he could save things from dying. He desperately scans the last notebook, flicking through pages of mundane, miraculous moments. Then, as he continues to read about the plants and the dying, he feels a seasick hope that his existence mattered. To Milly, to Audrey — to every person who enjoyed the orchids.

As the sun rises, he is wearing a moss-covered suit and humble shoulders. Harry tears out the pages from his last two notebooks. He then fumbles in his pocket for the crumpled photograph of a day in Buffalo, New York. With trembling hands, he creases the falling limbs, the billboard signs, the bricks of a hotel, until he has made the base of a black-and-white bird. He does this with his writing too. He unfolds and refolds the stories he has been telling himself.

Master Yoshizawa said he tried to express with paper the joy of life, and the last thought before a man dies. And this is Harry's attempt, his love letter. Perhaps someone visiting these redwoods will find it. They'll toss the paper birds into the air, watch as they drop then are taken by a gust of wind. Their flimsy wings will fly over the city.

As dawn becomes day he stands in front of the Ruined Arch and takes a look at his choices. It's going to be a beautiful winter; he can smell it. He picks some ivy and rubs it between his fingers. Taking in its scent, he remembers lying on the ground, that blue sky winking at him like a long-lost lover. Feeling the familiar seizure in his heart, he tries to retain his composure. Barefoot and suited, his hands are folded, as if he is standing in a pew at Sunday service. The thought of church reminds him of his first kiss as a ten-year-old behind the gravestones — her sherbety lips. Then the gravestones crumble into baking powder, the doughy scent of his mother. She wipes the flour from her hands and brings her mouth to his. What kiss is this? He's forgotten so many. Here's his six-year-old brother wrestling him to the ground, then giving him a slobbery kiss on his kneecap. Look, there he is, in his uniform, with Harry's dying comrades. How they clung to his collar, their whispering lips caressing his earlobes. Then he sees Au. The surprises of that smile, the many weathers in her kiss. But these memories are making him dizzy, unsure. He stands at the threshold, trying to gather the balls. He doesn't know what is next but he does know this. All it takes is one step.

In the space where he stood, there's just smoke and rain. A puddle. Now Jonah is standing at the threshold — but not this threshold, the door of our flat. The story begins again, with a world rearranged.

The images repeat, like a record skipping, the scratch scratch of the same second. It always ends at the point where Harry stands in front of the Arch — or is it my bare feet, waiting to step forward?

Then I return to the beginning, to my husband staring at tulips.

Joe? Why are the flowers wilting?

Why do I keep thinking of kisses?

Credits

A Note on Kew Gardens

The Royal Botanic Gardens, Kew is a major character in this novel. As a living entity, it is constantly changing. *A Thousand Paper Birds* is an impressionist painting of the Gardens rather than a realistic representation. For narrative purposes I have, at times, compacted dates or let fiction overrule. For instance, the pagoda was opened to the public in 2006, not 2005. The clay sculpture of Mother Earth was the focal point of a biodiversity garden designed by Mary Reynolds as part of Kew's *Go Wild* summer festival in 2003. Kew's summer concerts are centred around modern, not classical, music. I have not included the draining of the lake and the opening of the Sackler Crossing in May 2006. In reality, the lake is pretty shallow.

The wonderful *Wounded Angel I* sculpture by Emily Young was in Kew Gardens from 2003. Also referenced is the bronze sculpture *The Profile of Time* by Salvador Dalí. Sadly, both have since been removed. The inscription on Audrey's bench was inspired by the Franz Schubert quote: "Some people come into our lives, leave footprints on our hearts, and we are never the same."

I am indebted to Kew's magazine and website for being a constant source of exceptional information. The many books written about the Gardens have also been a valuable resource and the BBC series, *A Year at Kew*, helped me understand a little more about the daily experience of working there. Any inaccuracies are entirely my own. I hope that all horticulturists and Kew enthusiasts will forgive my mistakes — I can only hope that my love for the Gardens shines through.

I would like to thank all the staff at Kew for their brilliant and important work. They are not only striving to sustain one particular garden, but the beauty of the world. You can find out more about this extraordinary place at www.kew.org.

Acknowledgements

Thank you to . . .

Jan and Steve Udall for your unwavering faith. You have supported me in so many ways. Without your love, and your belief in me, this book would not exist.

The entire Currie family for your encouragement throughout.

nowhere for your generous support during the writing of this book — in particular Nick Udall, Marc Cornwell and Andrea Turner. Also thanks to Joe Knowles for filming the book trailer, and to Boz Kay, Jane James and Judith Hemming for your friendship and phenomenal wisdom.

Francesca Main, Hannah Griffiths, Rachel Malig, Jonathan Pegg, Arabella Pike and Alice Williams — your early support kept me going.

Andrew Gordon, Judith Murray, Carrie Kania, Carrie Plitt and Jo Unwin for falling in love with this novel and for your invaluable insights on earlier drafts.

The Festival of Writing in York for being the catapult that fired me into an agent frenzy, and to Andrew Wille for being such an astute guide. Your sensitivity and general cheerleading are both tonic and balm. Thanks also to the great writers I met at the Festival, especially Deborah Install, Amanda Saint and Sadie Hanson. And to Shelley Harris for being absolutely gorgeous!

The inimitable Sam Bain for brilliant advice, and the mesmerising Ben Okri for an enchanting afternoon in Soho House discussing the power of stories while a snowstorm swirled outside.

My fellow writers, Deborah Andrews and Eleanor Anstruther, for being on the journey with me. For picking me up, for cheering me on, for understanding that each day when we leave the boxing ring, the only person we have been fighting with are ourselves. You are such talented and inspiring beauties.

Dr Annette Steele for medical advice and for making her life a work of art. Philip Raby for reading early drafts and for teaching me the word *mudita*. Jean Littlejohn and the late Julia Caprara for being, like my mum, inspiring examples of what it is to be a creative woman.

All my friends for your support over many decades, especially Mita Pujara, Josh Towb, Sean Blair, Nizami Cummins, Caroline Udall, Julie Paul, Manuela Harding, Medan Gabbay and Jenny Lenhart.

Julie McBride and Simon Massey for sharing your experience of grief so vividly. Mass — you are loved beyond words.

The many teams involved in helping me obtain permission for "Oh! You Pretty Things": a rather daunting task! In particular, I would like to thank Leah Mack for your generous guidance throughout and the brilliant Richard Palk and Mich Gadvhi for making initial introductions. What fine gentlemen you are!

Everyone at the Royal Botanic Gardens, Kew, particularly Richard Deverell and Magda North. My thanks also to Nina Davies and Aurelie Grail for showing me around the herbarium so gracefully.

Peter Engel for his book *Origami from Angelfish to Zen*. His interview with Master Akira Yoshizawa inspired many of my thoughts regarding origami and was also where I found the wood-block print by Katsushika Hokusai that inspired Chloe's tattoo: *A Magician Turns Sheets of Paper into Birds*.

To the artists who have inspired me — including Tori Amos, Mary Reynolds, and Emily Young for creating the *Wounded Angel* series. And, of course, a big thank you to David Bowie for enriching our world.

Special thanks to everyone at Andrew Nurnberg Associates — you are such a brilliant team. And to my wonderful agent, Jenny Savill, I am so glad that you are on this journey with me. Your love of this book, and your friendship, have been true gifts.

A huge thank you to my incredibly talented and wise editor, Alexa von Hirschberg — and a bow of gratitude to the entire Bloomsbury team, especially the amazing Imogen Denny, Cal Kenny, Philippa Cotton, Joe Thomas, Lea Beresford and Alexandra Pringle. I would also like to thank my copy editor, Sarah-Jane Forder, for her immaculate work (love really is in the detail), Emma Ewbank for her exquisite jacket design, and Livi Gosling for her beautiful map of Kew.

A final thank you to . . .

My grandmother, Audrey Beaney, for encouraging me to write. I'm so glad that just before she died, at the ripe old age of a hundred and one, I was able to tell her that *A Thousand Paper Birds* would fly.

My children, Willow and Theo — for teaching me all the shades of love, and all the different shapes of laughter.

And to Tom, for all the kisses past and present — and for all the kisses that are to come.